SEQUOYAH REGIONAL LIBRARY
3 8749 0074 84064

Redeployment

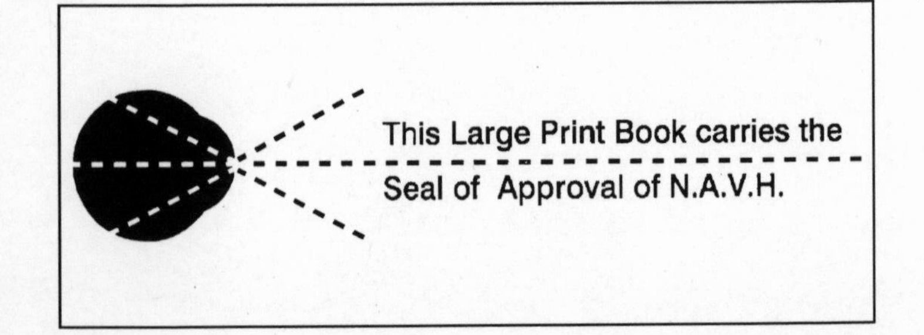
This Large Print Book carries the
Seal of Approval of N.A.V.H.

REDEPLOYMENT

PHIL KLAY

THORNDIKE PRESS
A part of Gale, Cengage Learning

Farmington Hills, Mich • San Francisco • New York • Waterville, Maine
Meriden, Conn • Mason, Ohio • Chicago

"Redeployment" first appeared in *Granta,* "After Action Report" in *Tin House,* and a portion of "Ten Kliks South" in *Guernica.*
Thorndike Press, a part of Gale, Cengage Learning.

Thorndike Press® Large Print Reviewers' Choice.
The text of this Large Print edition is unabridged.
Other aspects of the book may vary from the original edition.
Set in 16 pt. Plantin.

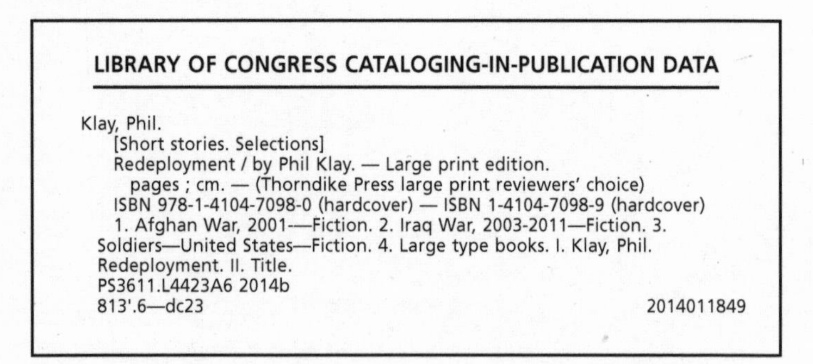
LIBRARY OF CONGRESS CATALOGING-IN-PUBLICATION DATA

Klay, Phil.
[Short stories. Selections]
Redeployment / by Phil Klay. — Large print edition.
pages ; cm. — (Thorndike Press large print reviewers' choice)
ISBN 978-1-4104-7098-0 (hardcover) — ISBN 1-4104-7098-9 (hardcover)
1. Afghan War, 2001—Fiction. 2. Iraq War, 2003-2011—Fiction. 3. Soldiers—United States—Fiction. 4. Large type books. I. Klay, Phil. Redeployment. II. Title.
PS3611.L4423A6 2014b
813'.6—dc23 2014011849

Published in 2014 by arrangement with The Penguin Press, a member of Penguin Group (USA) LLC, a Penguin Random House Company.

Printed in Mexico
1 2 3 4 5 6 7 18 17 16 15 14

FOR MY MOTHER AND FATHER,

WHO HAD THREE SONS
JOIN THE MILITARY
IN A TIME OF WAR

CONTENTS

Redeployment

We shot dogs. Not by accident. We did it on purpose, and we called it Operation Scooby. I'm a dog person, so I thought about that a lot.

First time was instinct. I hear O'Leary go, "Jesus," and there's a skinny brown dog lapping up blood the same way he'd lap up water from a bowl. It wasn't American blood, but still, there's that dog, lapping it up. And that's the last straw, I guess, and then it's open season on dogs.

At the time, you don't think about it. You're thinking about who's in that house, what's he armed with, how's he gonna kill you, your buddies. You're going block by block, fighting with rifles good to 550 meters, and you're killing people at five in a concrete box.

The thinking comes later, when they give you the time. See, it's not a straight shot back, from war to the Jacksonville mall.

When our deployment was up, they put us on TQ, this logistics base out in the desert, let us decompress a bit. I'm not sure what they meant by that. Decompress. We took it to mean jerk off a lot in the showers. Smoke a lot of cigarettes and play a lot of cards. And then they took us to Kuwait and put us on a commercial airliner to go home.

So there you are. You've been in a no-shit war zone and then you're sitting in a plush chair, looking up at a little nozzle shooting air-conditioning, thinking, What the fuck? You've got a rifle between your knees, and so does everyone else. Some Marines got M9 pistols, but they take away your bayonets because you aren't allowed to have knives on an airplane. Even though you've showered, you all look grimy and lean. Everybody's hollow-eyed, and their cammies are beat to shit. And you sit there, and close your eyes, and think.

The problem is, your thoughts don't come out in any kind of straight order. You don't think, Oh, I did A, then B, then C, then D. You try to think about home, then you're in the torture house. You see the body parts in the locker and the retarded guy in the cage. He squawked like a chicken. His head was shrunk down to a coconut. It takes you a while to remember Doc saying they'd shot mercury into his skull, and then it still doesn't make any sense.

You see the things you saw the times you nearly died. The broken television and the hajji corpse. Eicholtz covered in blood. The lieutenant on the radio.

You see the little girl, the photographs Curtis found in a desk. First had a beautiful Iraqi kid, maybe seven or eight years old, in bare feet and a pretty white dress like it's First Communion. Next she's in a red dress, high heels, heavy makeup. Next photo, same dress, but her face is smudged and she's holding a gun to her head.

I tried to think of other things, like my wife, Cheryl. She's got pale skin and fine dark hairs on her arms. She's ashamed of them, but they're soft. Delicate.

But thinking of Cheryl made me feel guilty, and I'd think about Lance Corporal Hernandez, Corporal Smith, and Eicholtz. We were like brothers, Eicholtz and me. The two of us saved this Marine's life one time. A few weeks later, Eicholtz is climbing over a wall. Insurgent pops out a window, shoots him in the back when he's halfway over.

So I'm thinking about that. And I'm seeing the retard, and the girl, and the wall Eicholtz died on. But here's the thing. I'm thinking a lot, and I mean a lot, about those fucking dogs.

And I'm thinking about my dog. Vicar. About the shelter we'd got him from, where Cheryl said we had to get an older dog because nobody takes older dogs. How we could never teach him anything. How he'd throw up shit he shouldn't have eaten in the first place. How he'd slink away all guilty, tail down and head low and back legs crouched. How his fur started turning gray two years after we got him, and he had so many white hairs on his face that it looked like a mustache.

So there it was. Vicar and Operation Scooby, all the way home.

Maybe, I don't know, you're prepared to kill people. You practice on man-shaped targets so you're ready. Of course, we got targets they call "dog targets." Target shape Delta. But they don't look like fucking dogs.

And it's not easy to kill people, either. Out of boot camp, Marines act like they're gonna play Rambo, but it's fucking serious, it's professional. Usually. We found this one insurgent doing the death rattle, foaming and shaking, fucked up, you know? He's hit with a 7.62 in the chest and pelvic girdle; he'll be gone in a second, but the company XO walks up, pulls out his KA-BAR, and slits his throat. Says, "It's good to kill a man with a knife." All the Marines look at each other like, "What the fuck?" Didn't expect that from the XO. That's some PFC bullshit.

On the flight, I thought about that, too.

It's so funny. You're sitting there with your rifle in your hands but no ammo in sight. And then you touch down in Ireland to refuel. And it's so foggy you can't see shit, but, you know, this is Ireland, there's got to be beer. And the plane's captain, a fucking civilian, reads off some message about how general orders stay in effect until you reach the States, and you're still considered on duty. So no alcohol.

Well, our CO jumped up and said, "That makes about as much sense as a goddamn football bat. All right, Marines, you've got three hours. I hear they serve Guinness." Oo-fucking-rah.

Corporal Weissert ordered five beers at once and had them laid out in front of him. He didn't even drink for a while, just sat there looking at 'em all, happy. O'Leary said, "Look at you, smiling like a faggot in a dick tree," which is a DI expression Curtis loves.

So Curtis laughs and says, "What a horrible fucking tree," and we all start cracking up, happy just knowing we can get fucked up, let our guard down.

We got crazy quick. Most of us had lost about twenty pounds and it'd been seven months since we'd had a drop of alcohol. MacManigan, second award PFC, was rolling around the bar with his nuts hanging out of his cammies, telling Marines, "Stop looking at my balls, faggot." Lance Corporal Slaughter was there all of a half hour before he puked in the bathroom, with Corporal Craig, the sober Mormon, helping him out, and Lance Corporal Greeley, the drunk Mormon, puking in the stall next to him. Even the Company Guns got wrecked.

It was good. We got back on the plane and passed the fuck out. Woke up in America.

Except when we touched down in Cherry Point, there was nobody there. It was zero dark and cold, and half of us were rocking the first hangover we'd had in months, which at that point was a kind of shitty that felt pretty fucking good. And we got off the plane and there's a big empty landing strip, maybe a half dozen red patchers and a bunch of seven tons lined up. No families.

The Company Guns said that they were waiting for us at Lejeune. The sooner we get the gear loaded on the trucks, the sooner we see 'em.

Roger that. We set up working parties, tossed our rucks and seabags into the seven tons. Heavy work, and it got the blood flowing in the cold. Sweat a little of the alcohol out, too.

Then they pulled up a bunch of buses and we all got on, packed in, M16s sticking everywhere, muzzle awareness gone to shit, but it didn't matter.

Cherry Point to Lejeune's an hour. First bit's through trees. You don't see much in the dark. Not much when you get on 24, either. Stores that haven't opened yet. Neon lights off at the gas stations and bars. Looking out, I sort of knew where I was, but I didn't feel home. I figured I'd be home when I kissed my wife and pet my dog.

We went in through Lejeune's side gate, which is about ten minutes away from our battalion area. Fifteen, I told myself, way this fucker is driving. When we got to McHugh, everybody got a little excited. And then the driver turned on A Street. Battalion area's on A, and I saw the barracks and I thought, There it is. And then they stopped about four hundred meters short. Right in front of the armory. I could've jogged down to where the families were. I could see there was an area behind one of the barracks where they'd set up lights. And there were cars parked everywhere. I could hear the crowd down the way. The families were there. But we all got in line, thinking about them just down the way. Me thinking about Cheryl and Vicar. And we waited.

When I got to the window and handed in my rifle, though, it brought me up short. That was the first time I'd been separated from it in months. I didn't know where to rest my hands. First I put them in my pockets, then I took them out and crossed my arms, and then I just let them hang, useless, at my sides.

After all the rifles were turned in, First Sergeant had us get into a no-shit parade formation. We had a fucking guidon waving out front, and we marched down A Street. When we got to the edge of the first barracks, people started cheering. I couldn't see them until we turned the corner, and then there they were, a big wall of people holding signs under a bunch of outdoor lights, and the lights were bright and pointed straight at us, so it was hard to look into the crowd and tell who was who. Off to the side there were picnic tables and a Marine in woodlands grilling hot dogs. And there was a bouncy castle. A fucking bouncy castle.

We kept marching. A couple more Marines in woodlands were holding the crowd back in a line, and we marched until we were straight alongside the crowd, and then First

Sergeant called us to a halt.

I saw some TV cameras. There were a lot of U.S. flags. The whole MacManigan clan was up front, right in the middle, holding a banner that read: OO-RAH PRIVATE FIRST CLASS BRADLEY MACMANIGAN. WE ARE SO PROUD.

I scanned the crowd back and forth. I'd talked to Cheryl on the phone in Kuwait, not for very long, just, "Hey, I'm good," and, "Yeah, within forty-eight hours. Talk to the FRO, he'll tell you when to be there." And she said she'd be there, but it was strange, on the phone. I hadn't heard her voice in a while.

Then I saw Eicholtz's dad. He had a sign, too. It said: WELCOME BACK HEROES OF BRAVO COMPANY. I looked right at him and remembered him from when we left, and I thought, That's Eicholtz's dad. And that's when they released us. And they released the crowd, too.

I was standing still, and the Marines around me, Curtis and O'Leary and MacManigan and Craig and Weissert, they were rushing out to the crowd. And the crowd was coming forward. Eicholtz's dad was coming forward.

He was shaking the hand of every Marine he passed. I don't think a lot of guys recognized him, and I knew I should say something, but I didn't. I backed off. I looked around for my wife. And I saw my name on a sign: SGT PRICE, it said. But the rest was blocked by the crowd, and I couldn't see who was holding it. And then I was moving toward it, away from Eicholtz's dad, who was hugging Curtis, and I saw the rest of the sign. It said: SGT PRICE, NOW THAT YOU'RE HOME YOU CAN DO SOME CHORES. HERE'S YOUR TO-DO LIST. 1) ME. 2) REPEAT NUMBER 1.

And there, holding the sign, was Cheryl.

She was wearing cammie shorts and a tank top, even though it was cold. She must have worn them for me. She was skinnier than I remembered. More makeup, too. I was nervous and tired and she looked a bit different. But it was her.

All around us were families and big smiles and worn-out Marines. I walked up to her and she saw me and her face lit. No woman had smiled at me like that in a long time. I moved in and kissed her. I figured that was what I was supposed to do. But it'd been too long and we were both too nervous and it felt like just lip on lip pushed together, I don't know. She pulled back and looked at me and put her hands on my shoulders and started to cry. She reached up and rubbed her eyes, and then she put her arms around me and pulled me into her.

Her body was soft and it fit into mine. All deployment, I'd slept on the ground or on canvas cots. I'd worn body armor and kept a rifle slung across my body. I hadn't felt anything like her in seven months. It was almost like I'd forgotten how she felt, or never really known it, and now here was this new feeling that made everything else black and white fading before color. Then she let me go and I took her by the hand and we got my gear and got out of there.

She asked me if I wanted to drive and hell yeah I did, so I got behind the wheel. A long time since I'd done that, too. I put the car in reverse, pulled out, and started driving home. I was thinking I wanted to park somewhere dark and curl up with her in the backseat like high school. But I got the car out of the lot and down McHugh. And driving down McHugh it felt different from the bus. Like, This is Lejeune. This is the way I used to get to work. And it was so dark. And quiet.

Cheryl said, "How are you?" which meant, How was it? Are you crazy now?

I said, "Good. I'm fine."

And then it was quiet again and we turned down Holcomb. I was glad I was driving. It gave me something to focus on. Go down this street, turn the wheel, go down another. One step at a time. You can get through anything one step at a time.

She said, "I'm so happy you're home."

Then she said, "I love you so much."

Then she said, "I'm proud of you."

I said, "I love you, too."

When we got home, she opened the door for me. I didn't even know where my house keys were. Vicar wasn't at the door to greet me. I stepped in and scanned around, and there he was on the couch. When he saw me, he got up slow.

His fur was grayer than before, and there were weird clumps of fat on his legs, these little tumors that Labs get but that Vicar's got a lot of now. He wagged his tail. He stepped down off the couch real careful, like he was hurting. And Cheryl said, "He remembers you."

"Why's he so skinny?" I said, and I bent down and scratched him behind the ears.

"The vet said we had to keep him on weight control. And he doesn't keep a lot of food down these days."

Cheryl was pulling on my arm. Pulling me away from Vicar. And I let her.

She said, "Isn't it good to be home?"

Her voice was shaky, like she wasn't sure

of the answer. And I said, "Yeah, yeah, it is." And she kissed me hard. I grabbed her in my arms and lifted her up and carried her to the bedroom. I put a big grin on my face, but it didn't help. She looked a bit scared of me, then. I guess all the wives were probably a little bit scared.

And that was my homecoming. It was fine, I guess. Getting back feels like your first breath after nearly drowning. Even if it hurts, it's good.

I can't complain. Cheryl handled it well. I saw Lance Corporal Curtis's wife back in Jacksonville. She spent all his combat pay before he got back, and she was five months pregnant, which, for a Marine coming back from a seven-month deployment, is not pregnant enough.

Corporal Weissert's wife wasn't there at all when we got back. He laughed, said she probably got the time wrong, and O'Leary gave him a ride to his house. They get there and it's empty. Not just of people, of everything: furniture, wall hangings, everything. Weissert looks at this shit and shakes his head, starts laughing. They went out, bought some whiskey, and got fucked up right there in his empty house.

Weissert drank himself to sleep, and when he woke up, MacManigan was right next to him, sitting on the floor. And MacManigan, of all people, was the one who cleaned him up and got him into base on time for the classes they make you take about, Don't kill yourself. Don't beat your wife. And Weissert was like, "I can't beat my wife. I don't know where the fuck she is."

That weekend they gave us a ninety-six, and I took on Weissert duty for Friday. He was in the middle of a three-day drunk, and hanging with him was a carnival freak show filled with whiskey and lap dances. Didn't get home until four, after I dropped him off at Slaughter's barracks room, and I woke Cheryl coming in. She didn't say a word. I figured she'd be mad, and she looked it, but when I got in bed she rolled over to me and gave me a little hug, even though I was stinking of booze.

Slaughter passed Weissert to Addis, Addis passed him to Greeley, and so on. We had somebody with him the whole weekend until we were sure he was good.

When I wasn't with Weissert and the rest of the squad, I sat on the couch with Vicar, watching the baseball games Cheryl'd taped for me. Sometimes Cheryl and I talked about her seven months, about the wives left behind, about her family, her job, her boss. Sometimes she'd ask little questions.

Sometimes I'd answer. And glad as I was to be in the States, and even though I hated the past seven months and the only thing that kept me going was the Marines I served with and the thought of coming home, I started feeling like I wanted to go back. Because fuck all this.

The next week at work was all half days and bullshit. Medical appointments to deal with injuries guys had been hiding or sucking up. Dental appointments. Admin. And every evening, me and Vicar watching TV on the couch, waiting for Cheryl to get back from her shift at Texas Roadhouse.

Vicar'd sleep with his head in my lap, waking up whenever I'd reach down to feed him bits of salami. The vet told Cheryl that's bad for him, but he deserved something good. Half the time when I pet him, I'd rub up against one of his tumors, and that had to hurt. It looked like it hurt him to do everything, wag his tail, eat his chow. Walk. Sit. And when he'd vomit, which was every other day, he'd hack like he was choking, revving up for a good twenty seconds before anything came out. It was the noise that bothered me. I didn't mind cleaning the carpet.

And then Cheryl'd come home and look at us and shake her head and smile and say,

"Well, you're a sorry bunch."

I wanted Vicar around, but I couldn't bear to look at him. I guess that's why I let Cheryl drag me out of the house that weekend. We took my combat pay and did a lot of shopping. Which is how America fights back against the terrorists.

So here's an experience. Your wife takes you shopping in Wilmington. Last time you walked down a city street, your Marine on point went down the side of the road, checking ahead and scanning the roofs across from him. The Marine behind him checks the windows on the top levels of the buildings, the Marine behind him gets the windows a little lower, and so on down until your guys have the street level covered, and the Marine in back has the rear. In a city there's a million places they can kill you from. It freaks you out at first. But you go through like you were trained, and it works.

In Wilmington, you don't have a squad, you don't have a battle buddy, you don't even have a weapon. You startle ten times checking for it and it's not there. You're safe, so your alertness should be at white, but it's not.

Instead, you're stuck in an American Eagle Outfitters. Your wife gives you some clothes to try on and you walk into the tiny dressing room. You close the door, and you don't want to open it again.

Outside, there're people walking around by the windows like it's no big deal. People who have no idea where Fallujah is, where three members of your platoon died. People who've spent their whole lives at white.

They'll never get even close to orange. You can't, until the first time you're in a firefight, or the first time an IED goes off that you missed, and you realize that everybody's life, everybody's, depends on you not fucking up. And you depend on them.

Some guys go straight to red. They stay like that for a while and then they crash, go down past white, down to whatever is lower than "I don't fucking care if I die." Most everybody else stays orange, all the time.

Here's what orange is. You don't see or hear like you used to. Your brain chemistry changes. You take in every piece of the environment, everything. I could spot a dime in the street twenty yards away. I had antennae out that stretched down the block. It's hard to even remember exactly what that felt like. I think you take in too much information to store so you just forget, free up brain space to take in everything about the next moment that might keep you alive. And then you forget that moment, too, and focus on the next. And the next. And the next. For seven months.

So that's orange. And then you go shopping in Wilmington, unarmed, and you think you can get back down to white? It'll be a long fucking time before you get down to white.

By the end of it I was amped up. Cheryl didn't let me drive home. I would have gone a hundred miles per hour. And when we got back, we saw Vicar had thrown up again, right by the door. I looked for him and he was there on the couch, trying to stand on shaky legs. And I said, "Goddamn it, Cheryl. It's fucking time."

She said, "You think I don't know?"

I looked at Vicar.

She said, "I'll take him to the vet tomorrow."

I said, "No."

She shook her head. She said, "I'll take care of it."

I said, "You mean you'll pay some asshole a hundred bucks to kill my dog."

She didn't say anything.

I said, "That's not how you do it. It's on me."

She was looking at me in this way I couldn't deal with. Soft. I looked out the window at nothing.

She said, "You want me to go with you?"
I said, "No. No."
"Okay," she said. "But it'd be better."
She walked over to Vicar, leaned down, and hugged him. Her hair fell over her face and I couldn't see if she was crying. Then she stood up, walked to the bedroom, and gently closed the door.
I sat down on the couch and scratched Vicar behind the ears, and I came up with a plan. Not a good plan, but a plan. Sometimes that's enough.
There's a dirt road near where I live and a stream off the road where the light filters in around sunset. It's pretty. I used to go running there sometimes. I figured it'd be a good spot for it.
It's not a far drive. We got there right at sunset. I parked just off the road, got out, pulled my rifle out of the trunk, slung it over my shoulders, and moved to the passenger side. I opened the door and lifted Vicar up in my arms and carried him down to the stream. He was heavy and warm, and he licked my face as I carried him, slow, lazy licks from a dog that's been happy all his life. When I put him down and stepped back, he looked up at me. He wagged his tail. And I froze.
Only one other time I hesitated like that.

Midway through Fallujah, an insurgent snuck through our perimeter. When we raised the alarm, he disappeared. We freaked, scanning everywhere, until Curtis looked down in this water cistern that'd been used as a cesspit, basically a big round container filled a quarter way with liquid shit.

The insurgent was floating in it, hiding beneath the liquid and only coming up for air. It was like a fish rising up to grab a fly sitting on the top of the water. His mouth would break the surface, open for a breath, and then snap shut, and he'd submerge. I couldn't imagine it. Just smelling it was bad enough. About four or five Marines aimed straight down, fired into the shit. Except me.

Staring at Vicar, it was the same thing. This feeling, like, something in me is going to break if I do this. And I thought of Cheryl bringing Vicar to the vet, of some stranger putting his hands on my dog, and I thought, I have to do this.

I didn't have a shotgun, I had an AR-15. Same, basically, as an M16, what I'd been trained on, and I'd been trained to do it right. Sight alignment, trigger control, breath control. Focus on the iron sights, not the target. The target should be blurry.

I focused on Vicar, then on the sights. Vicar disappeared into a gray blur. I switched off the safety. There had to be three shots. It's not just pull the trigger and you're done. Got to do it right. Hammer pair to the body. A final well-aimed shot to the head.

The first two have to be fired quick, that's important. Your body is mostly water, so a bullet striking through is like a stone thrown in a pond. It creates ripples. Throw in a second stone soon after the first, and in between where they hit, the water gets choppy. That happens in your body, especially when it's two 5.56 rounds traveling at supersonic speeds. Those ripples can tear organs apart.

If I were to shoot you on either side of your heart, one shot . . . and then another, you'd have two punctured lungs, two sucking chest wounds. Now you're good and fucked. But you'll still be alive long enough to feel your lungs fill up with blood.

If I shoot you there with the shots coming fast, it's no problem. The ripples tear up your heart and lungs and you don't do the death rattle, you just die. There's shock, but no pain.

I pulled the trigger, felt the recoil, and focused on the sights, not on Vicar, three times. Two bullets tore through his chest, one through his skull, and the bullets came fast, too fast to feel. That's how it should be done, each shot coming quick after the last so you can't even try to recover, which is when it hurts.

I stayed there staring at the sights for a while. Vicar was a blur of gray and black. The light was dimming. I couldn't remember what I was going to do with the body.

Frago

LT says drop the fucking house. Roger that. We go to drop the fucking house.

I gather my guys, make a sand-table diagram. I've got a dip in while I brief, and the dip spit's evaporating as soon as it hits the ground.

HUMINT says the place is an IED factory filled with some bad motherfucking hajjis, including one pretty high up on the BOLO list. SALUTE report says there's a fire team–sized element armed with AKs, RPKs, RPGs, maybe a Dragunov.

I make 2nd Fire Team the main effort. That's Corporal Sweet's team, and Sweet's a fucking rock star. Stellar NCO. Sweet's SAW gunner is PFC Dyer, and Dyer's excited because here's a chance to finally pop his cherry and shoot somebody. He's nineteen, one of our baby-wipe killers, and all he's killed so far in the Corps has been paper.

I put 1st Fire Team in support. Corporal Moore's team. Moore's a bit of a motard, always thinks his fire team should be main effort, like it's a fucking prize. He could be less oo-rah, but he's good to go.

I put 3rd Fire Team in reserve, as usual. They're Malrosio's, and he's dumber than Fabio on two bottles of NyQuil. 3rd's had an easy deployment so far because I don't give his team anything too complicated. Sometimes it helps to be led by an idiot.

When we get to the house, the other squads set a cordon and we tear down the road and bust in the back door. M870 with lockbuster shells. Boom, and we go.

Back door leads to the kitchen. Right, clear. Left, clear. Overhead, clear. Rear, clear. Kitchen, clear. We roll through, don't stack, just roll. Slow is smooth. Smooth is fast. Corporal Sweet's fire team clears houses like water running down a stream.

Next room there's AK fire as soon as we go through the doorway, but we're better shots. End state is two hajjis, no survivable wounds, no injuries on our side, just another day in paradise. Except Corporal Sweet leads 2nd Fire Team to the bedroom and hajji jumps out shooting blind from the hip and plugs lucky into Corporal Sweet. Two get stopped by his SAPI plate, but one goes through the nut protector and into his thigh. PFC Dyer's on Sweet's ass, second man through the door, and he fires a burst of 5.56 into hajji's face. We clear the bedroom, call, Corpsman up, and Dyer drops down to pack Sweet's wound. It's bleeding bright red, maybe hit the femoral.

We keep moving. 1st Fire Team steps up and Doc P's in with Dyer on Corporal Sweet now and, oh, hajji's still breathing, so Doc tells Dyer, Go pack the wound in hajji's face, do the four life-saving steps, restore the breathing, stop the bleeding, protect the wound, treat for shock. I get on the IISR to the LT to call for CASEVAC.

We keep moving. Bedroom, clear. Head, clear. Pantry, clear. Whatever the fuck this room is, clear. First deck, clear.

LT gets on and says they've got a CH-46 in the air coming to save Sweet's life. He asks for status, so I shoot Doc P a look like, WIA or KIA? Doc says, Urgent, no joke, and I tell the LT as we stack outside the door to the basement.

We drop a flashbang, and when it goes off we flow downstairs. There's three down there. One's al-Qaeda, but he's shook by the flashbang and there's no weapon in his hands. He looks like he's seventeen and scared, and when we flexcuff him and start to go through all the usual EPW shit, he pisses himself. That happens sometimes.

No threat from the other two in the basement, a policeman and a *jundi* from the 1st Iraqi Army Division. They're tied to a chair in front of a video camera on a tripod. They're beat to hell, and there's a nice pool of blood working the floor.

Corporal Moore sees the camera and the two guys who've been tortured. Real quiet he says, Whiskey Tango Foxtrot. But we all know what this is.

Lance Corporal McKeown looks at the camera and says, Al-Qaeda makes the worst pornos ever.

Moore looks over at the EPW, who we've got facedown on the deck, flexcuffed and blindfolded, and says, You son of a bitch cunt-ass SOB. Moore takes a step forward, but I stop him.

1st Fire Team unties the two guys and starts first aid. AQI used wire to strap them to the chairs and it's dug into their skin, so getting them loose is tricky without stripping off more flesh. Also, something's wrong with their feet. I say, Bring 'em to the CCP Doc's set up on the first deck. The house is clear now, whole thing took under two mikes, so pretty good except for Sweet, and that's a real motherfucker. Any groin injury's a nightmare wound.

In the basement there's a weapons cache, usual shit, AKs and RPKs, homemade explosive, RPGs, some rusty 122 mm arty shells. I leave that to Moore and go check on Sweet.

Upstairs, I see Doc's already pulled out the QuikClot and put it on the wound. A bad sign, and that QuikClot shit burns, but Sweet forces a grin. He gives me a thumbs-up, looks down at Doc working on his thigh, and says, Hey, Doc, you wanna give me a BJ while you're down there? Doc doesn't look up.

PFC Dyer's working on the hajji he shot in the face. I see he's pulled apart his own IFAK to get gauze for the hajji. Not supposed to do that. Your IFAK is for you.

Hajji's bad. It looks like half the jaw is gone. There's bits of the beard, still attached to skin, sitting on the other side of the room. Dyer's holding down hard on the gauze to stop the bleeding, and I can see he's got the look. So I grab Lance Corporal Weber and tell him to take over from Dyer, give him a break.

CH-46 touches down in under ten mikes. That's enough time for Sweet to stop joking and start saying the usual shit people say when they've been hit bad. I tell him we won't let him die. I don't know if I'm lying or not.

We take Sweet out with the hajji and the IP and the *jundi* and load 'em all up and they're off to TQ. I tell the squad Sweet's got a good shot. You make it to Surgical with a pulse, you'll probably leave with one.

Once the CASEVAC leaves, it's mostly waiting. I give the LT my SITREP. He passes it on to Ops and they tell him that the CO said, Bravo Zulu, whatever the fuck that means.

I make sure security's posted and that nobody's in a post-combat slump. I'm definitely not. Normally after a raid the adrenaline taps out and I want to curl up in a ball and take a nap. Not with Sweet up in the air, though.

The guys are posted right. Malrosio's team, God help us, in overwatch. Sweet's team is not in a good way.

Dyer's at one of the main room windows, but he's not really there. Not tactical. First, he's too close. Second, not even really scanning. An insurgent could probably walk up and grab his balls before he noticed. And Dyer's covered in blood, Sweet's and the hajji's, probably. Packing a wound isn't pretty. The sleeves of his flight suit are drenched.

I tell him, Come here. And since the main room's got two bodies, I tell Moore he's in charge for a second and walk Dyer to the kitchen and say, Strip.

He looks at me.

You can't wear those, I say.

He strips and I do too. I see the huge Superman *S* he got tattooed on his chest before deployment. Everyone makes fun of him for that, but I don't say anything now. I take off my flight suit and give it to him. I put my PPE back on, roll up Dyer's suit under my arm, and walk back out into the main room wearing just my boots, my flak, my skivvy shorts, and my Kevlar. My legs and arms haven't seen the sun in a while and are pale as pigeon shit. Moore sees me and starts smiling. McKeown sees Moore smiling and starts cracking up. I'm like, Fuck you, I look sexy.

LT's in a corner with Doc. He takes in my legs sticking out of my flak and doesn't smile, just says, Good thing you wore skivvies today.

I say, Hey, Doc, what the fuck? And I nod toward the door to the basement.

Doc shakes his head. Beat up pretty bad, he says. I think with hoses. A lot of lacerations all over their skin and the bottoms of their feet especially. And they took a power drill through their ankles, right at the joint, so they're pretty much fucked for life. Not life-threatening, though.

LT says, They were gonna videotape them.

Doc says, They put them up in front of the camera, like, "Get ready to die, *kuffar,*" and then realized they were out of film.

LT says, There's two more out there. The ones they sent to get film. Probably never see them again, but keep an eye. One might get stupid and try something.

Sir, I hope so, I say.

I go to tell the Marines, but the LT puts a hand on my shoulder. He says quietly, Sergeant, you ever seen anything like this before?

Sometimes I forget it's his first deployment. I shrug. Adrenaline's gone now, and I've got that deep tired. Not this, exactly, I say, but there's not much that'd surprise me. At least it's not kids.

LT nods.

Sir, I say, don't let yourself think about it until we're back in the States.

Right, he says. He looks out to the road and adds, Well, EOD's coming for the cache. They said don't fuck with anything.

I say, I don't play with bombs, sir.

He says, As soon as they're done, we go check on Sweet. He's at TQ.

He okay? I say.

He will be, he says.

I go check on my men. EOD comes pretty quick, and I see it's Staff Sergeant Cody's team. Cody's a down-home Tennessee boy, and he points to my bare legs and gives me a big old country grin.

When you're done fucking these hajjis, he says, you're supposed to put your pants back on.

While his team is dealing with the UXO, I deal with Dyer's flight suit. Moore gets me some gasoline from the basement, and we douse it and set it on fire. These things are supposed to be flame resistant, it's why we wear them, but it goes up fine.

Looking at the flames, I ask Moore, Were you gonna stomp that hajji downstairs?

Would've deserved it, he says.

Not the point, I say. Your Marines see you fucked up over this, then they start thinking about how fucked up it all is. And we don't have time to deal with that. We've got another patrol tomorrow.

LT walks over with a spare flight suit. Change, he says. We're going straight to TQ. Sweet's stabilized, but they're gonna fly him to Germany soon. IP and *jundi* are stabilized, too. Hajji didn't make it.

I take the flight suit and tell Moore, Pass

to the squad that Sweet's okay, and don't mention hajji dying.

I go back to the kitchen and change over, and by that time EOD's done, so we all roll.

As we're driving to TQ, McKeown says, Hey, at least we saved those guys' lives.

I say, Yeah, Second Squad to the motherfucking rescue.

Except I've got their eyes in my head. I don't think they wanted to be saved. After al-Qaeda sets you up in front of the video camera? And you've been beaten and tortured and drilled through and you think, Finally. Just let the head come off in one slice. That's what I'd be thinking. But then, guess what? Ha-ha, motherfucker. No film. So you're sitting, in pain, waiting to die, for who knows how long. There isn't exactly a Walmart nearby.

I didn't see any tears of joy when we burst in, M4s at the ready. They were dead men. Then we doped them up, CASEVAC'd them out, and they had to live again.

I think, for a second, maybe we should all breathe out tonight as a squad. Get drunk off Listerine and deal with this shit. But I don't want to pull that trigger unless I have to, and Sweet's still alive. Today's a good day. Save that shit for a bad day.

We roll into TQ, which is a huge FOB, all

U.S. and Coalition Forces. We all clear our weapons, bring them to Condition 4 at the gate. FOBs are basically safe. And crawling with contractors.

The road signs to the hospital are just like you'd see in the U.S., a blue square with a white H in the middle. And there's Marines driving civilian-type vehicles in their cammies, without body armor, just like you'd see in any base in the U.S. TQ Surgical's in the middle of the FOB, next to the Dark Tower, which is what the logistics guys call their command post. The road circles us around the tower, slowly edging closer. I've been here before.

We're quiet as we get close, and then McKeown says, Sergeant, that was really fucked up.

But now's not the time to have that conversation, so I say, Yeah, that's the most blood I've seen since I fucked your mom on her period. And then the guys laugh and bullshit a bit, and it breaks the mood that was settling. We get out of the Humvees and walk to TQ Surgical in the right head space.

Inside TQ Surgical, Sweet's awake but on an IV drip of the good stuff.

I feel good, he says, I've got my leg.

Another Marine had come in while Sweet was in surgery and things didn't go so well for him. Still, it was a good day for us.

Except while we're joking with Sweet, Dyer grabs a doc walking past and asks him how the hajji he shot in the face is doing. I try to catch Doc's eye so I can signal, Don't tell him hajji's dead, but it's not a problem. Doc's like, I have no idea which one you shot. Besides, al-Qaeda gets flown out to a high-security hospital after we stabilize 'em. Right now you won't find any here.

Then Dyer's standing there, off to the side. He's still in my flight suit, and he's swimming in it. I put a hand on his shoulder and say, You did good today, PFC. You took out the guy that shot Sweet.

Next ward over from Sweet, they've got the IP and the *jundi* we saved. I step out into the hall and peek in and there they are, fucked up, drugged up, and knocked out. It's nice in the hospital, not the blood and dust over everything like in the basement, but those two, even cleaned up, their bodies don't look like bodies should. Seeing them stops me for a second. I don't call the squad over because they don't need to see this.

After that, there's not much left to do but hit the DFAC. We're on a FOB, might as well get that good chow while we can. My guys deserve it. Maybe they need it. Besides, everyone says TQ's got the best chow hall in Anbar, and soon we'll be back in the COP.

The DFAC's about a klik away. It's a huge white barn of a building, two hundred meters long at least, a hundred wide, surrounded by a ten-foot fence topped with barbed wire. We show the Ugandan guards our IDs and walk through the gate. Inside, there's sinks you wash your hands at first, no eating with dirty fingers, and then there's a huge cafeteria line with KBR workers serving all kinds of shit. I'm not hungry, but I get some prime rib with horseradish sauce.

We sit down at a big table. The DFAC is pretty full, there's probably a thousand people eating there, and we're sitting between some Ugandans and some Marines and sailors from the TQ BOS.

I'm across from PFC Dyer, and he's not eating much. I'm next to some Navy O4 from the BOS, and he's chowing down. When he sees we aren't exactly FOBbits, he starts talking. I don't tell him what we're here for, I just say a little about our COP and how it's good to eat something that's not an MRE or the Iraqis' red shit and rice. He says, Y'all are lucky. You came here on a good day. It's Sunday. Sunday is cobbler day. And he points to a serving table in the rear of the DFAC where they're serving cobbler with ice cream.

So fuck it, when we finish we all get up to get some cobbler, except for Dyer. He says he's not hungry, but I tell him, "Eric. Get your ass up and get some fucking cobbler." So we go.

KBR's laid out all kinds. Cherry cobbler. Apple cobbler. Peach.

The O4 says cherry's the best. Roger that. I get the cherry. Dyer gets the cherry. We all get the fucking cherry.

Sit back down, I'm across from Dyer and he's looking at his ice cream melting into the cobbler. No good. I put a spoon in his hand. You've got to do the basic things.

After Action Report

In any other vehicle we'd have died. The MRAP jumped, thirty-two thousand pounds of steel lifting and buckling in the air, moving under me as though gravity was shifting. The world pivoted and crashed while the explosion popped my ears and shuddered through my bones.

Gravity settled. There'd been buildings before. Now headlights in the dust. Somewhere beyond, Iraqi civilians startling awake. The triggerman, if there even was one, slipping away. My ears were ringing and my vision was a pinpoint. I crawled my eyes up the length of the barrel of the .50-cal. The end was warped and blasted.

The vehicle commander, Corporal Garza, was yelling at me.

"The fifty's fucked," I screamed. I couldn't hear what he was saying.

I got down and climbed through the body of the MRAP. I went on my hands and knees across the seats and opened the back hatch. Then I stepped out.

Timhead and Garza were out already, Timhead posted on the right side of the vehicle while Garza checked the damage. Vehicle Three came up with Harvey in the turret to provide security. It was a tight street, just getting into Fallujah, and they parked off to the left of the MRAP, which was slumped down in the front like a wounded animal.

The mine rollers weren't even attached anymore. Their wheels were spread out everywhere, surrounded by bits of metal and other debris. One of the vehicle's tires was sitting a few feet out, cloaked in dust, looking like the big granddaddy of all the little baby mine roller wheels around it.

I wasn't quite steady on my feet, but training kicked in. I put my rifle in front, scanning the dark, trying to do my fives and twenty-fives, but the dust would have to settle before I could see more than five feet in front of me.

A light in one house glowed through the haze. It flickered, quickly dimming and brightening. My head rang and my back hurt. I must have slammed into the side of the turret.

Timhead and I stood on the right side of

the MRAP, oriented outboard. When the dust settled I saw Iraqi faces in a few shitty one-stories, looking out at us. One of them was the bomber, probably, waiting to see if there was gonna be a CASEVAC. They get paid extra for that.

The civilians were probably watching for it, too. You can't plant a bomb that big without the neighborhood knowing.

Since my heart was pumping fast, the pain throbbed in my back in superquick spurts.

Corporal Garza circled to the other side of the MRAP, assessing the damage. We stayed where we were.

"Fuck," I said.

"Fuck," said Timhead.

"You all right?" I said.

"Yeah."

"Me too."

"I feel fucking . . ."

"Yeah?"

"I don't know."

"Yeah. Me too."

There was a crack of rounds, like someone repeatedly snapping a bullwhip through the air. AK fire, close, and we were exposed. I had no turret to crouch down in, and only my rifle, not the .50. I couldn't see where the rounds were coming from, but I dropped back behind the side of the MRAP to get cover. I snapped back to training, but there was nothing to see as I scanned over my sights.

Timhead fired from the front of the MRAP. I fired where he was firing, at the side of the building with the flickering light, and I saw my rounds impact in the wall. Timhead stopped. So did I. He was still standing, so I figured he was okay.

A woman screamed. Maybe she'd been screaming the whole time. I stepped out from behind the MRAP and felt my balls tighten up close to my body.

As I approached Timhead, I could see more and more around the wall of the building. Timhead had his rifle at the ready, and that's where I kept mine. On the other side there was a woman in black, no veil, and maybe a thirteen- or fourteen-year-old kid lying on the ground and bleeding out.

"Holy shit," I said. I saw an AK lying in the dust.

Timhead didn't say anything.

"You got him," I said.

Timhead said, "No. No, man, no."

But he did.

We figured that the kid had grabbed his dad's AK when he saw us standing there and thought he'd be a hero and take a potshot at the Americans. If he'd succeeded, I guess he'd have been the coolest kid on the block. But apparently he didn't know how to aim, otherwise me and Timhead would have been fucked. He was firing from under fifty meters, a spray and pray with the bullets mostly going into the air.

Timhead, like the rest of us, had actually been trained to fire a rifle, and he'd been trained on man-shaped targets. Only difference between those and the kid's silhouette would have been the kid was smaller. Instinct took over. He shot the kid three times before he hit the ground. Can't miss at that range. The kid's mother ran out to try to pull her son back into the house. She came just in time to see bits of him blow out of his shoulders.

That was enough for Timhead to take a big step back from reality. He told Garza it wasn't him, so Garza figured I shot the kid, who everybody was calling "the insurgent" or "the hajji" or "the dumbshit hajji," as in, "You are one lucky motherfucker, getting fired on by the dumbest dumbshit hajji in the whole fucking country."

When we finished the convoy, Timhead helped me out of the gunner's suit. As we peeled it off my body, the smell of the sweat trapped underneath hit us, thick and sour.

Normally, he'd make jokes or complain about that, but I guess he wasn't in the mood. He hardly said anything until we got it off, and then he said, "I shot that kid."

"Yeah," I said. "You did."

"Ozzie," he said, "you think people are gonna ask me about it?"

"Probably," I said. "You're the first guy in MP platoon to . . ." I stumbled. I was gonna say "kill somebody," but the way Timhead was talking let me know that was wrong. So I said, "To do that. They'll want to know what it's like."

He nodded. I wanted to know what it was like, too. I thought about Staff Sergeant Black. He was a DI I'd had in boot camp, and the rumor was he'd beat an Iraqi soldier to death with a radio. He'd turned a corner and run smack into a hajji so close he couldn't bring his rifle around and he'd freaked, grabbed his Motorola, and bashed the guy's head in until it was pulp. We all thought that was badass. Staff Sergeant Black used to chew us out and say crazy shit like, "What you gonna do when you're taking fire and you call in arty and it blows that fucking building to fuck and you walk through and find pieces of little kids, tiny arms and legs and heads everywhere?" Or he'd ask, "What you gonna tell a nine-year-old girl who don't know her daddy's dead 'cause his legs is still twitching, but you know 'cause his brains is leaking out his head?" We'd say, "This recruit does not know, sir." Or, "This recruit does not speak Iraqi, sir."

Crazy shit. And crazy cool, if you're getting ready to face what you think will be real-deal no-shit war. I'd always wanted to get hold of Staff Sergeant Black after boot camp and ask him what had been bullshit and what was really in his head, but I never got a chance.

Timhead said, "I don't want to talk about it."

"So don't," I said.

"Garza thinks you did it."

"Yeah."

"Can we keep it that way?"

Timhead looked serious. I didn't know what to say. So I said, "Sure. I'll tell everyone I did it." Who could say I didn't?

That made me the only sure killer in MP platoon. Before the debrief, a couple guys came by. Jobrani, the only Muslim in the platoon, said, "Good job, man."

Harvey said, "I'd have got that motherfucker if fucking Garza and Timhead hadn't been in the way."

Mac said, "You okay, man?"

Sergeant Major came over to the MP area while we were debriefing. I guess she'd heard we had contact. She's the sort of sergeant major that always calls everybody "killer." Like, "How's it going, killer?" "Oo-rah, killer." "Another day in paradise, right, killer?" That day, when she walked up, she said, "How's it going, Lance Corporal Suba?"

I told her I was great.

"Good work today, Lance Corporal. All of you, good work. Oo-rah?"

Oo-rah.

When we were done, Staff Sergeant pulled me, Timhead, and Corporal Garza aside. He said, "Outstanding. You did your job. Exactly what you had to do. You good?"

Corporal Garza said, "Yeah, Staff Sergeant, we good," and I thought, Fuck you, Garza, on the other side of the fucking MRAP.

The lieutenant said, "You need to talk, let me know."

Staff Sergeant said, "Oo-rah. Be ready to do it tomorrow. We got another convoy. Check?"

Check.

Me and Timhead went right back to the can we shared. We didn't want to talk to anybody else. I got on my PSP, played *Grand*

Theft Auto, and Timhead pulled out his Nintendo DS and played *Pokémon Diamond.*

The next day, I had to tell the story.

"Then it was like, crack crack crack" — which it was — "and rounds off the fucking blown-up fucking mine rollers and me and Timhead see hajji with an AK and that was it. Box drill. Like training."

I kept telling the story. Everybody asked. There were follow-up questions, too. Yeah, I was like here, and Timhead was here . . . let me draw it in the sand. See that, that's the MRAP. And hajji's here. Yeah, I could just see him, poking around the side of the building. Dumbass.

Timhead nodded along. It was bullshit, but every time I told the story, it felt better. Like I owned it a little more. When I told the story, everything was clear. I made diagrams. Explained the angles of bullet trajectories. Even saying it was dark and dusty and fucking scary made it less dark and dusty and fucking scary. So when I thought back on it, there were the memories I had, and the stories I told, and they sort of sat together in my mind, the stories becoming stronger every time I retold them, feeling more and more true.

Eventually, Staff Sergeant would roll up

and say, "Shut the fuck up, Suba. Hajji shot at us. Lance Corporal Suba shot back. Dead hajji. That's the happiest ending you can get outside a Thai massage parlor. Now it's over. Gunners, be alert, get positive ID, you'll get your chance."

A week later, Mac died. MacClelland.

Triggerman waited for the MRAP to go past. Blew in the middle of the convoy.

Big Man and Jobrani were injured. Big Man enough to go to TQ and then out of Iraq. They say he stabilized, though he's got facial fractures and is "temporarily" blind. Jobrani just got a little shrapnel. But Mac didn't make it. Doc Rosen wouldn't say anything to anybody about it. The whole thing was fucked. We had a memorial service the next day.

Right before the convoy, I'd been joking with Mac. He'd got a care package with the shittiest candy known to man, stale Peeps and chocolate PEZ, which Mac said tasted like Satan's asshole. Harvey asked how he knew what Satan's asshole tasted like and Mac said, "Yo, son. You signed your enlistment papers. Don't act like you ain't have a taste." Then he stuck his tongue out of his mouth and waggled it around.

The ceremony was at the Camp Fallujah

chapel. The H& S Company first sergeant did the roll call in front of Mac's boot camp graduation photo, which they'd had Combat Camera print out and stick on poster board. They also had his boots, rifle, dog tags, and helmet in a soldier's cross. Or maybe it wasn't his stuff. Maybe it was some boots, rifle, and helmet they keep in the back of the chapel for all the memorials they do.

First Sergeant stood up front and called out, "Corporal Landers."

"Here, First Sergeant."

"Lance Corporal Suba."

"Here, First Sergeant," I said, loud.

"Lance Corporal Jobrani."

"Here, First Sergeant."

"Lance Corporal MacClelland."

Everybody was quiet.

"Lance Corporal MacClelland."

I thought I heard First Sergeant's voice crack a bit.

Then, as if he were angry that there was no response, he shouted, "Lance Corporal James MacClelland."

They let the silence weigh on us a second, then they played Taps. I hadn't been close with Mac, but I had to hold both my forearms in my hands to stop from shaking.

Afterward, Jobrani came up to me. He had a bandage on the side of his head where he got peppered with shrapnel. Jobrani's got a baby face, but his teeth were gritted and his eyes were tight and he said, "At least you got one. One of those fucks."

I said, "Yeah."

He said, "That was for Mac."

"Yeah."

Except I killed hajji first. So it was more like Mac for hajji. And I didn't even kill hajji.

In our can, Timhead and I never talked much. We'd get back and I'd play *GTA* and he'd play *Pokémon* until we were too tired to stay up. Not much to talk about. Neither of us had a girlfriend and we both wanted one, but neither of us was dumb enough to marry some forty-year-old with two kids in Jacksonville, like Sergeant Kurtz did two weeks before deployment. So we didn't have anybody waiting for us at home other than our moms.

Timhead's dad was dead. That's all I knew about that. When we did talk, we talked mostly about video games. Except there was a lot more to talk about now. That's what I figured. Timhead figured different.

Sometimes I'd look at him, focused on the Nintendo, and I'd want to scream, "What's going on with you?" He didn't seem different, but he had to be. He'd killed somebody. He had to be feeling something. It weirded me out, and I hadn't even shot the kid.

The best I could get were little signs. One time in the chow hall we were sitting with Corporal Garza and Jobrani and Harvey when Sergeant Major walked up. She called me "killer," and after she passed, Timhead said, "Yeah, killer. The big fucking hero."

Jobrani said, "Yo? Jealous?"

Harvey said, "It's okay, Timhead. You just ain't quick enough on the draw. Ka-pow." He made a pistol with his thumb and finger and mimed shooting us. "Man, I'd have been up there so fast, bam bam, shot his fuckin' hajji mom, too."

"Yeah?" I said.

"Yeah, son. Ain't no more terrorist babies be poppin' out of that cunt."

Timhead was gripping the table. "Fuck you, Harvey."

"Yo," said Harvey, the smile dropping from his face. "I was just playing, man. I'm just playing."

I wasn't getting good sleep. Neither was Timhead.

Didn't matter if we had a mission in four hours, we'd be in our beds, on the video games. I'd tell myself, I need it to come down. Some brainless time on the PSP.

Except it was every day, time I could be sleeping spent coming down. Being so tired all the time makes everything a haze.

One convoy we stopped for two hours for an IED that turned out to just be random junk, wires not going anywhere but looking suspicious as hell. I was chugging Rip Its, jacked up so much on caffeine that my hands were shaking, but my eyelids kept sliding down like they were hung with weights. It's a crazy feeling when your heart rate is 150 miles per hour and your brain is sliding into sleep and you know when the convoy gets going that if you miss something, it will kill you. And your friends.

When I got back I smashed my PSP with a rock.

I told Timhead, "I never even liked people calling me 'killer' before this bullshit."

"Okay," he said, "so suck it up, vagina."

I tried a different tack. "You know what? You owe me."

"How's that?"

I didn't answer. I stared him down, and he looked away.

"You owe me," I said again.

He laughed a weak little laugh. "Well, I

ain't gonna let you suck my dick."

"What's going on with you?" I said. "You okay?"

"I'm fine. What?"

"You know."

He looked down at his feet. "I signed up to kill hajjis."

"No, you fucking didn't," I said. Timhead signed up because his older brother had been in the MPs and got blown up in 2005, burns over his whole body, and Timhead joined to take his place.

Timhead looked away from me. I waited for him to respond.

"Yeah," he said. "Okay."

"You fucked in the head, man?"

"No," he said. "It's just weird."

"What do you mean?"

"My little brother's in juvie."

"I didn't know that."

There was a loud boom somewhere outside our can. Probably artillery going off.

"He's sixteen," said Timhead. "He set a couple fires."

"Okay."

"That's some dumb shit. But he's a kid, right?"

"Sixteen's only three years younger than me."

"Three years is a big difference."

"Sure."

"I was crazy when I was sixteen. Besides, my brother did it when he was fifteen."

We didn't say anything for a bit.

"How old you think that kid I shot was?"

"Old enough," I said.

"For what?"

"Old enough to know it's a bad fucking idea to shoot at U.S. Marines."

Timhead shrugged.

"He was trying to kill you. Us. He was trying to kill everybody."

"Here's what I see. Everything dust. And the flashes from the AK, going wild in circles."

I nod my head.

"And then I see the kid's face. Then the mom."

"Yeah," I said. "That's the shit, right there. I see that too."

Timhead shrugged. I didn't know what to say. After a minute, he went back to his game.

Two days later Jobrani and me opened up on a house after a SAF attack in Fallujah. I don't think I hit anything. I don't think Jobrani did either. When the convoy was done, Harvey gave Jobrani a high five and said, "Yeah, Jobrani. Jihad for America."

Timhead laughed and said, "I'm pretty sure you're still sleeper cell, Jobrani."

Afterward, I went and talked to Staff Sergeant. I told him everything Timhead said about the kid, but like it was me.

He said, "Look, it fucking sucks. Firefights are the scariest fucking thing you'll ever fucking face, but you handled it, right?"

"Right, Staff Sergeant."

"So, you're a man. Don't worry about that. Now all this other shit" — he shrugged — "it don't get easier. Fact you can even talk about it is a good thing."

"Thanks, Staff Sergeant."

"You want to go see the wizard about it?"

"No." There was no way I was going to let myself be seen going to Combat Stress over Timhead's bullshit. "No, I'm fine. Really, Staff Sergeant."

"Okay," he said. "You don't have to. Not a bad thing, but you don't have to." Then he gave me a grin. "But maybe you get religious, start hanging with the chaplain."

"I'm not religious, Staff Sergeant."

"I'm not saying really get religious. Just, Chaps is a smart guy. He's good to go. And hey, you start hanging with him, everybody's just, maybe you found Jesus or some bullshit."

■ ■ ■ ■

A week later another IED hit. I heard the explosion and turned back. Garza was listening to the lieutenant screaming something on the radio. I couldn't see to where they were. Could have been a truck in the convoy, could have been a friend. Garza said Gun Truck Three, Harvey's. I swiveled the .50-cal. around, looking for targets, but nothing.

Garza said, "They're fine."

That didn't make me feel better. It just meant I didn't have to feel worse.

Somebody said combat is 99 percent sheer boredom and 1 percent pure terror. They weren't an MP in Iraq. On the roads I was scared all the time. Maybe not pure terror. That's for when the IED actually goes off. But a kind of low-grade terror that mixes with the boredom. So it's 50 percent boredom and 49 percent normal terror, which is a general feeling that you might die at any second and that everybody in this country wants to kill you. Then, of course, there's the 1 percent pure terror, when your heart rate skyrockets and your vision closes in and your hands are white and your body is humming. You can't think. You're just an animal, doing what you've been trained to do. And then you go back to normal terror, and you go back to being a human, and you go back to thinking.

I didn't go to the chaplain. But a few days after Harvey got hit the chaplain came to me. That day, we'd waited three hours outside of Fallujah while EOD defused a bomb I'd spotted. The whole time I sat there thinking, Daisy chains, daisy chains, ambush, even though we were in the middle of fuck-all nowhere desert with nowhere to ambush us from and if the IED had been daisy-chained to another one, it would have gone off already. Still, I was stressed by the end. More than usual. When Corporal Garza reached up to grab my balls, which he sometimes does to fuck with me, I threatened to shoot him.

Then we got back and the Chaps just happened to drop by the can, and I thought, I'm gonna shoot Staff Sergeant, too. We went and talked by the smoke pit, which is a little area sectioned off with cammie netting. Somebody'd put a wooden bench there, but neither of us sat down.

Chaplain Vega's a tall Mexican guy with a mustache that looks like it's about to jump off his face and fuck the first rodent it finds. Kind of mustache only a chaps could get away with in the military. Since he's a Catholic chaplain and a Navy lieutenant, I wasn't sure whether to call him "sir," "Chaps," or "Father."

After he tried to get me to open up for a bit, he said, "You're being unresponsive."

"Maybe," I said.

"Just trying to have a conversation."

"About what? That kid I shot? Did Staff Sergeant ask you to talk to me about it?"

He looked at the ground. "Do you want to talk about it?"

I didn't want to. I thought about telling him that. But I owed it to Timhead. "That kid was sixteen, Father. Maybe."

"I don't know," he said. "I know you did your job."

"I know," I said. "That's what's fucked with this country." I realized, a second too late, I'd used profanity with a priest.

"What's fucked?" he said.

I kicked at a rock in the dirt. "I don't even think that kid was crazy," I said. "Not by hajji standards. They're probably calling him a martyr."

"Lance Corporal, what's your first name?" he said.

"Sir?"

"What's your first name?"

"You don't know?" I said. I wasn't sure why, but I was angry about that. "You didn't, I don't know, look me up before you came over here?"

He didn't miss a beat. "Sure I did," he said. "I even know your nickname, Ozzie. And I know how you got it."

That stopped me. "Ozzie" came from a bet Harvey made after Mac's lizard died in a fight with Jobrani's scorpion. Fifty bucks that I wouldn't bite its head off. Stupid. Harvey still hadn't paid me.

"Paul," I said.

"Like the apostle."

"Sure."

"Okay, Paul. How are you?"

"I don't know," I said. How was Timhead doing? That was what he was really about, even though he didn't know it. "I usually don't feel like talking to anyone about it."

"Yeah," said the Chaps, "that's pretty normal."

"Yeah?"

"Sure," he said. "You're a Catholic, right?"

That's what's listed on my dog tags. I wondered what Timhead was. Apathetic Protestant? I couldn't tell him that. "Yeah, Father," I said. "I'm Catholic."

"You don't have to talk to me about it,

but you can talk to God."

"Sure," I said, polite. "Okay, Father."

"I'm serious," he said. "Prayer does a lot."

I didn't know what to say to that. It sounded like a joke.

"Look, Father," I said. "I'm not that much for praying."

"Maybe you should be."

"Father, I don't even know if it's that kid that's messing with me."

"What else is there?"

I looked out at the row of cans, the little trailers they give us to sleep in. What else was there? I knew how I was feeling. I wasn't sure about Timhead. I decided to speak for myself. "Every time I hear an explosion, I'm like, That could be one of my friends. And when I'm on a convoy, every time I see a pile of trash or rocks or dirt, I'm like, That could be me. I don't want to go out anymore. But it's all there is. And I'm supposed to pray?"

"Yes." He sounded so confident.

"MacClelland wore a rosary wrapped into his flak, Father. He prayed more than you."

"Okay. What does that have to do with it?"

He stared at me. I started laughing.

"Why not?" I said. "Sure, Father, I'll pray. You're right. What else is there? Keep my fingers crossed? Get a rabbit's foot, like

Garza? I don't even believe in that stuff, but I'm going crazy."

"How so?"

I stopped smiling. "Like, I was on a convoy, stretched my arms out wide, and a minute later a bomb went off. Not in the convoy. Somewhere in the city. But I don't stretch out like that anymore. And I patted the fifty, once, like a dog. And nothing happened that day. So now I do it every day. So, yeah, why not?"

"That's not what prayer is for."

"What?"

"It will not protect you."

I didn't know what to say to that. "Oh," I said.

"It's about your relationship with God."

I looked at the dirt. "Oh," I said again.

"It will not protect you. It will help your soul. It's for while you're alive." He paused. "It's for while you're dead, too, I guess."

We took different routes all the time. Don't be predictable. It's up to the convoy commander, and they're all lieutenants, but most of them are pretty good. There's one who can't give an Op Order for shit but tends not to fuck up too bad on the road. And there's one female lieutenant who's tiny and real cute but tough as balls and knows her shit cold, so it evens out. Still, there's only so many routes, and you got to use one.

It was at night and I was in the lead vehicle when I spotted two hajjis, looked like they were digging in the road. I said, "Hajjis digging," to Garza. They saw us and started running.

This was just getting into Fallujah. There were buildings on the left side of the road, but they must have been spooked stupid because they ran the other way, across a field.

Garza was on the radio, getting confirmation. I should have just shot them. But I waited for an order.

"They're running," Garza was saying, "yes . . ." He twisted and looked up at me. "Light 'em up."

I fired. They were on the edge of the field by then, and it was dark. The flash of the .50 going off killed my night vision. I couldn't see anything, and we kept driving. Maybe they were dead. Maybe they were body parts at the edge of the field. The .50 punches holes in humans you could put your fist through. Maybe they got away.

There's a joke Marines tell each other.

A liberal pussy journalist is trying to get

the touchy-feely side of war and he asks a Marine sniper, "What is it like to kill a man? What do you feel when you pull the trigger?"

The Marine looks at him and says one word: "Recoil."

That's not quite what I felt, shooting. I felt a kind of wild thrill. Do I shoot? They're getting away.

The trigger was there, aching to be pushed. There aren't a lot of times in your life that come down to, Do I press this button?

It's like when you're with a girl and you realize neither of you has a condom. So no sex. Except you start fooling around and she gets on top of you and starts stressing you out. And you take each other's clothes off and you say, We're just gonna fool around. But you're hard and she's moving and she starts rubbing against you and your hips start bucking and you can feel your mind slipping, like, This is dangerous, you can't do this.

So that happened. It wasn't bad, though. Not like the kid. Maybe because it was so dark, and so far away, and because they were only shadows.

That night, I got Timhead to open up a bit. I started talking to him about how maybe I killed somebody.

"I'm bugging a little," I said. "Is this what it's like?"

He was quiet for a bit, and I let him think.

"For me," he said, "it's not that I killed a guy."

"Yeah?"

"It's like, his family was there. Right there."

"I know, man."

"Brothers and sisters in the window."

I didn't remember them. I'd seen all sorts of people around, eyes out of windows. But I hadn't focused in.

"They saw me," he said. "There was a little girl, like nine years old. I got a kid sister."

I definitely didn't remember that. I thought maybe Timhead had imagined it. I said, "It's a fucked-up country, man."

"Yeah," he said.

I almost went to the Chaps, but I went to Staff Sergeant instead.

"It's not that I killed a guy," I told him. "It's that his family was there."

Staff Sergeant nodded.

"There was this nine-year-old girl," I said. "Just like my sister."

Staff Sergeant said, "Yeah, it's a son of a

bitch." Then he stopped. "Wait, which sister?"

Both my sisters had been at my deployment. One's seventeen and the other's twenty-two.

"I mean . . ." I paused and looked around. "She reminded me of when my sister was little."

He had this look, like, "I don't know what to say to that," so I pressed.

"I'm really bugging."

"You know," he said, "I went and saw the wizard after my first deployment. Helped."

"Yeah, well, maybe I'll go after my first deployment."

He laughed.

"Look," he said, "it ain't like your sister. It's not the same."

"What do you mean?"

"This kid's Iraqi, right?"

"Sure."

"Then this might not even be the most fucked-up thing she's seen."

"Okay."

"How long we been here?"

"Two and a half months."

"Right. And how much fucked-up shit have we seen? And she's been here for years."

I supposed that was true. But you don't

just shrug off your brother getting shot in front of you.

"Look, this isn't even the wildest Fallujah's been. Al-Qaeda used to leave bodies in the street, cut off people's fingers for smoking. They ran torture houses in every district, all kinds of crazy shit, and you don't think the kids see? When I was a kid I knew about all the shit that was going on in my neighborhood. When I was ten this one guy raped a girl and the girl's brother was in a gang and they spread him out over the hood of a car and cut his balls off. That's what my brother said, anyway. It was all we talked about that summer. And Fallujah's way crazier than Newark."

"I guess so, Staff Sergeant."

"Shit. There's explosions in this city every fucking day. There's firefights in this city every fucking day. That's her home. That's in the streets where she plays. This girl is probably fucked up in ways we can't even imagine. She's not your sister. She's just not. She's seen it before."

"Still," I said. "It's her brother. And every little bit hurts."

He shrugged. "Until you're numb."

In the can the next night, after about thirty minutes of me staring at the ceiling while

Timhead played *Pokémon,* I tried to bring it up again. I wanted to talk about what Staff Sergeant had said, but Timhead stopped me.

"Look," he said, "I'm over it."

"Yeah?"

He put both his hands in the air, like he was surrendering.

"Yeah," he said. "I'm over it."

A week later a sniper shot Harvey in the neck. It was crazy, because he wasn't even hurt bad. The bullet barely grazed him. A quarter inch to the right, he'd be dead.

Nobody got positive ID. We kept driving, primed and ready to kill, but no targets.

As we moved down the road, my hands jittery with adrenaline, I wanted to scream, *"Fuck!"* as loud as I could, and keep screaming it through the whole convoy until I got to let off a round in someone. I started gripping the sides of the .50. When my hands were white, I would let go. I did that for a half hour, and then the rage left me and I felt exhausted.

The road kept turning under our wheels, and my eyes kept scanning automatically for anything out of place, signs of digging or suspicious piles of trash. It doesn't stop. Tomorrow we would do this again. Maybe get blown up, or get injured, or die, or kill somebody. We couldn't know.

At the chow hall later that day, Harvey pulled the bandage back and showed everyone his wound.

He said, "Purple fucking Heart, bitches! You know how much pussy I'm gonna get back home?"

My mind was whirling, and I made it stop.

"This is gonna be a badass scar," he said. "Girls'll ask and I'll be like, 'Whatever, I just got shot one time in Iraq, it's cool.' "

When we got back to the can that night, Timhead didn't even pull out his Nintendo DS.

"Harvey's so full of shit," he said. "Mr. Tough Guy."

I ignored him and started pulling off my cammies.

"I thought he was dead," said Timhead. "Shit. *He* probably thought he was dead."

"Timhead," I said, "we got a convoy in five hours."

He scowled down at his bed. "Yeah. So?"

"So let it go," I said.

"He's full of shit," he said.

I got under the covers and closed my eyes. Timhead was right, but it wouldn't do either of us any good to think about it.

"Fine," I said. I heard him moving around the room, and then he turned off the light.

"Hey," he said, quiet, "do you think —"

That did it. I sat up straight. "What do you want him to say?" I said. "He got shot in the neck and he's going out tomorrow, same as us. Let him say what he wants."

I could hear Timhead breathing in the dark. "Yeah," he said. "Whatever. It doesn't matter."

"No," I said. "It doesn't."

Bodies

For a long time I was angry. I didn't want to talk about Iraq, so I wouldn't tell anybody I'd been. And if people knew, if they pressed, I'd tell them lies.

"There was this hajji corpse," I'd say, "lying in the sun. It'd been there for days. It was swollen with gases. The eyes were sockets. And we had to clean it off the streets."

Then I'd look at my audience and size them up, see if they wanted me to keep going. You'd be surprised how many do.

"That's what I did," I'd say. "I collected remains. U.S. forces, mostly, but sometimes Iraqis, even insurgents."

There are two ways to tell the story. Funny or sad. Guys like it funny, with lots of gore and a grin on your face when you get to the end. Girls like it sad, with a thousand-yard stare out to the distance as you gaze upon the horrors of war they can't quite see.

Either way, it's the same story. This lieutenant colonel who's visiting the Government Center rolls up, sees two Marines maneuvering around a body bag, and decides he'll go show what a regular guy he is and help.

As I tell the story, the lieutenant colonel's a large, arrogant bear of a man with fresh-pressed cammies and a short, tight mustache.

"He's got huge hands," I'd say. "And he comes up to us and says, 'Here, Marine, let me help you with that.' And without waiting for us to respond or warn him off, he reaches down and grabs the body bag."

Then I'd describe how he launches up, as though he's doing a clean and jerk. "He was strong, I'll give him that," I'd say. "But the bag rips on the edge of the truck's back gate, and the skin of the hajji tears with it, a big jagged tear through the stomach. Rotting blood and fluid and organs slide out like groceries through the bottom of a wet paper bag. Human soup hits him right in the face, running down his mustache."

If I'm telling the story sad, I can stop there. If I'm telling it funny, though, there's one more crucial bit, which Corporal G had done when he'd told the story to me for the first time, back in 2004, before either of us had collected remains or knew what we were talking about. I don't know where G heard the story.

"The colonel screamed like a bitch," G had said. And then he'd made a weird, high-pitched keening noise, deep in his throat, like a wheezing dog. This was to show us precisely how bitches scream when covered in rotting human fluids. If you get the noise right, you get a laugh.

What I liked about the story was that even if it had happened, more or less, it was still total bullshit. After our deployment there wasn't anybody, not even Corporal G, who talked about the remains that way.

Some of the Mortuary Affairs Marines thought the spirits of the dead hung about the bodies. It'd creep them out. You could feel it, they'd say, especially when you look at the faces. But it got to be more than that. Midway through the deployment, guys started swearing they could feel spirits everywhere. Not just around the bodies, and not just Marine dead. Sunni dead, Shi'a dead, Kurd dead, Christian dead. All the dead of all Iraq, even all the dead of Iraqi history, the Akkadian Empire and the Mongols and the American invasion.

I never felt any ghosts. Leave a body in the sun, the outer layer of skin detaches from the lower, and you feel it slide around in your hands. Leave a body in water, everything swells, and the skin feels waxy and thick but recognizably human. That's all. Except for me and Corporal G, though, everybody in Mortuary Affairs talked about ghosts. We never said any different.

In those days I used to think, Maybe I'd handle it better if Rachel'd stayed with me. I didn't fit in at Mortuary Affairs, and nobody else would want to talk to me. I was from the unit that handled the dead. All of us had stains on our cammies. The smell of it gets into your skin. Putting down food is hard after processing, so by the end of the deployment we were gaunt from poor nutrition, sleep deprived from bad dreams, and shambling through base like a bunch of zombies, the sight of us reminding Marines of everything they know but never discuss.

And Rachel was gone. I'd seen it coming. She was a pacifist in high school, so once I signed my enlistment papers the thing we had going went on life support.

She would have been perfect. She was melancholy. She was thin. She always thought about death, but she didn't get off on it like the goth kids. And I loved her because she was thoughtful and kind. Even now, I won't pretend she was especially good-looking, but she listened, and there's a beauty in that you don't often find.

Some people love small towns. Everybody knows everybody, there's a real community you don't get in other places. If you're like me, though, and you don't fit in, it's a prison. So our relationship was half boyfriend/girlfriend, half cell mates. For my sixteenth birthday, she blindfolded me and drove me twenty miles out of town, to a high point off the interstate where you could watch the roads stretch out forever across the plains toward all the places we'd rather be. She told me her gift was this, the promise to come back here with me someday and keep going. We were so close for two years, and then I signed up.

It was a decision she didn't understand much more than I did. I wasn't athletic. I wasn't aggressive. I wasn't even that patriotic.

"Maybe if you'd joined the Air Force," she'd said. But I was tired of doing the weaker thing. And I knew that her talk about the future was just that, talk. She'd never leave. I didn't want to stay with her, work in a veterinarian's office, and be wistful. My ticket out of Callaway was what passed in our town for first class. The Marine Corps.

I told her, "What's done is done." It made

me feel like a tough guy from a movie.

Even still, we stayed together through boot camp. She wrote me letters while I was there, even sent me naked photos of herself. A few weeks earlier another guy'd gotten a package like that and the DIs had put the photos up in the bathroom stalls. The guy's girlfriend had worn a cheerleading uniform and stripped it off picture by picture. I remember thinking how glad I was that Rachel wasn't the kind of girl to send me something like that.

Mail call in boot camp works like this. One of the DIs stands at the front of the squad bay with all the platoon's mail while the platoon stands at attention in front of their racks. The DI calls out names one by one, and recruits run up and take their mail. If it's a package or an envelope that feels suspicious, the DI makes him open it right there. So when I opened Rachel's letter it was in front of the whole platoon and with Sergeant Kuba, my kill hat, glaring at me.

This wasn't the first time I'd had to open a letter with him watching. My parents had sent me photos of their vacation to Lakeside. That was no big deal, and I hadn't been worried. I didn't think my parents would send me naked photos. Rachel's name on the envelope, though, terrified me.

I opened it slowly, trying to come up with a plan if the photos turned out to be contraband.

The envelope had three glossy four-by-six prints that Rachel had developed herself in our high school's darkroom. When I pulled them out and saw her thin, pale, and very naked body, I didn't even look up for Sergeant Kuba's reaction. I stuffed the prints into my mouth, closed my eyes, and hoped for the best.

It's impossible to swallow three photographs at once, especially if you've only got two seconds before your kill hat has one hand on your face and the other on your throat while he screams and sprays spit at you.

The senior drill instructor, Staff Sergeant Kerwin, came running and broke us up. When Sergeant Kuba released my neck, I spat the pictures on the floor. Staff Sergeant Kerwin looked at me and said, "You must be fucking crazy, and I must be on the Marine Corps shit list if they give me a worthless fuck like you to turn into a Marine." Then he leaned in close and said, "Maybe I'll just kill you instead."

He told me to pick up the photos. It was hard because I was shaking and because all the other DIs were screaming at me. I tried to hold them so my hands covered Rachel's body. Only her face stared out, and her face in the photo seemed scared. She often looked like that in photos, because she didn't like how she looked when she smiled. There's no way she'd ever taken shots like that before.

"Rip them up," he said. It was a kindness.

I tore them, slowly, into smaller and smaller pieces, twisting and tearing them, making sure no one could put them back together. When they were in shreds, he turned and walked away, leaving me to the other DIs.

I had to eat the torn pieces while Sergeant Kuba delivered a lecture to all of us on how a true Marine wouldn't just share naked photos of his girlfriend with his platoon, but would let them run a train on her as well. Then he told them they were all fucked up if they'd tolerate an individual like me in their platoon, somebody who thought he was special, and he took them out back and thrashed them for a good twenty minutes while I stood at the position of attention and watched. Every night that week, he made me stand at the mirror and scream, "I'm not crazy, you are!" at my reflection for a half hour, and he hated me from then on and thrashed me pretty much continuously while I was there.

The next time I saw Rachel was after I graduated from boot camp. I showed up at her parents' place in my uniform. Dress blues are supposed to get you laid, but she started crying. She told me she didn't think she could stay with me if I went on a deployment, and I asked her to give me at least until I went to Iraq. She said yes. Ten months later, I was heading out. They'd given me the opportunity to deploy if I deployed with Mortuary Affairs, and I took it.

Rachel came to see me off. She gave me a sad little blow job the night before and told me we were done. In the military, the thing women are supposed to do if they love you is stay with you at least through deployment. Maybe divorce you a few months after you get back, but not before. Which meant, to my simple little mind, that she didn't love me. That she'd never loved me and that everything I'd felt so strongly about in high school was just me being childish. Which was okay, because I was going somewhere that would definitely make me a man.

Except what happened in Iraq was just what happened, nothing more. I don't think it made me any better than anyone else. It was months and months of awful. And the first weekend back we got a ninety-six, and Corporal G convinced me to go with him to Las Vegas.

"We need to get away from Iraq," he said, "and you don't get much more American than Vegas."

We didn't go to Vegas proper. We drove an extra thirty minutes to go to some local bar where, according to Corporal G, the drinks would be cheaper. If we struck out there, we could always leave and find some tourists looking to party.

I never liked G, but for clubbing he's the one to go out with if you want to get laid. He's got a whole system. He scopes the bar and talks to lots of girls early on. "Quantity is better than quality," he says. "It's all about planting seeds." In that first hour, he doesn't try to seal any deals or even stay with a group of girls for more than five minutes. "Make them think you've got better options," he says, "so they'll want to prove you wrong." He knows which girls to hit on at which parts of the night, which girls to say hi to but then bounce and leave wondering, and which girls to keep hitting on. Late in the night, when everyone's a bit looser and it doesn't take much to push them over the edge, he starts buying lots of shots. He never drinks any himself, though.

Girls like Corporal G. He's a tall workout freak with a trapezoid chest, a slew of shiny dress shirts, and dance moves right out of a music video. He avoids carbs, overloads on red meat, and shoots steroids immediately after any unit drug test. He can be charming, too, and he's ruthless when he gets going. If he likes a girl, he lets her know right away. "What's your name again?" he'll stop and say in the middle of a conversation. "I want to know for sure because I'm getting your number in two hours." It doesn't work every time, but it doesn't have to. Once a night is enough.

At the local bar, he did his best to set me up with a girl. She was thirty-eight years old. I know that for sure because she kept repeating it like it made her guilty, being with a bunch of twenty-somethings just old enough to drink. And she had a fifteen-year-old daughter who at that very moment was babysitting the son of this plump brunette Corporal G was targeting by the end of night.

"Fat girls fuck better 'cause they have to," he'd said as though dispensing great wisdom. "And they're easier, too, so it's a win-win."

I could tell the brunette liked him because she tried to convince her friend to like me, too. They'd talk off to the side, the brunette pointing at me from time to time. And when I'd ask Thirty-eight to dance, the brunette would give her an approving nod. None of that worked so well. Even on slow songs we'd dance so far apart I could picture her fifteen-year-old daughter standing in the open space between us. Then Corporal G bought her enough shots to get a grizzly bear wasted, and it was on.

Late in the evening, the brunette told us we were all too young, then asked how much we worked out and felt our pecs. She slipped her hand underneath my shirt and cupped my pec and squeezed, smiling at me the whole time with this drunk smile.

To me, that was crazy. I hadn't touched a woman since Rachel, let alone been touched by one. Just being close enough to a girl to smell her was enough. And then she touched me like that. And then she touched G, too. If she'd asked us to fight each other for her, I'm sure we would have done it.

Thirty-eight had her arm around me when we left the bar, but the cold air sobered her up a bit and she unhooked herself and walked to her friend, who was talking with G. He motioned to me.

"You get in their car," he said.

"What?"

He shot me an angry look, walked over, gripped his hand on my shoulder, and said into my ear, "You get in their car, deal's sealed."

The thing had a drunk logic to it, so I followed the two women to a lime green sedan and got in the backseat without asking if it was all right. The brunette got in and sat at the wheel. She wasn't sober enough to have any business driving, but she was sober enough to know it was weird having me in the back. Thirty-eight got in the passenger side, and we drove off, G behind us following in his car.

"So, where do you live?" I asked from my hostage's position in the backseat.

The brunette said a street name that meant nothing to me.

"Nice place?"

Neither bothered to answer. Thirty-eight fell asleep and smeared her cheek down the window of the car until she leaned forward enough that her head dropped and she startled and woke up again.

After about ten minutes we arrived at a one-story in a nice street filled with houses just like it, long ranch houses with big lawns and cactuses along the driveways. It confused me. I wouldn't have thought any woman who'd fuck some Marine on a one-night stand would have the money for a house like that.

G parked in the street, got out, and walked over. The brunette smiled when he put his arm around her, and then she opened the door and let us all into a big room with a huge L-shaped couch in front of the TV. She said I could sleep in the room off to the right, and while she was in the bathroom, G pushed me and Thirty-eight into it.

There was a low bed with Transformers sheets, toys on the dresser, and small shirts and pants on the floor. Thirty-eight looked drunk and tired and confused, and also like she might bolt. Now that we were out of the club, I could smell her perfume. She had a slender body, a dancer's body, and I thought I remembered her saying she taught ballet, but that could have been another woman. She had long black hair and small breasts, and her friend had touched me on the chest earlier, and I wanted her to touch me too.

I shut the door. She looked up at me like she was scared, and I was also scared, but I knew what I was supposed to do.

After Rachel, she was the second woman I'd ever slept with. The next morning we woke up, hung over, on those Transformers sheets, and she looked disgusted. Like I was unclean. Being in Mortuary Affairs, I knew that look well.

We didn't stay long. The brunette had to pick up her kid, so G and I went off to get breakfast at Waffle House. G's friend Haiti arrived in town later that morning, and I went off by myself and let G and Haiti do their thing. They ended up double-teaming some tourist, or at least they said they did. Either way, I'm glad I wasn't there.

It was another three weeks before I got home and everybody thanked me for my service. Nobody seemed to know exactly what they were thanking me for.

I called Rachel up and asked if we could hang out. Then I drove out to her parents' place. It's in a development on the edge of town that's full of shitty cookie-cutter houses laid out in twirly roads and cul-de-sacs. Rachel was living in their basement, which had been made out into a separate apartment. I went around to the back and down the stairs to the basement. Within a second of me knocking, she opened the door.

"Hi," I said.

"Hi."

She looked different from what I remembered. She'd gained weight, in the best way. Her shoulders had fleshed out. She had curves. She looked healthier, stronger, better. I was greyhound lean, and she'd never seen me like that.

"It's good to see you," she said, and then she smiled like it'd just occurred to her that that was the right thing to do. "You want to come in?"

"Yeah. I do," I said. The words came quick and nervous. I forced a smile and she backed away as I walked through the door, but then changed her mind and stepped forward to hug me.

I held on and she tensed, after a second. She moved out of range and then spread her hands apart, as if to say, "This is my place."

It was all one room, a bed with sky blue sheets and a desk shoved in a corner, exposed pipes running down the ceiling, and water damage streaking the walls, but she had a kitchen and a bath and, I guess, no rent. Better than the barracks, anyway. It looked completely different from when her parents had used it as a game room and we'd used it as a place to make out.

On the floor by the fridge, I saw a small water and food bowl. "That's Gizmo's," she said. Then she called out, "Gizmo."

She turned away from me. I looked around, too. We couldn't see him, so I got down on my hands and knees and peeked under the bed and saw eyes. A slender gray cat edged forward. I put out my hand for him to sniff and waited.

"Come on, cat," I said, "I've been defending your freedom. At least let me pet you."

"Come on, Gizmo," Rachel said.

"Is he a pacifist, too?" I asked.

"No," she says. "He kills cockroaches. I can't get him to stop."

Gizmo edged a little toward my hand and sniffed.

"I like you, cat," I said. I scratched him behind the ears and then stood up and grinned at her.

"Well," she said.

"Right." I looked for a place to sit. The basement had only one chair. Optimistically, I sat on the bed. She pulled the chair over and faced me.

"So," she said. "How you doing? Okay?"

I shrugged. "Okay."

"What was it like?"

"I'm glad you wrote," I said. "Letters from home mean a lot."

She nodded. I wanted to tell her more. But I'd just got there, and she looked so much more beautiful than I remembered, and I didn't know what would happen if I started talking for real.

"So," I said, "any new boyfriends or anything?" I gave her a smile to let her know it'd be okay if there were.

She frowned. "I don't think that's a fair question."

"Really?" I said.

"Yeah," she said. She folded down her skirt with her hands and left them resting in her lap.

"You look great," I said.

I leaned over, closer to her, and put my hand over hers. She pulled her hands back.

"I didn't shave my legs today," she said.

"Neither did I," I said.

And then, since I wanted to and since I'd been to Iraq and since why not, I put my hand on her thigh, just by her knee. She put her hand on my wrist and gripped it. I thought she was going to pull my hand off, but she didn't.

"It's just," she said, "so I wouldn't, you know —"

"Yeah yeah yeah," I said, stopping her. "Absolutely. Me too."

I have no idea what I meant by that, but it felt like agreeing with her was the right thing to do. She let go of my wrist, at least.

The warmth of her thigh under my hand was killing me. That deployment, I'd spent a lot of time being cold. Most people don't think you'd be cold in Iraq, but the desert's got nothing to keep the heat in, and not every month is summer. I felt there was something important I had to say to her, or something she had to say to me. Maybe tell her about the rocks.

"It's good to see you," she said.

"You said that already."

"Yeah." She looked down at my hand, but I wasn't about to take it off her thigh. Back in high school, she'd said she loved me. I still deserved that much. Besides, I was exhausted. Talking to her had never been this difficult, but touching her felt as nice as it always had.

"Listen," I said, "do you want to lie down?" I nodded toward the bed and she drew back, so I added, "Not to do anything. Just . . ." I didn't know what.

I looked at her and thought, She's going to say no. I could taste it, hanging in the air.

"Listen," I said again, and ran out of words. The room got narrower and tighter, the way the world does when you're pumping adrenaline.

"Listen," I said again, "I need this."

When I said it, I didn't look at her. Just at my hand on her thigh. I didn't know what I'd do if she said no.

She got up from her chair. I let out a long breath. She walked to the side of the bed, stood there a second, and then lay down, facing away from me. She'd agreed.

Crazy thing was, now I didn't want to. I mean, to curl up with this girl, who'd made me beg? I was a veteran. Who was she?

I sat there for a second. But there was nothing else to do in that room but get down on the bed.

I lay on my side, next to her, and spooned her body, fitting my hips against hers and resting my right arm across her waist. There was a warmth to her that flowed into me, and though she was tense at first, like she'd been earlier, she relaxed after a bit and it stopped feeling like I was grabbing her and more like we were fitting into each other. I relaxed, too, all the sharp edges of my body lost in the feel of her. Her hips, her legs, her hair, the nape of her neck. Her hair smelled like citrus, and her neck smelled softly of sweat. I wanted to kiss her there, because I knew I'd taste salt.

There were times, after dealing with the remains, when I'd grab a piece of my flesh and pull it back so I could see it stretch, and I'd think, This is me, this is all I am. But that's not always so bad.

We stayed on the bed for maybe five

minutes, me saying hardly anything, just breathing, buried in her hair. The cat jumped up on the bed and joined us, pacing about at first and then settling down near her head and watching us. Rachel started telling me about him in a quiet voice — how long she'd had him, how she got him, and the funny things he did. She was talking about something she loved, so the words came easy, and it was nice to hear a sound so natural. I listened to her voice and felt her breathe. When she ran out of things to say, we lay there and I thought, How long can we stay like this?

That close to her, I was afraid I'd get hard. I wanted to kiss her. There was no one but me and her in that room, and I knew she didn't want me. In that little system of me and her, I was the nothing. I had this sense of looking at myself from above, like all of my wanting her was there in my body and I was outside of it, watching. I knew if I crawled back into my skull, I'd start begging.

I rolled onto my back and looked at the ceiling. The cat got up, too, and walked to the headboard, rubbing himself against it. Rachel turned toward me.

"I've got to go," I said, even though I didn't have to go or even have anywhere I'd rather be.

She said, "How long are you around?"

"Not long," I said. "Mostly seeing family."

I wanted to hurt her, somehow. Maybe tell her about the woman in Vegas. But I said, "It was great seeing you."

And she said, "Yeah, it was great."

I sat up and put my feet over the side of the bed, facing away from her. I waited, hoping she'd say something else. The cat jumped off the bed and over to his food bowl, sniffed, and turned away.

Then I got up and walked out the door without looking back. As I went up the steps and through her backyard, I tried not to think about anything. And when that didn't work, I tried to remember the name of the woman in Vegas, like if I did, it would protect me.

That woman, Thirty-eight, had seemed so unwilling. I was almost certain that what happened with her couldn't be called rape. She made no complaint, never said, "No," never resisted. She never said anything. After a few minutes, she even started bucking her hips toward me in a sort of mechanical way. She was so drunk, I guess it'd be hard to say if she wanted it one way or the other, but if she had really objected, I think she'd have said something to try to stop me.

How drunk the girl was, whether she really wanted you or whether she let you, or was scared of you, that doesn't bother most Marines when they get laid on a Friday night. Not as far as I can tell. I doubt it bothers college frat kids, either. But walking back from Rachel's, it started to really bother me.

I was quiet when I got home, and I was quiet later that night when I went out drinking with a few friends from high school. They weren't close friends. I didn't have close friends from high school. I'd spent all my time with Rachel. But they were good guys to share a beer with.

As the night wore on, more and more people came into the bar, and it got to be a regular high school reunion. I kept wondering if maybe Rachel would show, but of course she didn't. I drank more than I usually do. It made me start wanting to tell stories.

One of the guys there, who was a few years older, told me he had a cousin who'd died in Iraq. At first I thought, Maybe I processed him. But the cousin died before I got in country.

The guy was a mechanic, and he seemed like a sympathetic sort of guy. He didn't talk about killing hajjis or act like it was so awesome I'd been over there. He just said, "That must have been rough," and left it at that. I don't remember his name. Once I got drunk enough, I told him what I'd wanted to tell Rachel.

It was a story about the worst burn case we ever had. Worst not in charring or loss of body parts, just worst.

This Marine had made it out of his vehicle only to die in flames beside it. The other MPs from his unit had taken his remains from the pile of trash and gravel where he died and brought him to us. We documented his wounds, distinguishing marks, and missing body parts. Most of what made it through the fire was standard. He had the Rules of Engagement in his left breast pocket. The flak had protected it, although the laminate had melted and the words were illegible. He had charred boots and dog tags and bits of uniform. Some plastic mess in a butt pack we couldn't identify. A wallet where the credit cards and IDs had melted into a solid block. There was no Kevlar, which he must have been wearing but which didn't make it to us.

Some of the remains we dealt with would have very personal items, like a sonogram or a suicide note. This one had nothing.

The hands, though, were clenched around

two objects. We had to work at them carefully to pry them out. Corporal G had the left hand. I had the right. "Careful," he said. "Careful. Careful. Careful." He was saying it to himself.

While I worked, I tried to avoid looking at the face. We all did that. I focused on the hands and what might be inside. Personal effects are important to the families.

We worked, slowly, carefully loosening the fingers. Corporal G finished first. He held up a small rock, probably from the gravel pile. After a minute, that's the same thing I found in the right hand. A little gray rock, mostly round, but with a few rough edges. It was embedded into his palm. I tore skin getting it out.

A few days later, Corporal G talked to me about it. We'd had more remains come through since then, and normally Corporal G never said anything about any of the remains once we'd finished processing them. We were smoking outside the chow hall, looking toward Habbaniyah, and he said, "That guy could have been holding on to anything."

I tried to tell the story to the mechanic. I was very drunk, and the guy tried very hard to listen.

"Yeah," he said softly, "yeah. It's crazy." I

could tell he was searching for the right thing to say. "Look, I'm gonna tell you something."

"Okay," I said.

"I respect what you've been through," he said.

I took a sip of my beer. "I don't want you to respect what I've been through," I said.

That confused him. "What do you want?" he said.

I didn't know. We sat and drank beer for a bit.

"I want you to be disgusted," I said.

"Okay," he said.

"And," I said, "you didn't know that kid. So don't pretend like you care. Everybody wants to feel like they're some caring person."

He didn't say anything else, which was smart. I waited for him to say something wrong, to ask me about the war or the Marine that died or the rocks that G and me had kept with us, that I still had in my pocket that night at the bar. But he didn't say another word, and neither did I. And that was that for me telling people stories.

I hung out in my parents' house for another week, and then I went back to Twentynine Palms and the Marine Corps. I never saw Rachel again, but we're Facebook friends. She got married while I was on my third deployment. She had her first kid while I was on my fourth.

OIF

EOD handled the bombs. SSTP treated the wounds. PRP processed the bodies. The 08s fired DPICM. The MAW provided CAS. The 03s patrolled the MSRs. Me and PFC handled the money.

If a sheikh supported the ISF, we distributed CERP. If the ESB destroyed a building, we gave fair comp. If the 03s shot a civilian, we paid off the families. That meant leaving the FOB, where it's safe, and driving the MSRs.

I never wanted to leave the FOB. I never wanted to drive the MSRs or roll with 03s. PFC did. But me, when I got 3400 in boot camp, I thought, Great. I'd work in an office, be a POG. Be the POG of POGs and then go to college for business. I didn't need to get some, I needed to get the G.I. Bill. But when I was training at BSTS, they told me, You better learn this, 3400s go outside the wire. A few months later, I was strapped up, M4 in Condition 1, surrounded by 03s, backpack full of cash, twitchiest guy in Iraq.

I did twenty-four missions, some with Marine 03s, some with National Guardsmen from 2/136. My last mission was to AZD. A couple of Iraqis had driven up fast on a TCP. They ignored the EOF, the dazzlers and the warning shots, and died for it. I'd been promoted to E4, so PFC was taking over consolation payments, but I went with him to give a left-seat right-seat on working off the FOB. PFC always needed his hand held. In the HMMWV it was me, PFC, PV2 Herrera, and SGT Green. Up in the turret on the 240G was SPC Jaegermeir-Schmidt, aka J-15.

There wasn't a lot to look at on the MSR south of HB. We scanned for all the different types of IEDs AQI would throw at us. IEDs made of old 122 shells, or C4, or homemade explosives. Chlorine bombs mixed with HE. VBIEDs in burned-out cars. SVBIEDs driven by lunatics. IEDs in drainage ditches or dug into the middle of the road. Some in the bodies of dead camels. Others daisy-chained together — one in the open to make you stop, another to kill you where you stand. IEDs everywhere, but most missions, nothing. Even knowing how bad the MSRs were, knowing we could die, we got bored.

PFC said, "It'd be cool to get IED'd, 'long as no one got hurt."

J-15 snapped, said, "That's bad juju, that's worse than eating the Charms in an MRE."

Temp was 121, and I remember bitching about the AC. Then the IED hit.

PV2 swerved and the HMMWV rolled. It wasn't like the HEAT trainer at Lejeune. JP-8 leaked and caught fire, burning through my MARPATs. Me and SGT Green got out, and then we pulled PV2 out by the straps of his PPE. But PV2 was unconscious, and I ran back for PFC, but he was on the side where the IED hit, and it was too late.

PFC's Eye Pro cracked and warped in the heat. The plastic snaps on his PPE melted. And even though J-15 left his legs behind, at least he got CASEVAC'd to the SSTP and died on the table. PRP had to wash PFC out with Simple Green and peroxide.

The MLG awarded me a NAM with a V. Don't see too many 3400s got a NAM with a V. It's up there next to my CAR and my Purple Heart and my GWOT Expeditionary and my Sea Service and my Good Cookie and my NDS. Even 03s show respect when they see it. But give me a NAM with a V, give me the Medal of Honor, it doesn't change that I'm still breathing. And when people ask what the NAM is for, I say it's so I don't feel bad that I was too slow for PFC.

In boot camp, the DIs teach you Medal of Honor stories. Most recipients were KIA. Their families didn't get a homecoming, they got a CACO knocking on their door. They got SGLI. They got a trip to Dover to see Marines lift the remains out of a C-130. They got a closed casket, because IEDs and SAF don't leave pretty corpses. The DIs tell you these stories over and over, and even a POG like me knows what they mean.

So I tell my family, "I'm staying in — the G.I. Bill can wait." And I tell my OIC, "Sir, I want to go to OEF. OEF's where the fight is now." And I tell my girlfriend, "Okay, leave me." And I tell PFC, "I wish it'd been me," even though I don't mean it.

I'm going to OEF. As a 3400. As a POG, but a POG with experience. I'll distribute CERP again. I'll roll with 03s again. And maybe I'll get IED'd again. But this time, out on the MSRs, I will be terrified.

I will remember the sounds PFC made. I will remember that I was his NCO, so he was my responsibility. And I will remember PFC himself as though I loved him. So I won't really remember PFC at all — not why I gave him low PRO/CONs, not why I told him he'd never make E4.

Instead I will remember that our HMMWV had 5 PX. That the SITREP was 2 KIA, 3 WIA. That KIA means they gave everything. That WIA means I didn't.

Money as a Weapons System

Success was a matter of perspective. In Iraq it had to be. There was no Omaha Beach, no Vicksburg Campaign, not even an Alamo to signal a clear defeat. The closest we'd come were those toppled Saddam statues, but that was years ago. I remember Condoleezza Rice declaring that civil administration and police functions had no part in a military campaign. "We don't need to have the 82nd Airborne," she said, "escorting kids to kindergarten." In 2008, around the time I got there, the 82nd Airborne was building greenhouses near Tikrit. It was a brave new world, and as a Foreign Service Officer heading an embedded Provincial Reconstruction Team, I was right at the heart of it.

Touching down in Camp Taji, I was nervous, and not simply because of the danger. I wasn't sure I belonged. I hadn't believed in the war when it started, though I did believe in government service. I also knew my career would be helped by time in Iraq. The team I'd be leading had already been in country for a while. I was the only Foreign Service Officer of the group, but the sum total of my experience doing reconstruction consisted of a few college summers in Alabama working for Habitat for Humanity. I didn't think it would help.

My colleagues had, theoretically, been hired for actual skills. As I exited the helicopter and headed toward a heavyset man holding a piece of paper with my name scrawled on it, I had the nagging impression that he would see through me to what I feared I was — a fraud and a war tourist.

It came as a surprise, then, when the man holding the sign — Bob, our ePRT's one ex-military team member — cavalierly informed me that he'd signed up on a 3161 as a lark. He laughed about it, as though his lack of commitment were funny, while he escorted me to the Nissan pickup truck the ePRT used to get around base. "I never did anything like this before," he said. "I never even figured I'd pass the physical. I've got a heart murmur. But there was no physical. There wasn't even an interview. They called me up and told me I was hired, straight off the résumé."

Bob, I quickly learned, had an existential view of the Iraq war. We were fighting in Iraq because we were fighting in Iraq. His was not to reason why, his was but to receive a $250,000 salary with three paid vacations and little expectation of tangible accomplishments.

"Cindy's a true believer," Bob said as he drove us to the ePRT office. "Fighting the fight of good versus evil. Democracy versus Islam. All that Sunday school shit. Careful with her."

"What is she working on?"

"She's our women's initiative adviser," said Bob. "She used to be on a local school board back in wherever the fuck she's from. Kansas or Idaho or something. She handles our women's business association, and she's starting an agricultural project for widows."

"She knows about farming?" I said hopefully.

"Nope, but I taught her how to Google."

He parked the car outside a rickety hut made of plywood, which, he announced, was our office. Inside were two rooms, four desks, a long series of power strips, and a skinny little woman in her mid-fifties, peering intently at her computer screen.

"There's two hundred fifty squirts in a gallon of milk!" she said.

Bob silently mouthed the word *Google.* Then he announced, "Cindy. Our fearless leader is here."

"Oh my," she said, springing out of her seat and walking over to shake my hand. "Sure glad to meet you!"

"I hear you're working on an agricultural initiative," I said.

"And a health clinic," she said. "That'll be tough, but it's what the women tell me they need."

I looked around the room.

"You can take either of the empty desks," said Bob. "Steve won't be using his."

"Who's Steve?" I said.

"The other contractor we were supposed to have," said Cindy. She made a sad face. "He got pretty badly injured on his first day."

"His first day?" I said. I looked over at the eerily empty desk in the back room. This was, I thought, a war zone. Death and disfigurement were possibilities for all of us.

"When he flew in to Taji," Bob said, smirking, "he jumped out of the Black Hawk action-movie style, like he was gonna have to sprint through machine-gun fire to get to safety. Shattered his ankle with his very first step."

■ ■ ■ ■

After I'd settled in, Bob oriented me to the AO, taking me to the large map hanging in our office and breaking down the region.

"Here's us," he said, pointing at Camp Taji. "To the east you've got the Tigris. There's a few old palaces on the western banks, and the other side is farming. Fruit groves. Oranges. Lemons. That weird fruit. What's it called?"

"Pomegranate?" I said.

"No. I like pomegranate. That stuff —" He waved his hands and grimaced, then pointed back to the east side of the Tigris on the map. "This section's all Sunni, so during Saddam, they did all right. It's less slummy."

"Less slummy?" I said.

"Until the highway. Route Dover" — Bob pointed to a road running north and south — "that's the dividing line. West of Dover, Sunnis. East of Dover, slums, shit land, a little farming irrigated by the canal." He pointed to a thin blue line running out of the Tigris, forming the southern border of the map. "Above that there's not much good farming. There's a water treatment plant here" — he pointed to a black spot on the map unconnected to any marked roads — "there's an oil refinery out to the east, and here's JSS Istalquaal."

"JSS," I said. "That means there's Iraqi units there."

"National Police," he said. "And two companies from the BCT. Sunni police stay on the Sunni side, Shi'a stay on the Shi'a side, but the National Police cross over."

"What are the National Police like?" I said.

"They're Shi'a death squads," he said, smirking.

"Oh."

"South of the canal is Sadr City. No one goes there except U.S. SpecOps looking to kill somebody. Istalquaal is the closest JSS in our AO to it."

I looked up at the map. "USAID claims agriculture should be employing thirty percent of the population," I said.

"Right," said Bob, "but the whole system broke down after we trashed the state-run industries."

"Fantastic," I said.

"It wasn't my idea," said Bob. "We remade the Ministry of Agriculture on free market principles, but the invisible hand of the market started planting IEDs."

"Okay," I said, "but this region" — I pointed to the Shi'a areas — "needs water for irrigation."

"West of Dover, too," he said. "Irrigation systems need maintenance, and nobody's been doing much of that."

I tapped the dark spot he'd said was a water treatment plant. "Is this operational?"

Bob laughed. "We sunk about 1.5 million dollars' worth of IRRF2 funds into it a couple years back."

"What'd that buy us?"

"No idea," Bob said. "But the chief engineer has been asking for a meeting."

"Great," I said. "Let's do it."

Bob shook his head and rolled his eyes.

"Look," I said, "I know there's a limit to what I can do. But if I can do one small thing —"

"Small?" said Bob. "A water treatment plant?"

"It's probably the best thing we could —"

"I've been here longer than you," said Bob.

"Okay."

"If you want to succeed, don't do big ambitious things. This is Iraq. Teach widows to raise bees."

"Raise bees?" I said.

"Beekeep?" he said. "Whatever. Grow honey. Get five widows some beehives —"

"What are you talking about?"

"I've got an Iraqi who can sell us the

hives, and an Iraqi local council saying they'll support the project —"

"Bob," I said.

"Yes?" he said.

"What the hell are you talking about?"

"The embassy likes completed projects supporting Lines of Engagement."

"Which has what to do with getting five widows beekeeping?"

Bob folded his arms and looked me over. He pointed to the opposite wall, where we had a poster outlining the LOEs. "Give someone a job. That's economic improvement. Give women a job. That's women's empowerment. Give a widow a job. That's aiding disenfranchised populations. Three LOEs in one project. Widow projects are gold. With the council supporting it, we can say it's an Iraqi-led project. And it'll cost under twenty-five thousand dollars, so the funding will sail through."

"Five widows with beehives."

"I think it's called an apiary," he said.

"Beekeeping," I said, "is not going to help."

"Help what?" said Bob. "This country is fucked whatever you do."

"I'm going to focus on water," I said. "Let's get that plant running."

"Okay," he said. He shook his head, then

looked up and smiled amiably. He seemed to have decided I could go to hell my own way. "Then we should get you to one of the companies at Istalquaal."

"Istalquaal," I said, trying out the sound of the word, eager to get it right.

"I think that's how you say it," Bob said. "It means freedom. Or liberation. Something."

"That's nice," I said.

"They didn't name it," he said. "We did."

It took six weeks to get to the plant. Three weeks alone trying to get Kazemi, the chief engineer, on the phone. Another three trying to nail down the specifics. Kazemi had an annoying habit of answering questions about dates and times the way a Zen master answers questions about enlightenment. "Only the mountains do not meet," he'd say, or, "The provisions for tomorrow belong to tomorrow."

Meanwhile, Cindy's women's health clinic took off. She set it up on the Sunni side of the highway, and the number of patients increased steadily each week. I didn't have much to do on the water front, and sitting around waiting for Kazemi to get back to me was enough to drive me insane, so I decided to get myself personally involved in the clinic. I didn't really trust Cindy with it. I thought she was too earnest to handle something important, and the more she told me, the more I thought the project was genuinely worthwhile.

In Iraq, it's hard for women to see a doctor. They need a man's permission, and even then a lot of hospitals and small clinics won't serve them. You'll see signs reading, "Services for Men Only," sort of like the old "Irish Need Not Apply" signs that my great-great-grandfather had to deal with.

Health services were the hook to draw people in, but key to the broader functioning of the clinic were Najdah, a dogged social worker, and her sister, the on-staff lawyer. Every woman who came in was interviewed first, ostensibly for the clinic to find out what health services they needed but actually to allow us to find out what broader services we could provide. The problems of women in our area went far beyond untreated urinary tract infections, though those were often quite severe — women's problems were usually not sufficient pretext for a man to allow his wife or daughter or sister to go see the doctor, and health issues we think of as minor in the United States had a tendency to snowball. One woman's UTI scarred her kidneys so badly, she was risking organ failure.

The clinic also helped women needing divorces, women suffering domestic violence, women not getting the public assistance they were entitled to, and women who wanted to file claims against Coalition Forces to get compensation for relatives they'd accidentally killed. One girl, a fourteen-year-old victim of gang rape, came in because her family planned to sell her to a local brothel. This wasn't uncommon for girls whose rapes destroyed their marriage prospects. It was actually a kinder option than the honor killings that still sometimes happened.

Najdah and the staff lawyer would do their best to help these women out, occasionally raising their concerns with the local councils and power brokers. They didn't try to "liberate" the Iraqi women — whatever that means — or turn them into entrepreneurs. Najdah and her staff listened to them and helped them with their actual problems. In the case of the fourteen-year-old, Najdah had a friend on the police force raid the girl's home as well as the brothel. The girl went to prison. For her, it was the best alternative.

I made a few trips out to the clinic and had started thinking about expanding the idea to other communities when Kazemi finally got back to us with concrete ideas for a meeting. I arranged things with him and then tried to set up a convoy with one of the units at Istalquaal.

"Nobody's been that way in a long time," one company commander told me over the phone. "There's probably IEDs there from '04. We have no idea what we might hit."

That's not something you want to hear from a hardened soldier. I'd already done a couple convoys by the time I got to Istalquaal, but the memory of that assessment and the wary nervousness of the soldiers there gave me what, in the military, they refer to as a "high pucker factor." The platoon that eventually took me out had clearly drawn the last straw. They all knew it. "Let's go get blown up," I overheard one soldier saying to another. When we got on the road, my only comfort was the obvious boredom of my translator, a somewhat short and pudgy Sunni Muslim everybody referred to as "the Professor."

"Why do they call you the Professor?" I asked him.

"Because I was a professor," he said, taking off his glasses and rubbing them as if to emphasize the point, "before you came and destroyed this country."

We were getting off to an awkward start. "You know," I said, "when this all started I opposed the war. . . ."

"You have baked Iraq like a cake," he said, "and given it to Iran to eat."

He sniffed and folded his arms over his belly and closed his eyes. I pretended something on the side of the road had caught my eye. Most translators would never say anything like that to an American. We sat in silence for a while.

"Istalquaal," I finally said, trying to draw him out. "Does it mean freedom, or liberation?"

He opened his eyes a crack and looked at me sidelong. "Istalquaal? *Istiqlal* means independence," he said. "Istalquaal means nothing. It means Americans can't speak Arabic."

It was rumored the Professor had blood on his hands from the Saddam days. Whether that was true or not, he was our best interpreter. On the road, though, he wasn't much company. He sat with his hands folded and his eyes closed, possibly sleeping, possibly avoiding conversation.

The landscape out there was desolate. No trees, no animals, no plants, no water — nothing. Often, when people try to describe Iraq, you hear a lot of references to *Mad*

Max, the post-apocalyptic film trilogy where biker gangs in S&M gear drive across the desert, killing one another for gasoline. I've never found the description particularly apt. Aside from that weird Shi'a festival where everybody beats themselves with chains, you won't find much fetish gear in country. And out there, not seeing a single living thing, I'd have welcomed the sight of other humans, even a biker gang in leather face masks and assless chaps. But war, unfortunately, is not like the movies.

Kazemi wasn't there when we got to the plant, a large, blockish structure with a row of enormous concrete cylinders topped by metal pipes. We went to the main building, but when we tried to get inside and out of the sun, we couldn't open the front door. It was large, metal, and so rusted that it wouldn't budge.

"Here, sir," said a burly Army sergeant. He smiled at his fellow soldiers, no doubt thinking he'd show them how much stronger and better at door opening the Army was than the State Department. He pushed at it. Nothing. Still smiling, with the eyes of most of the soldiers on him, the sergeant backed up a step and launched himself into the door. The primary effect was a loud booming noise. Now red-faced, he started cursing, and with everybody, even the Professor, watching him, he backed up about fifteen feet and then ran into the door at full speed. The crash of his body armor against the steel was enormous, and the door opened with a screaming metallic creak. A few soldiers cheered.

Inside was dark and rusty.

"I don't think anyone's been here in a while, sir," said the sergeant.

I looked back at the convoy of soldiers. I'd risked all their lives bringing them here.

"Professor," I said, "we need to get Kazemi on the phone. Now."

While he called, I daydreamed about beekeeping. Images floated through my head of Iraqi Widow Honey in U.S. supermarkets, of Donald Rumsfeld helping out by doing TV ads: "Try the sweet taste of Iraqi freedom." After about thirty phone calls, the Professor assured me Kazemi was en route.

The Iraqis arrived from the south in a small convoy of pickup trucks. Chief Engineer Kazemi, a thin little Iraqi with a bushy mustache, waved and spoke in Arabic for about ten minutes. The Professor nodded and nodded and didn't translate a word until the end.

"He greets you, and wants to take you to

his office," he said.

I agreed, and we followed Kazemi through the dark hallways of the plant. This entailed a lot of backtracking.

"He would like you to believe," the Professor said after our ninth or tenth wrong turn, "that he normally comes in through another door and that is why he is not knowing where to go."

When we got to the office, one of the police officers with Kazemi made tea that he served in a dusty cup with a sludge of sugar congealed at the bottom. I tried, while drinking it, to come to the point in my best American manner.

"What do we need to get this plant operating?" I said.

The Professor reiterated the question, and Kazemi smiled and started fumbling under the desk. He mumbled something, and the Professor looked concerned and asked what sounded like a few sharp questions.

"What are you telling him?" I said.

The Professor ignored me. After a minute or so, Kazemi pulled something from under the desk, dislodging papers and spilling office supplies all over the floor.

"I do not think this man is very intelligent," said the Professor.

Kazemi held a large box in his hands. He

placed it on top of the desk, opened it, and carefully pulled out a scale model of the water treatment plant, constructed of cardboard and toothpicks. At the four corners of the plant, though, were thin cardboard towers. Kazemi pointed to one of these.

"Mah-sheen gaans," he said.

Then he smiled and cradled his hands as though holding a weapon.

"Rat-tat-tat-tat-tat," he said, shooting the imaginary gun. Then came another stream of Arabic.

"Your military," the Professor said after a pause, "failed to approve funds for the construction of machine-gun towers. They are not standard on U.S. water plants."

Kazemi said something else.

"Also, your military built the wrong pipes," said the Professor.

"What does he mean, the wrong pipes?" I said.

This time the discussion went on for some time, the Professor getting increasingly curt. He seemed to be berating Kazemi.

"Your military built pipes for the wrong water pressure," said the Professor, "and they built them across the highway."

"Is there a way to deal with the water pressure —"

"The water pressure is not the problem,"

said the Professor. "The ministry is Jaish al-Mahdi."

I looked at him blankly. "But water would be good for —"

"They will not turn on water for Sunnis." His accusing stare suggested that, somehow, this was my fault. Of course, given that the United States had split Iraqi ministries between political parties at the outset of the war, allowing the various factions to expel the old Baathist technocrats in favor of party hacks who carved the country up between them, it sort of was.

Kazemi spoke again.

"I am sure of it," said the Professor. "This man is not intelligent."

"What does he say?"

"He would like to pump water," said the Professor. "He has had this job for many years without pumping any water and he wants to see what it is like."

"If some of the water is going to Sunnis," I said, "he will need machine guns?"

"He will need them anyway," said the Professor.

"Okay," I said.

"He will get himself killed," said the Professor.

"Ask him what it will take to get the plant working," I said, "aside from machine guns."

They spoke in Arabic. I stared at the wall. When they were finished, the Professor turned to me and said, "He will have to assess. He has not been here in many weeks."

"Where has he been?" I said.

The Professor asked him, and Kazemi smiled, looked at me, and said, "Ee-ran."

Everyone knew that word. The American soldiers with me had looked tense from the outset; now they looked murderous. Iran was the major importer of EFPs, a particularly lethal IED that sends a hot liquid metal bullet crashing through the sides of even the most heavily armored vehicles, spraying everybody inside. One EOD tech told me that even if the metal didn't get you, the change in pressure caused by the sheer speed of the thing would.

Kazemi continued speaking. Occasionally the Professor would frown and say something back. At one point he took his glasses off and rubbed them while shaking his head.

"Ah," said the Professor. "He went to get marriages."

"Marriages?" I said. I turned to Kazemi. "Congratulations." I put my hand over my heart. I was smiling in spite of myself. The soldiers behind me all looked relieved.

"Iranian women are very beautiful," said the Professor.

Kazemi pulled out a cell phone. He fiddled with it for a bit, then showed it to me. On the screen was a picture of a pretty young woman's face.

"Madame," said Kazemi.

"Very lovely," I said.

He pushed a button and flipped to another picture of another woman, then flipped to another, and another, and another. "Madame. Madame. Madame. Madame," he said.

"Why is her face bruised?" I said.

The Professor shrugged, and Kazemi kept flipping through pictures.

We talked more about Iranian women and their beauty, I congratulated him on his marriages again, and then another forty minutes of discussion left us with the agreement that I'd figure out a security solution for Kazemi if he'd figure out what it'd take to get the plant on line.

On the drive back, the Professor explained the marriages to me in the tone you'd use to speak with a mentally deficient golden retriever.

"Nikah mut'ah," he said. "Shi'a allow temporary marriages. Shi'a marry a woman for an hour, the next day marry another."

"Oh," I said. "Prostitution."

"Prostitution is illegal under Islam," said

the Professor.

Two days later, I got back to Taji. As I turned down the road toward the plywood hut we called our office, I saw Major Jason Zima and one of his CAT teams unloading a bunch of boxes from the pickup truck they used to drive around the FOB. I immediately had the sick and certain realization that whatever was in those boxes, it was going to be my problem.

"Sir!" said Major Zima, smiling. "Just the man I wanted to see."

Zima ran the brigade's Civil Affairs Company and was thus my closest U.S. military counterpart. He was a stocky man with a bizarrely spherical head that he shaved to a smooth shine each morning. It gave him the appearance, in bright Iraqi sunshine, of a lovingly polished bowling ball resting on a sack of grain. With no hair on his head and eyebrows so fair they were invisible, Zima had no discernible age markers and could have been anywhere from thirty to fifty-five, his cherubic smile making him seem the former and his what-the-hell-is-this-civilian-telling-me frown the latter. In all my interactions with him thus far, he had projected an idiocy so pure it boggled the mind.

"What's this?" I said.

Major Zima dropped his box to the ground, sending up a dust cloud. Then, waving his right hand with a magician's flourish, he pulled a Leatherman out of his pocket, bent down, and proceeded to cut open the box.

"Baseball uniforms!" he said, pulling one out to show me. "Fifty of them. Some blue, some gray — like the Union and Confederacy in the Civil War."

I was still wearing my flak jacket and helmet. I took the helmet off. It felt like I'd need the maximum amount of blood circulation to my brain to make sense of this.

"They're for you," Zima said. "Somebody dropped them off with Civil Affairs by accident."

"What the hell do we need these for?" I said.

He smiled one of his stupidly beatific smiles at me. "They're for the Iraqis to play baseball in," he said.

"Iraqis don't play baseball," I said.

Zima frowned, as though this complication had just occurred to him. Then, as he looked at the uniform in his hand, his face lit up in a grin.

"Then they can play soccer in them!" he said. "They'll love it. They play on dirt fields anyway. The leggings will protect them."

"Okay," I said. "But why are they here? Why am I looking at fifty baseball uniforms in the middle of Camp Taji?"

Major Zima nodded, as if to let me know he thought it was a valid question. "Because Gene Goodwin sent them to us," he said. "Gene Goodwin thinks baseball is just the thing for Iraqis."

"Who is Gene — You know what? It doesn't matter. Am I supposed to take care of this?"

"Well," said the major, "are you going to teach the Iraqis baseball?"

"No," I said.

"That's a problem," said the major, frowning.

I put my face in my hands and rubbed my forehead. "Are *you* going to teach the Iraqis to play baseball?" I said.

"I don't think they'd be interested," he said.

We stood staring at each other, me scowling and Zima smiling angelically. I knelt and looked at the package. There was a sheet inside detailing the contents. It said the uniforms were sized for boys eight to ten. I figured the malnutrition in our area meant they'd fit best on thirteen- to fifteen-year-olds.

"There was a convoy just for this?" I said.

"No," he said. "I'm sure they were carrying other Class One supplies."

"So . . . energy drinks, Pop-Tarts, and those muffins nobody eats?"

"Fuel for the American soldier!"

I rubbed my forehead. "Who exactly is Gene Goodwin?" I said.

"The mattress king of northern Kansas," said Major Zima.

I wasn't sure how to respond to that.

"I've never met him," Zima continued, "but when Representative Gordon was here, he made a special point of telling me one of his key constituents had a spot-on idea for Iraqi democracy."

"Of course he did."

"He said it in front of everybody. Including Chris Roper."

"I see," I said. Chris Roper was my boss. He generally didn't make it out of the Green Zone but when a congressional delegation swung through, Roper tagged along to do a bit of war tourism. Nobody wants to do a year in Iraq and come back with nothing but stories about the soft-serve ice-cream machine at the embassy cafeteria.

"What did Chris Roper say?" I asked.

"Oh, he told the congressman how 'sports diplomacy' was the new thing, and they'd been setting up matches between Sunni and

Shi'a soccer teams. It's all the rage at the embassy, he said. It's been very effective."

"Very effective at what?"

"Well," said the major, beaming, "I'm not sure, but they make for some great photos."

I took a deep breath. "Chris Roper thinks this is a good idea?"

"Absolutely not," said the major, an expression of outrage on his face.

"Then Representative Gordon . . . ," I said.

"I don't think so," said Major Zima. "But he did tell me and the colonel what a key constituent Mr. Goodwin was, and how angry Mr. Goodwin was that no one seemed to take his baseball plan seriously."

"And you told him the ePRT guys could handle it."

"I said you'd be honored."

Bob thought the uniforms were hilarious. About twenty times a day he'd look up at them, crack a smile, and then go back to playing solitaire on his computer. Cindy was less amused, and she carefully pointed out that since they were boys' uniforms, they were not in her purview as women's initiative adviser. Also, she was too busy because her agricultural initiative had been taking off.

"Really?" I said.

"Yep," she said. "They don't have modern farm knowledge over here."

"And you do?"

"Well, I know getting the imam to tie a verse of the Koran to your cow's tail won't cure the poor thing's bloating problem. Besides, there's a reservist here on Taji who's a farmer in real life. He's helping me."

That made sense. I refused to believe that Cindy with her Googling could get an agricultural initiative off the ground on her own, though she did have a knack for networking. Najdah, the social worker at the women's clinic, spoke very highly of her.

"Membership is increasing," said Cindy. "A lot of the women's husbands have been showing up and telling their friends they can get good advice and medicine."

"I thought they were widows?"

Cindy shrugged and turned back to Google, occasionally blurting out fun facts like, "Nothin' doin' in chickens these days, not with the price of these Brazilian frozens." I stared at the boxes of uniforms until I couldn't stand it anymore. I left the office, slamming the flimsy wooden door behind me, and walked over to the Civil Affairs Company's offices to talk to Major Zima again — this time about the water plant and the pipeline to the Sunni community. I found him in the midst of moving various files to new and seemingly random locations.

"That pipeline is still in construction," Zima told me while shoving an overly large stack of paper into an overly small filing cabinet. He explained that before either of us had even gotten to Iraq, a provincial council had convinced the previous brigade's Civil Affairs Company to build the pipeline. He'd inherited the project and thought it should continue.

"Most local water's a mix of E. coli, heavy metals, and sulfuric acid," Zima said. "I wouldn't want to brush my teeth with that."

I explained to him the Sunni-Shi'a difficulties. Then I tried to tell him about how the pipes were for the wrong water pressure. "Even if you finish it and the plant gets on line and the ministry somehow allows it to start operating," I said, "the pipeline will pump water at such high pressure that all the toilets and sinks and spigots west of Route Dover will simultaneously explode."

"Really?" he said, looking up from the problematic filing cabinet.

"That's what you're building," I said. "Or, what the Iraqi firm you're hiring is."

"They're Jordanians," he said. "There's only one Iraqi." He leaned back, lifted a leg, and kicked at the filing cabinet's drawer. The thing closed, but with bits of paper sticking out the sides. Satisfied, he looked up and said, "I'll handle it." When I pressed him for his solution, though, he only smiled and told me to wait.

Having the uniforms in the office meant I had to look at them all the time. It's no surprise I snapped.

"Do you really want me to start a goddamn baseball team in Iraq?" I practically screamed into the phone. Chris Roper was not the sort of man you screamed at. With him, it tended to be the other way around. For a career diplomat, he was surprisingly undiplomatic. Too much time spent around the Army, probably.

"The fuck are you talking about?" he said. He had the slightest hint of a Brooklyn accent.

I told him what Major Zima had told me about the uniforms.

"Oh," said Roper, "that. That doesn't matter. I want to talk about the women's business association."

"The women's business association is a scam," I said. "Starting an Iraqi baseball league, though, is a joke."

"Isn't the Civil Affairs Company handling that?" Roper said. "I didn't pony up for responsibility, that's for sure."

"You didn't tell them about how 'sports diplomacy' was all the rage at the embassy?"

There was a long pause.

"Well," he said, drawing the word out, "it kind of is."

"Jesus, Chris."

"And you can't cut the women's business association."

"Why not? It's been going a year already and has yet to start a business. The last meeting, we rented a 'conference and presentation room' for fifteen thousand dollars which turned out to be an unused room in an abandoned school *we* built back in 2005." I paused and took a breath. "Actually, 'abandoned' is the wrong word. No one ever used it."

"Women's empowerment is a huge mission goal for the embassy."

"That's why the women's health clinic —"

"Women's empowerment," he said, "means jobs. Trust me when I tell you that was a key takeaway of the past ten meetings I've been to. The health clinic is not providing jobs."

"It's providing local women what they

actually want and —"

"We're sinking, what, sixty thousand into it?" he said.

"They're not going to start —"

"There is a direct link," Roper intoned, "between the oppression of women and extremism."

There was brief silence.

"And it's not like I don't think it's hard," he continued. "All of this is hard. Doing anything in Iraq is hard."

"The clinic —"

"Is not jobs," he said. "Give me Rosie the Riveter. Not Suzie the Yeast Infected."

"Suzie the Cured of Yeast Infection," I said.

"Right now the business association is the only thing your ePRT has going for women's empowerment," he said. "That's not good. Not good at all. And you want to shut that down? No. Fucking no. Keep it going. Use it better. Start some fucking jobs. Do you have anything, anything at all, even in planning, for women?"

I could hear him breathing heavy over the phone.

"Sure . . . ," I said, racking my brains, "we've got things."

"Like?"

There was an awkward silence. I looked

around the office, as if I might find an answer hanging on the wall somewhere. And then my eyes settled on Bob's desk.

"How much do you know about beekeeping?" I said.

"You're going to have women beekeepers?" he said.

"Not just women," I said. "Widows."

There was another pause. He sighed.

"Yeah," he said. His voice sounded resigned. "A lot of ePRTs are doing that one."

"Wait a minute," I said. "Do you . . . do you know this is bullshit?"

The e-mail popped up as soon as I got off the phone. The subject was: IRAQ'S SOON TO BE NATIONAL PASTIME. The sender was: GOODWIN, GENE GABRIEL. I thought, Who gave this asshole my e-mail address? That was answered almost immediately.

> Dear Nathan (I hope I can call you Nathan? Major Zima told me you were a very approachable guy),
>
> I'm glad to get a hold of someone who's finally willing to give this a shot. You won't believe the amount of BS you've got to go

through to get anything done with the US Army.

Here's the idea: The Iraqi people want democracy, but it's not taking. Why? They don't have the INSTITUTIONS to support it. You can't build anything with a rotten foundation, and Iraqi culture is, I'm sure, as rotten as it gets.

I know this sounds crazy, but there are few better institutions than the institution of BASEBALL. Look at the Japanese. They went from Emperor-loving fascists to baseball-playing democracy freaks faster than you can say, Sayonara, Hirohito!

What I'm saying is, you've got to change the CULTURE first. And what's more AMERICAN than baseball, where one man takes a stand against the world, bat in hand, ready to make history, every moment a one-on-one competition. Batter versus pitcher. Runner versus first baseman. Runner versus second baseman. Third baseman. If he's lucky, against the catcher himself. And yet! And YET!!! It's a team sport! You're nothing without the team!!!!

I guess they play soccer over there now.

Figures. There's a sport that teaches kids all the wrong lessons. "Pretend you're hurt and the ref might help you out!" "You'll never make it on your own, kick the ball to your friend!" And worst of all, nobody ever scores. It's like, "Go ahead, kids, but don't expect much! Even if you're near the goal, you're probably not gonna make it!" And they can't use their hands. What the heck is that all about?

I know this probably sounds silly to you, but remember: Great ideas always sound silly. People told me my Grand Slam Discounts were silly too, but I went and did it and nobody calls me silly anymore. It's like we say in the mattress business: SUCCESS = DRIVE + DETERMINATION + MATTRESSES. And here I'm supplying the materials. All I'm asking from you is a little effort to give these Iraqi kids a chance for the future.

Yours Truly,
GG Goodwin

Reading the e-mail was like getting an ice pick to the brain. I stared blankly at my computer, all higher mental functions short-circuited, and resisted the urge to punch the screen. This, I thought, was bullshit. I composed a terse note explaining that while we appreciated his generosity, baseball wasn't likely to catch on, and while the kids would certainly make use of the uniforms, I couldn't promise him they'd be playing baseball in them. Then I clicked "send."

Within an hour, I found myself cc'd on an e-mail to none other than Representative Gordon. Also cc'd were a host of military and civilian personnel. Chris Roper. Some brigadier general. Major Zima. *And* the colonel in charge of the BCT I was attached to. The sight of his name alone was enough to let me know I'd seriously screwed up. I was new to the cc game, a game played with skill by staff officers throughout the military, but I knew enough to know that the more senior people you could comfortably cc on your e-mails, the more everyone had to put up with whatever bullshit your e-mails were actually about.

The message began, "I am continually amazed by the lack of foresight I have found . . . ," and got uglier from there. Within five minutes, I had a new e-mail in my in-box, this from Lieutenant Colonel Roux, the brigade XO. It was addressed not to me, but to Major Zima. Roux hadn't been cc'd on the initial e-mail, but scanning down through the document, I saw the colonel had forwarded it with the terse message

"Jim. Deal with this."

Lieutenant Colonel Roux was not quite as laconic. His message read, "Can someone explain to me why the Colonel is getting cc'd on angry letters to members of Congress? I want this unfucked. Now." Below that was his signature block: "Very Respectfully, LTC James E. Roux."

I started sweating over a response e-mail to the XO. It seemed important to convey the sheer idiocy of G. G. Goodwin, and I wasn't sure I had the skill to get it across. But before I'd even put down the first paragraph, Major Zima beat me to the punch with what was clearly the right reply. "Sir," it read, "I'll handle it immediately."

Five minutes later came another e-mail, this also from Major Zima. Lieutenant Colonel Roux and I were cc'd, as was the congressman and the random brigadier general, but not the colonel.

"Sir," it began. "There's been a little miscommunication on our part. I actually just finished talking with a schoolteacher who would be glad to take the uniforms and teach the children baseball."

That seemed highly unlikely, but Major Zima went on to give a rather dizzying account of all the logistical hoops he was jumping through to get the project fast-tracked.

The e-mail continued: "We talked about having the children write you thank-you notes, but unfortunately most children in our area of operations are illiterate." Then Zima urged patience, using Gene Goodwin's very own reference to Japan as an example. He explained how baseball was actually introduced in 1872 and took about fifteen years to become firmly entrenched in Japanese culture. This bit was surprisingly long and technical, which made sense, since it turned out Zima had simply copied and pasted the Wikipedia entry for "Baseball in Japan" right into the text to make it seem like he was as engaged with the sport as Gene himself.

A little later, another e-mail popped up, this one strictly from Zima to me, no one else cc'd.

"Hey, Nathan," it read. "Maybe you should let me handle this guy. No need to kick the hornets' nest."

About two weeks later, I ran into Major Zima doing push-ups in his cammies. Between grunts, he told me that if I wanted to start funding repairs for the water plant, the ministry wouldn't go out of their way to roadblock us or steal more than the usual amount of reconstruction dollars.

"How many dollars are we talking?" I said. "Didn't we already sink 1.5 million dollars into it?"

He stopped, put a cheerful grin on his face, and said, "Yep."

"Where'd that money go?"

"I don't know," he said, dropping down for another push-up, "I wasn't here then."

I watched him for a bit. His torso was round enough that even with his arms fully extended, his belly was still hovering less than an inch above the ground. He dropped down and used his stomach to trampoline back up. I said, "How'd you get them to agree?"

"Seventy-nine," he said. *"Ahhhhh. . . . Eighty!"*

He collapsed to the ground. There was no way he'd done eighty push-ups. My guess was closer to twenty-five. He looked up.

"I told them what you told me," he said between big breaths, lying belly down on the ground with one cheek in the dirt.

"What did I tell you?"

"That if we turned on the water, it'd make all the Sunnis' toilets explode." Zima slowly rolled onto his back. "Ahhhh," he said.

"And that was enough?"

"No," he said. "But they double-checked

and it turns out you're right. Those pipes are designed off the Nasiriyah Drainage Pump pipes, so they'll push out twenty cubic meters a second. That's way too much. There's something that you need to reduce the pressure. I forget what it's called."

"A pressure reducer?" I said.

"Yeah, a pressure reducer," he said. "We're not building that."

"You told them the United States would purposely destroy all the plumbing in a Sunni community in order to get the water plant on line."

"Yep."

"And they believed you?"

"I told them I get promoted for completing projects, which is sort of true, and that the plant wouldn't be operational until well after I was out of Iraq, which is definitely true, and that I wasn't going to go through with the nine-hundred-thousand-dollar open-air market one of the ministry guys' cousins is supposed to build for us if they keep cock-blocking us on water."

I stared at the major in awe. Initially, I had thought the man stupid. Now, I wasn't sure if Zima was brilliant or insane.

"But," I said, "we can't destroy a Sunni village. . . ."

"It's okay," he said. "For now, we keep moving forward. The Sunnis aren't going to let overpressurized water destroy their homes. That'd be a silly thing to happen in the desert. They'll keep track of it, even if we don't."

Zima's confidence didn't reassure me. "Do they know about the pressure?" I said.

"No," he said. "But I put a reminder on my Outlook calendar for the week the BCT's scheduled to leave Iraq. It says, 'Tell Sheikh Abu Bakr that the pipes we built for him will make his house explode.' "

Sheikh Abu Bakr was, in addition to being an important item on Zima's to-do list, a major player west of Route Dover. The first time I met him, the lieutenant commanding my convoy told me, "Sheikh Abu Bakr is, literally, Tina Turner from *Mad Max.*" Bob also claimed the sheikh was the man to see about widows, so a little after my water conversation with Zima, I headed out to try to get the beekeeping project off the ground. I needed to see Abu Bakr anyway, as we were shifting monetary support to the *qada'a,* or provincial council. Previously we'd given funds directly to him and he'd pay Iraqis to man security checkpoints instead of fight in the insurgency. Since Abu

Bakr ran the *qada'a,* shifting payments to the council was somewhere between a shell game and a method of helping the Iraqis develop government institutions capable of managing budgets.

As we drove into town, I saw a couple of kids in baseball uniforms going through garbage on the side of the road. One kid was in gray, the other in blue. Blue had cut the leggings off to turn them into impromptu shorts.

"Stop the convoy," I said. Nobody paid any attention, and I didn't press the matter.

Given the squalor all around, I was always shocked coming to Abu Bakr's home. It was an enormous estate, with five separate buildings and the only real lawn I'd seen in Iraq outside of the U.S. embassy. The creation of the embassy lawn had been ordered by the ambassador himself and had involved sod imported from Kuwait, armored convoys to bring in lawn supplies, intense efforts to keep birds away from the seed, and a casual disregard for the rules of nature. Estimates for the cost varied from two to five million taxpayer dollars. What Abu Bakr's cost, I had no idea. Given the sheer number of pots he had his fingers in, it was likely U.S. taxpayer dollars had gone into his lawn as well.

When we arrived at his home, the U.S. soldiers and the Iraqi police and Iraqi army set up a defensive perimeter. There was a uniformed Iraqi police officer already there who was in the midst of detailing the car in the driveway, a black Lexus. We walked inside and were escorted through rooms filled with mahogany furniture, crystal vases, and the occasional flat-screen TV hooked up to an Xbox. Our guide brought us to a dining room where Abu Bakr was waiting. We exchanged pleasantries and sat down, and he had his men serve me, the Professor, the convoy commander, the police lieutenant, and a couple of the Iraqi army guys lamb and rice. They brought the lamb out in a big slimy pile on a large plate and set it down next to an equally large plate of rice. There was no silverware. One of the IA guys, thinking I didn't know how to eat, elbowed me, smiled, and grabbed a bunch of lamb in his right hand, grease oozing through his fingers. He then slapped the lamb on the rice plate and mashed it up with his hand until he had a little ball of rice and lamb, which he picked up and dropped on my plate.

"Thanks," I said.

He stared at me, smiling. Abu Bakr was looking at me, too. He seemed faintly amused. The Professor was openly amused. I took it and ate it. Hygiene questions aside, it was delicious.

With that, real discussion began. Abu Bakr was a fat, jovial man who claimed to have three bullets lodged in his torso. Doctors had told him it'd be more dangerous to take them out than to leave them in, but, he'd say, "Every night I feel them worming closer to my heart."

The Professor claimed that three years ago a Shi'a death squad had attempted to kidnap Abu Bakr. As they were pulling him to their vehicle, he saw that one of the gunmen had a pistol lodged in his belt. The sheikh pulled it out, shot two of his captors, and sustained two nonfatal gunshots himself. The final gunman was captured by his men. If you wanted to see what happened to that guy, you could apparently buy the torture tape at most kiosks in the area. I never had any interest.

The conversation shifted into a long discussion of the local *nahiyas* and provincial *qada'as.* Abu Bakr claimed it would be much easier to give him the money. I maintained they needed to learn how to manage the money themselves. After about an hour, we started talking widows.

"Yes," said the Professor. "He can get

them for you. Sheikh Umer will handle this matter."

Sheikh Umer was considerably lower in the local hierarchy. No Lexus in his driveway. He was a player in one of the *nahiyas*.

"The widows will learn to grow bees if you provide the hives and training," said the Professor, "but they also will need you to pay for their taxis to the training, as the area is very dangerous."

"Taxis don't cost a tenth of what he's asking," I said. "Tell him this would be a very personal favor."

The Professor and Abu Bakr talked. I was certain that Abu Bakr spoke English. He always seemed to know what I was saying and would cut the Professor off sometimes before he could fully translate. But Abu Bakr never fully let on.

Eventually the Professor looked at me and said, "There are other fees he may not anticipate, but which may complicate this matter." He paused and added, "It is as they say. A rug is never fully sold."

"Tell him," I said, "we want real widows this time. At the last women's agricultural meeting, Cindy said she thought they were all married women."

The Professor nodded, then spoke some more.

"This will not be a problem," he said. "Iraq is short of many things, but not widows."

The baseball bats and mitts arrived not long after the Abu Bakr meeting.

"I'll take care of these, too," said Major Zima.

"Don't just dump the bats like you did the uniforms," I said.

"I would never!" he said.

"Every time I go outside the wire," I said, "I see different kids in the uniforms, but I have yet to see a baseball game."

"Of course not," said Major Zima, "they don't have bats yet."

"I don't want to see U.S.-supplied equipment in a torture video," I said.

"Too late for that," said Major Zima. "Besides, if there's one thing I've learned doing Civil Affairs in Iraq, it's that it's hard to come in and change people's culture."

"What do you mean?" I said.

"Right now," he said, "the Shi'a are pretty set in their ways of drilling people to death. And the Sunnis like to cut off heads. I don't think we'll manage to change that with baseball bats."

"Jesus," I said. "I don't want to be a part of it."

"Too late," said Major Zima, frowning, "you're here."

The next day, I visited the women's health clinic for what I feared would be the last time. I didn't look forward to telling Najdah, the social worker there, that I'd failed her again.

"I am Iraqi," she'd said on my previous visit. "I am used to promises that are good but not real."

Visiting the women's clinic was always odd, since I wasn't allowed inside. I'd meet Najdah in a building across the street, and she'd tell me what was going on.

The clinic was, perhaps, the thing I felt most proud of. That and the farming education program, though the farming stuff was mostly Cindy's work. Najdah seemed to know what the clinic meant to me, and she'd always push me hard for more help whenever I showed up. She also thought I was somewhat crazy.

"Jobs?" she said.

"Yeah," I said. "Is there any way we could use this as a platform for starting businesses?"

"Platform?"

"Or maybe we could have a bakery attached to the clinic, and women could . . ."

She looked so puzzled, I stopped.

"My English is not so good, I think," she said.

"Never mind," I said. "It's a bad idea anyway."

"Will our funding be continued?"

I looked out at the clinic across the street, the love I had for it feeling like a weight in my chest. Two women walked in, followed by a group of children, one of them wearing a blue baseball shirt with sleeves longer than the child's arms.

"Inshallah," I said.

I made another trip out to JSS Istalquaal with the intent of meeting with Kazemi, but as soon as I arrived the mission was canceled. Kazemi, I was told, was dead.

"Suicide bomber on a motorcycle," said the S2 over the phone.

"Oh, my God," I said. "All he wanted to do was pump water."

"For what it's worth," said the S2, "I don't think he was the target. Just in the wrong place at the wrong time."

The S2 didn't know when the funeral would be, and he strongly suggested that it would be unwise to attend in any case. There was nothing to do but try to get on a convoy back to Taji. I arranged for travel in a sort of haze. I ate a Pop-Tarts and muffins dinner. I waited.

At one point, I called my ex-wife on an MWR line. She didn't pick up, which was probably a good thing but didn't feel like it at the time. Then I went outside and sat down in a smoke pit with a staff sergeant. His body, with armor on, formed an almost perfect cube. I wondered how much time, as a career military man, he must have spent here already.

"Can I ask you something?" I said. "Why are you here, risking your life?"

He looked at me as though he didn't understand the question. "Why are you?" he said.

"I don't know," I said.

"That's a shame," he said. He dropped his cigarette, which was only halfway done, and ground it out.

Major Zima was doing jumping jacks when I got back to Taji, his belly bouncing in counterpoint to the rest of his body. He would go down and the belly would stay up, then his feet would leave the ground and his stomach would come crashing down. I'd never seen a man work out so much and achieve so little.

"How're things?" he said breathlessly.

"They're breaking my heart," I said. And then, because Bob didn't care, and Cindy was outside the wire, and there was no one else to talk to, I told Major Zima what was happening. He already knew about Kazemi. It was old news at this point. But he hadn't heard about the clinic's funding. He stood and smiled at me, nodding encouragingly, a look of pure idiocy on his face. It was like confessing your sins to Daffy Duck.

"How," I said at the end, "how do you deal with it? The bullshit?"

Major Zima shook his head sadly. "There is no bullshit."

"No bullshit?" I said. "In Iraq?" I cracked the sort of cynical smile Bob was always shooting in Cindy's direction.

Zima kept shaking his head. "There's a reason for everything," he said, sounding almost spiritual. "Maybe we can't see it. But if you were here two years ago . . ." His face was blank.

"If I was here two years ago what?"

"It was madness," he said. Zima wasn't looking at me. He wasn't looking at anything. "Things are getting better. What you're dealing with, it isn't madness."

I looked away, and we stood there in silence until I couldn't put off going to work any longer. I went to the ePRT office, he went back to jumping jacks. When I got to my computer, I sat and stared at it, unsettled. It felt as though Zima's mask had slipped and given me a glimpse of some incomprehensible sadness, the sadness you saw all around you every time you left the FOB. This country had a history that didn't reset when a new unit rotated in. This time, these problems, they were an improvement.

Two days later, Major Zima strolled into our office, whistling. He had a large green bag in one hand and a blank piece of paper in the other. He put the paper on my desk, pulled up a chair, and sat down.

He said, "I'm not really sure how you State boys write these things up, but here goes."

Then he pulled out a pen with a flourish, hunched over the paper, and started writing, reading aloud what he put down.

"Our women's business association," he said, "has proved highly successful —"

"No, it hasn't," I said.

"Highly successful in sparking entrepreneurship among our AO's disenfranchised population."

Bob looked over, an eyebrow arched. Zima kept going, "In fact," he said, scribbling illegibly with great speed, "due to its growing membership and the increasingly key place it has taken within community power structures, it has, on its own initiative, begun expanding its operations to encompass —" He looked up. "That's a good word, right? *Encompass?*"

"*Encompass* is a great word," I said, curious.

"To encompass a more holistic approach."

"Have they now?" I said, smiling in spite of myself.

"Several promising businesses have failed, despite substantial opportunities for female employment, due to a lack of adequate child care and medical facilities. Providing these services is a prerequisite to a flourishing free market and represents a business opportunity in its own right."

"Oh," I said, getting it. "Very nice."

Bob scowled.

"We are still collecting broader metrics, but two projects have been hamstrung by a lack of health care. One female bakery closed after two workers, both widows, stopped coming due to complications from untreated yeast infections."

"There's no way that's true," I said.

"Maybe someone gave me bad information," the major conceded, "but I can't be held responsible for that. We get bad information all the time."

"I," said Bob, standing up, "am going outside for a smoke break."

"You don't smoke," I said. He ignored me.

"Statistics show," Zima continued as Bob walked out, "that countries which improve health care do a better job improving their economies than countries which focus exclusively on business development."

"Is that true?"

Major Zima put on his shocked face. "Of course it's true," he said. "I deal only in truth-hood." After a moment he added, "I saw it in a TED Talk."

"Okay," I said. I looked down at the paper. "Can you get me the name of the speaker? Let's see if we can do this."

"Good," said the major. "Glad we can work together on this. You know, I think I can even convince the colonel to throw in some CERP funds. . . ."

"That would be amazing," I said.

"Oh," he said, "and I was wondering. Could you help me with something?"

"What?" I said.

He pulled a blue baseball helmet out of the green bag and put it on my desk. "G. G. Goodwin wants a picture of kids playing baseball."

■ ■ ■ ■

The next two times I went outside the wire, I went out with a baseball helmet, mitt, and bat. No uniforms in sight, though.

"I know what you're doing," said Chris Roper over the phone, "and this bullshit is not going to stand."

"What?"

"You want to push the money for the clinic through the women's association? You know ninety percent of it, if not more, is gonna go right into Abu Bakr's pocket."

"You wanted me to keep them going," I said, "even knowing that. So why not have some of the money going to something real."

"Uh-huh," he said. "Very clever."

"Something is better than nothing," I said, "and funding for the clinic runs out next month."

"Wow," said Roper. "Honesty. How refreshing."

"The clinic is big in the community," I said. "It's not a bad thing if the sheikh takes ownership of it."

"It's big for the women," he said. "Have you met an Iraqi who gives a fuck about women?"

"There is a direct link," I said, "between the oppression of women and extremism."

"Don't give me that bullshit," he said.

"This is real," I said. "And he'll keep it going. It'll hurt his reputation if he stops it."

"Any buy-in from local councils?" he said.

"It says in the —"

"I know what it says," he snapped. "Is there real buy-in?"

"Yes," I said. "Minimal financial support. As long as we're funding something, the Iraqis don't want to step in and kill the goose that lays the golden eggs, but the bit in there about the distribution network —"

"Okay," he said. "I'm gonna sit on this and think it over."

It was more than I had any right to hope for.

The next week, while meeting with Sheikh Umer about the beekeeping project, I saw three children, two of them in uniforms. One gray, one blue. Perfect.

"Holy shit!" I said. "Professor, tell him I need to get a photograph with those children."

Much explaining later, along with the understanding that I now owed a favor, I had one extremely confused child wearing a baseball helmet and another with a glove on his hand. I also had one highly irritated translator.

"I hate you more than I have ever hated you right now," the Professor said, rubbing his glasses hard enough that I thought they might break.

"Why do you even work for us?" I said.

"Forty. Dollars. A day."

"Nonsense," I said. "You're risking your life for us."

He sized me up for a second. "There was hope at the beginning," he said. His face softened a bit. "Even without hope, you must try."

I smiled. Eventually, he smiled back.

After another bout of more or less patient explanations, we had the children lined up right, the one crouched like a pitcher and the other standing as if at bat. I saw a woman hurrying toward us out of the corner of my eye, but Sheikh Umer cut her off and began speaking to her in Arabic.

"Tell him to swing," I said.

The kid swung as though he were using the bat to beat someone to death, lifting it overhead and bringing it brutally down. I wanted to send that shot to G. G., but instead I showed the kid how to swing correctly and went back to taking photos. The timing was difficult, but after about twenty swings I got it perfect, the bat blurry, the batter's face pure concentration, and a look of worry from the catcher, as if the batter had just connected with a pitch. I turned the camera's display around and showed the picture to the Professor and the kids.

"Look at that," I said.

The Professor nodded. "There you are," he said. "Success."

In Vietnam They Had Whores

My dad only told me about Vietnam when I was going over to Iraq. He sat me down in the den and he took out a bottle of Jim Beam and a few cans of Bud and started drinking. He'd take long pulls of the whiskey and small sips of the beer, and in between sips he'd tell me things. The sweatbox humidity in the summers, the jungle rot in the monsoons, the uselessness of the M16 in any season. And then, when he was really drunk, he told me about the whores.

I guess at first the command organized monthly trips to town, but it didn't last because everybody'd get too crazy. Once the trips stopped, the brothels moved in next to base and Marines would either bust through the wire at night or invite girls in as "local national guests" during the day. Those girls, he said, you'd treat more like girlfriends, which made it better.

By his second tour, he said, the whole

thing was a pretty smooth machine and there was a wide range of services, even different brothels for white and black Marines. If a girl who worked in a white brothel ever got found out servicing a black man, she'd wind up dead or at least beat till she couldn't work anymore. He didn't agree with that, but it happened, and he said it amazed him, to think you could just do that to somebody.

Then he told me about one place where they had dancers and a stage where the girls would do this trick to make a little extra money. Customers would put a stack of quarters on the bar. Then the girls would squat down over the stack, drop their vag on top of it, and pick up as many quarters as they could. That was the thing at that bar.

Dad was pretty well gone at this point, but he didn't stop knocking them back, pulling on the whiskey and taking those small sips of beer. He looked so old, deep wrinkles running down his face and little gray spots on his hands.

"I had this friend," he said, and one time this friend goes to that bar and drinks, all night, not talking to anybody. And he takes out a stack of quarters and puts it on the bar, and then he hunches over with his arms around it so no one can see, and he takes out his lighter and holds the flame on those quarters till they're branding iron hot. Then he calls over a girl. "Just any girl," said my dad, "my friend, he didn't care which." My dad took another pull of the whiskey. "It smelled like sizzling steak," he said.

I was like, Jesus. All right. Well, thanks, Dad. That was helpful.

We didn't keep drinking much beyond that. Dad was too drunk to even sit right. Before I brought him to his bed, he mumbled to me about being careful and gave me a tiny metal cross, the sort you'd wear on a necklace. He said it carried him through Vietnam. A few weeks later I was overseas.

We weren't in Iraq long before I told Old Man my dad's story. In the team, Old Man was the one you'd go to with things like that. West, our team leader, would have thought badly of me. With West, you were either a hundred percent or you were a piece of shit. Old Man was different. He'd joined the Corps late in life, so he had age and, we thought, wisdom. When I told him, all Old Man did was laugh and say, "Yep. In Vietnam they had whores. I guess that's one thing they had over us."

I thought about that the first time I jerked off in a sandstorm. Being nineteen and seven months without getting laid makes you all kinds of crazy. I thought about it again when West died, and Old Man said he wished to God he knew where the Iraqi whorehouses were, 'cause he'd get himself a big fat whore who'd let him cry into her tits.

But we didn't know where the whores were, and that convinced me we didn't know anything about Haditha. In training we'd learned to observe our environment, get the rhythms of city life. A man who walks this way every day is suddenly avoiding a particular street, an unusually tall woman you've never seen before strolls through the market in a hijab and people get out of her way. A bunch of kids that used to play soccer in a dirt patch near the road don't play there anymore. I spent so much time looking at women through scopes. Sometimes I'd switch from eye to eye, closing one and then the other. Look at women through my bare eye. Look at women through the sights. Human, animal, human, animal. Me and my dad used to hunt.

But I never scratched the surface. I never had a chance to look at a woman and think, There is a whore.

First Platoon, though, in Kilo Company, we were sure they'd found a place. They got herpes all at once, and we thought, That's it. They're going on patrols and visiting a brothel when they're supposed to be meeting sheikhs and drinking tea.

Who would have done that, in those days, violent as things were? Only a crazy person. But half of them were at the BAS with their dicks oozing. They had to be fucking somebody. And the one thing everybody wanted to know was, Where is it? Where is it? I'll wear a condom, I'll be fine. But none of them said a word. They'd get mad, tell us to fuck off. I cornered one of the guys, this shifty-looking PFC. I told him, Everybody knows what you're doing, we just want to know where. He told me if I didn't quit asking, he'd face fuck me with his KA-BAR. I left him alone after that. I wasn't really serious anyway.

We shouldn't have bothered. The next day, the CO had all the herp cases called to the BAS and the doc said, "All right, guys, where's the whores? You ain't leaving till we figure out this goddamn dick epidemic."

They all looked at the ground and their faces turned red, and after a while one of them finally admitted, "Doc. Ain't no whores. We been sharing a pocket pussy."

"Jesus," said the doc. "Clean the fucking thing out, boys." And he got that platoon issued a pallet of hand sanitizer as a joke. For the rest of us, we had something to laugh about the next couple days.

Then the mortar attack came where the mortars wouldn't fucking stop, mortar after mortar after mortar, and we just cowered there, wondering, Aren't we getting place of origin on these fucks? Isn't somebody targeting them? West was still alive, then, and he started praying, freaking everyone out because you'd hear, "O Lord in heaven —" Boom. "Forgive us, God, us sinners —" Boom. "Sinners —" Boom. "West! Shut the fuck up!" Boom.

No injuries, and afterward I had an erection that could bust concrete. So hard, it hurt. And I went up to the roof, and Flores was up there with Old Man, and they looked the other way while I jerked off on the roof, looking out at Haditha, wondering, Is there a sniper out there, scoping in to shoot me, dick in hand?

At first I put some tits in my brain and the idea of me fucking someone, anyone, but toward the end my mind was blank, just me scratching an itch, and I heard small-arms fire off in another section of the city and I kept jerking, faster and faster, almost coming with the thought floating in, as it always did when I heard gunfire, that maybe somebody I knew was dying.

First female I saw after that, I smelled first. The whole table of us, at the chow hall at Al Asad, and the smell of her short-circuited our collective brain and the conversation stopped and we all turned to her at once and she walked right by, neither pretty nor ugly but a woman, not seen through a scope, close enough to reach out and touch. Close enough to smell.

Me and Flores got into a conversation about what we'd like to do to her. I mean, things we didn't even want to do, just us competing with each other for the dirtier thing. Flores won when he said, "I'd let her piss in my mouth just for a sniff of her snatch."

"Who wouldn't?" said Old Man.

"You guys are idiots," said West. Later, though, West got all motherly and told me how much he missed his family, and he asked me, "You got any girls back home you'd like to see?"

"Not really," I said.

"You know," he said, "sometimes, girls who wouldn't give you the time of day when you were in high school change their minds once you're a war hero."

I didn't feel like a war hero when I got back to Lejeune, especially not after the memorial service for West and for Kovite and for Zapata. It was a lot to take. Everybody got drunk afterward. Flores couldn't deal and went to the barracks to be alone. I wanted to go with him, but I stayed with Old Man. He needed looking after. And Old Man wanted to go to the Pink Pussycat, this strip club in a double-wide trailer, painted pink. The Pussycat was off-limits for Marines, but Old Man said it was the best place for what we wanted, and Old Man was the one to know.

"So there's whores in there?" I asked him when we pulled into the parking lot, which was nothing more than a mud-and-grass field. I thought I knew the answer to that. Whores was the whole purpose of the trip.

"They don't think they're whores," he said. "They think they're dancers who sometimes fuck their clients."

I laughed, but he stopped me.

"I'm serious," he said. "You fuck this up, you aren't getting laid. They don't see themselves as street whores."

"But . . ." I pointed at the trailer.

He laughed. "I bet there's girls that fuck

at the Driftwood, too. There's girls that fuck at the nicest strip clubs in the world. And there's a few girls here that don't."

"All right," I said. "So why're we here?"

He started counting out reasons on his fingers. "Most of the girls here fuck," he said. "It's less expensive. These girls treat you better because they aren't hot and they want repeat customers. You and I are just back from deployment, so really hot women are wasted on us. Also, there's no dress code." He pointed to his crotch. "There's a reason I'm wearing sweatpants."

Old Man saw me shudder at that, and he laughed again. If I'd felt like I had a choice, I would have walked away. Something about the sad little parking lot, with a few busted-up Buicks and trucks lined out in front of the pink trailer, it was too far away from what I hoped I'd get. Some hot young chick who was doing it for the money, yeah, but maybe one who really liked me, too. Old Man headed over to the door, and since he had the car keys, I followed him.

We walked in and there they were. Naked women. It was a small space, smelling of beer and sweat, with seventies rock blaring. There were only seven or eight customers in there, all but two of whom were definitely civilians. The chairs and couches all looked like they'd been picked up off the side of the road. We stood at the back for a few seconds, and then we went to the front and sat down together in a pleather, zebra-print love seat by the side of the stage, which was a little square about a foot off the ground at the end of the trailer. Old Man got me a beer and I drank it quick, taking small but quick sips and looking around at the girls and the customers, trying to figure how the whole thing worked. Then the dancer on-stage got down in front of me and I stared straight ahead, into the tiny strip of fabric between her legs. She was an older woman who didn't have the greatest body but didn't have any scars that I could see and who looked like she'd probably been pretty when she was younger. I didn't breathe for a bit. When she got up, I asked Old Man how we got the girls alone.

He could see how I was, and he smiled. He pulled two twenties out of his wallet and gave them to me. Then he pulled out a one, folded it, waved it in front of the dancer, and tucked it in her G-string.

"Relax," he said. "I'm gonna buy you a lap dance. Then you ask the girl to take you to the VIP room."

I looked around.

"It's in another trailer," he said. "You get

there, she gives you another lap dance, you ask her if there's anything else she could do. You tell her you like her so much and she's so great and you just got back and is there anything else." He pointed to the two twenties in my hand. "Don't give her more than that. And don't give it to her until after. And don't settle for her letting you grope her."

I looked down at the money. Two hours earlier, I'd spent more on whiskey at Alexander's.

"It's good here," he said. He pointed to the corner of the room, where a tired-looking woman was standing, waiting to take the stage. "That's my girl. She's real sweet. We're like an old married couple — we only fuck once every seven months." He paused for a second. "She's good. After I finish, she stays with me till the time is up."

I nodded. When the first girl got off the stage, Old Man paid for my lap dance. Then I did what Old Man had said.

The VIP lounge was a white trailer about fifty yards from the main one. We stepped out of the music into the fresh air, and I was excited, walking a step ahead of her. Inside, the trailer had a corridor and a bunch of little rooms. There was loud music in that trailer, too, so you mostly couldn't hear what was going on in the rooms around you.

The woman was very polite. We settled on forty. I felt bad arguing for less than that, and she pulled down my pants. I wasn't hard, but she took me in her mouth in a very professional way and then she put a condom on me and then we had sex and then I paid her the money Old Man had given me.

As I walked back to the main trailer, I didn't feel anxious anymore. She had been a little dry, which made sense, but it had felt great right until the moment that I came and the world crashed back into focus.

Inside the trailer, Old Man was getting a lap dance, his face buried in the stripper's tits. It wasn't from the one he'd called his girl. It was another woman. This one looked something like my mother, before she'd died. When she finished, he whispered to her and they got up. He nodded to me and walked over.

"How was Nancy?" he said.

"Nancy?" I said.

"That's her real name," he said. "She's good, but she can be kind of a bitch sometimes."

"It was good," I said.

He patted me on the shoulder. "Take your

time with it," he said. "Talk to the girls." And he went back to where he was sitting and motioned to the one who looked like my mother. She climbed on top of him again and I looked away.

Nancy walked back into the trailer and started working the room. She smiled at me as she passed and then climbed on the lap of some civilian. I looked away from that, too.

Old Man had the keys in the pocket of his sweatpants, and there was no easy way to get them, so I waited in the back while he had his fun. I had a whiskey, then another beer. I was pretty far gone at this point, but I kept drinking. I waited and waited and I looked at the sad women onstage. Some looked zoned out. On something for sure. Old Man took his time. When he went to the VIP trailer with his girl, I counted the money in my pocket. I had more than enough. If I let myself get into it again, it'd be almost as good as not being there.

PRAYER IN THE FURNACE

Rodriguez didn't approach me because he wanted to talk to a chaplain. I don't think he even recognized who I was until I stood up straight and he saw the cross on my collar. At first, he only wanted a cigarette.

He had blood smeared across his face in horizontal and diagonal streaks. His hands and sleeves were stained, and he wouldn't look at me directly, his eyes wild and empty. Violent microexpressions periodically flashed across his face, the snarling contortions of an angry dog.

I handed him a cigarette and lit it against mine. Rodriguez drew in, let the smoke out, glanced back to his squad, and his face again turned to violence.

Twenty years ago, well before I became a priest, I used to box light heavyweight. Rage is good for amping you up before a fight, but something different happens once the fighting begins. There's a kind of joy to it. A surrender. It's not a particularly Christian feeling, but it's a powerful one. Physical aggression has a logic and emotion of its own. That's what I was seeing on Rodriguez's face. The space between when rage ends and violence begins.

I didn't even know his name then. We were four months into our deployment, standing outside of Charlie Medical, where the surgeons had just called time of death for our battalion's twelfth KIA, Denton Tsakhia Fujita. I'd learned Fujita's name that day.

Rodriguez was wire thin, his body taut and electric. I was huddled against the wind, clutching my cigarette as if it could calm my nerves. Ever since my hospice days working with children, I've had difficulty with hospitals — the sight of needles turns me pale and weak, as if the blood is slowly draining out of all my limbs at once — and there was a leg amputation going on. Another of Rodriguez's friends, John Garrett, had been injured at the same time as Fujita. I'd just learned Garrett's name that day as well.

Rodriguez smiled. There was no warmth to it.

"Chaps," he said. He looked back at his squad, all of them waiting for word on their friend's condition. They were a few yards away, out of earshot. For a second, Rodriguez seemed nervous. "I want to talk with you."

After attacks, sometimes Marines will want to talk to the chaplain or to Combat Stress. They're enraged, or grieving, or oscillating between the two. But I'd never seen a Marine like this, and I didn't really want to be alone with him.

"I'll tell them I'm going to confession," he said. His eyes were pinpricks. It occurred to me that he might be on drugs. Alcohol, marijuana, heroin — these were available if you knew the right Iraqi.

Rodriguez smiled again, the corners of his mouth tight. "He was a pretty good shortstop," he said. At first I didn't realize who he was talking about. "Not great, but good."

"I should go in," I said, "see how the docs are doing."

"Okay, sir," he said, "I'll come find you."

After the amputation, though, Rodriguez had disappeared.

At Fujita's memorial service, I read from Second Timothy: "I have fought the good fight. I have finished the race. I have kept the faith." During memorials, I try as best I can to set an appropriate tone.

Captain Boden, the Charlie Company commander, came after me and told the assembled Marines that they'd "get them motherfuckers back for Fujita." The men listened with surly acceptance. Little more was expected from Boden. This was the man who would announce, straight-faced, that his idea of leadership was "taking my Marines to the field and beating the shit out of them." It's a leadership style that goes over well with nineteen-year-olds before they've actually been to war. When their lives are on the line, Marines learn to want more than pure, unthinking aggression. Unthinking aggression can get Marines killed. In this deployment, it had already killed more than a few.

Rodriguez spoke next, in the role of the best friend. He was calmer than when I'd last seen him, and he spoke of how Fujita actually liked the Iraqis. That he was the one guy in the squad who thought the country wouldn't be better off if we just nuked it until the desert turned into a flat plane of glass. Then Rodriguez gave a bitter smile, looked out at the crowd, and said, "Guys teased him, said Fuji'd been out fucking hajjis, and they could smell it." It felt like Rodriguez was berating the audience. Marines from his squad looked at each other uneasily. For a moment I wondered if I'd have to step in, but Rodriguez went on, the remainder of his remarks in a more traditional, hagiographic vein.

The rest of the service was standard, insofar as it was heartbreaking. When the first sergeant did the roll call, a number of Marines put their faces into their hands and a number openly wept.

When Fujita's squad approached the battle cross, they knelt close together, their arms over one another's shoulders, leaning into one another until it was one silent, weeping block. Geared up, Marines are terrifying warriors. In grief, they look like children. Then one by one they stood up, touched the helmet, and walked to where Captain Boden stood in the back, grim, stupid determination set on his thick, square face.

After the service, Staff Sergeant Haupert held court in the smoke pit behind the chapel. Haupert was the acting platoon commander of 2nd Platoon. Their original platoon commander, Lieutenant Ford, had been killed in an IED blast in the first month of the deployment.

From the smoke pit, you couldn't see to the city, but I turned away from Haupert and looked out toward it anyway. The men in Charlie Company spent every day in Ramadi. I went out regularly, too, but always to an outpost. Never on a combat mission. I ministered. Always busy, always overworked, but still, most days I woke up in my bed on base, prayed in relative safety, and only listened for violence in the distance. Augustine, sermonizing from safety about the sack of his beloved Rome, repeated only what he could not know for sure: "Horrible it was told to us; the slaughter, burning, pillaging, the torture of men. It is true, many things we have heard, all filled with bellowing, weeping, and hardly were we comforted, nor can I deny, no, I cannot deny we have heard many, many things were committed in that city." I had the same problem.

I turned back to Haupert, in the midst of his own sermon, a simple sermon but one buttressed by the experience of daily patrols. "What do we do?" Haupert was saying to the loose assembly of 2nd Platoon members. "We come here, we say, We'll give you electricity. If you work with us. We'll fix your sewage system. If you work with us. We'll provide you security. If you work with us. But no better friend, no worse enemy. If you fuck with us, you will live in shit. And they're like, Okay, we'll live in shit." He pointed off to the direction of the city, then swatted with his hand, as if at an insect. "Fuck them," he said.

I retreated back to the chapel, which was where Rodriguez found me. I was organizing all our candy in the walk-in closet off to the side, stacks of candy and jerky and Beanie Babies sent by grateful Americans to the troops, care packages I often ended up distributing to the platoons. Chaplains receive more care packages addressed to "Any Marine" than we know what to do with, but the excess can be useful because coming to get goodies is one inconspicuous way Marines can talk to the chaplain without announcing to their unit that they have an issue.

Rodriguez entered the small space silently. He didn't have the same level of intensity as the first time we talked, though it was there, in his eyes and in his hands, in the way he couldn't just stand still but had to always move. They say that on patrol in Ramadi, you don't walk, you run.

"You know what we were doing," he asked, "when Fuji got shot?"

"No."

"Nobody does," he said. He looked around suspiciously, as if someone might break in on us. "Nobody thought I should talk to you," he said. "What's a fucking Chaps gonna say? What's anybody gonna say? You know nobody respects chaplains, right?"

"Their mistake."

"I respect priests," he said. "Most priests. Not the little-boy fuckers. You ain't a little-boy fucker, right?"

Rodriguez was testing me. "Why? Are you?" I said. I folded my arms and made a point of sizing him up, giving him a look to let him know I wasn't impressed. Normally I'd be more aggressive, maybe even pull rank, but I couldn't after a memorial service.

Rodriguez held up a hand. "I respect priests," he said again. "Not the faggots and the boy fuckers, but, you know, priests."

Rodriguez looked around and took a breath.

"You know we get hit like every fucking day," he said.

"I know you've got a violent part of the city."

"Every day. Shit, they used to come at us in the Government Center three times a week. Suicide assaults. Crazy. It'd end with air strikes on Battleship Gray or Swiss Cheese. Allah's fucking Waiting Rooms. Killing motherfuckers. And you go out on the street, you go on a raid. You stop for a minute too long, you're getting lit the fuck up."

His face contorted into one of those quick snarls of rage I'd seen before. "You remember Wayne?" he said. "Wayne Bailey? You remember him?"

"Yes," I said quietly. I made a point of remembering the full names of all the dead. And Bailey was one of the fallen I'd actually interacted with before he died. That made it easier.

"We were checking on a fucking school. And they made us stay. We're on the radio telling them we gotta go and they're like, No, stay there. We're like, We stay here too long, something's *got* to happen. But the Iraqis are late and we got to follow orders. And there's a group of kids and the first RPG lands smack in the group of kids."

I could remember seeing the ComCam photos. I'd seen sick and dying children before, but that had shaken me. It's strange how a child's hand is so easily identifiable as a child's hand, even without a frame of reference for size or a recognizable body for it to be attached to.

"Then Wayne gets hit. Doc was pounding his chest and I was holding his nose, doing rescue breathing."

Wayne, everybody said, was a popular man in the platoon.

"My last deployment," Rodriguez said, "IEDs, IEDs, IEDs. Here there's still IEDs, but them suicide assaults are coming every week. We're getting shot at every week. More firefights than any unit I ever heard of. And Captain Boden, he puts up a board listing all the different squads. The Most Contact Board."

Rodriguez lifted a tightly clenched fist to his face and looked down, baring his teeth. "The Most Contact Board," he said again. "You get a hash mark every firefight. IEDs don't count. Even if somebody dies. Just firefights. And it's like, whoever has the most contact, they get respect. 'Cause they been through the most shit. You can't argue with that."

"I suppose not." Suffering, I thought, has always had its own mystique.

"Four months in, them suicide assaults stop coming. Hajjis got smart. We were chewing them up. And now it's just IEDs. And Second Squad" — he slapped his chest — "my squad, we were the leaders. Not just in the platoon, in the whole fucking company. Which means battalion, too. Probably the whole fucking Corps. We were top. Most fucking contact. Nobody could touch our shit."

"And then . . . ," he said, and stopped for a second, as though to gather courage. "Attacks fall off. Our squad's stats fall off, too. Staff Sergeant gave us shit for it." Rodriguez scowled and then, imitating Haupert's gruff, confident voice, said, "You pussies used to find the enemy." He spat at the ground. "Whatever. Fuck that. Fuck firefights. Firefights are fucking scary. I don't get off on that shit."

I nodded, trying to hold his eyes, but he looked away.

"What were you doing," I said, "when Fujita got hit?"

Rodriguez looked around at the stacked-up care packages all around him. Our closet was crammed with rows of wooden shelves filled with M&M's, Snickers bars, individually wrapped brownies, Entenmann's cakes, and other goodies. Rodriguez dug his hand into a bag of Reese's Peanut Butter Cups and pulled one out, inspecting it in his hand. "You know this is Sergeant Ditoro's first deployment?" he said.

"No," I said. I figured he was talking about his squad leader, though I wasn't sure and I didn't want to stop his flow of words by asking.

"Embassy duty." Rodriguez shook his head and tossed the candy back into the bag. Then he quickly wiped at his face. It took me a second to realize he was wiping away tears. In relation to what, I wasn't sure. "You know, if I hadn't been busted down after that DUI, I'd probably be leading this squad."

"What happened," I asked again, "when Fujita got hit?"

"About a month back," he said, "Corporal Acosta was buzzing off Ambien. That shit gives you a body high, and it's like being a little drunk. Maybe he'd taken something else, too."

"He get Ambien from the Combat Stress team?"

Rodriguez laughed. "What you think?" He pulled a plastic sandwich bag full of little pink pills out of his cargo pockets and held it at eye level. "How you think any of us sleep?"

I nodded my head.

"We set up an OP," he said, "and we just trash it. I mean, insurgents like to destroy any place we use as an OP anyway, so might as well go crazy. And Ditoro, he doesn't have respect. Acosta, though, he's good to go."

"Even on drugs?"

Rodriguez kept going. "Last deployment, I saw what he did. Suicide bomb, and Acosta was helping wounded and the motherfucker was on fire. He didn't even realize. He was actually burning and he was running around helping wounded kids and shit. Man could have gotten a medical discharge, one hundred percent disability, but after burn unit he stayed in to do another deployment. Man's got fucking respect."

"Sure. Of course."

"So Ditoro ain't saying shit to Acosta. And Acosta is buzzing. We're not even looking and he strips to his underwear and Kevlar and goes out on the roof like that, dick hanging out, and he starts doing jumping jacks, screaming every Arabic curse word he knows."

It wasn't the craziest thing I'd heard of Marines doing.

Rodriguez smiled, his eyes dead. "They started shooting at us within five minutes."

"Who's they?" I said.

"What?"

"Who's shooting at you?"

He shrugged. "Insurgents, I guess. I don't know. Honestly, Chaps, I don't care. They're all the same to me. They're all enemy." He shrugged again. "We lit them fuckers up.

And we get back and it was, you know, another hash mark. On the Most Contact Board. We went out and found the enemy, instead of waiting for him to IED us. And our stats went up."

"Ah," I said. "So you did it again."

"Sergeant Ditoro would make the junior Marines play rock-paper-scissors, see who goes."

It was starting to make sense. "Fujita was a junior Marine."

"When he got here," he said, "Ditoro used to make him sing, 'I am the new guy and I am fucking gay.' " Rodriguez laughed. "It was funny as shit. Fuji took it well. He played the game. It's why we liked him. But he didn't like us setting up contact bait. He said it was fucked up. That if it was his neighborhood, he'd take a shot at some asshole on the roof. But we did it anyway."

Rodriguez paused. "Fuji played the game," he repeated. "You know we're back up top for most contact?"

"And the day Fujita died . . ."

"There was a sniper. There wasn't shooting. There was one shot. I helped Ditoro put Fuji's pants back on while Acosta tried to stop the bleeding."

"And then Garrett . . ."

"They IED'd us while we were bringing

Fuji back."

Rodriguez lowered his head and stared at the ground, clenching and unclenching his fists. He grimaced, then looked straight at me, challenging.

"If you killed somebody," he said, "that means you're going to hell."

Marines had asked me about that before, so I thought I had an answer. "Killing is a serious thing," I said, "no doubt about that. And —"

"I mean" — Rodriguez looked away, down at the candy — "somebody you're not supposed to."

That brought me up short. At first I didn't understand what he was talking about, though I suppose it should have been obvious. "You're not responsible for Fujita's death —"

"That's not what I'm talking about," Rodriguez snapped, eyes back on me, angry. "I mean, not Marines. I mean, out in the city." He took a breath. "And, if other people did it, too, when you're out there, and you don't stop them. Do you go to hell, too?"

The silence held for a moment. "What are you telling me, Lance Corporal?" I said it in an officer voice, not in a pastoral voice. Immediately, I knew it was a mistake.

"I ain't telling anything," he said, drawing back. "Just asking."

"God always offers forgiveness," I said, softening my tone, "to those who are truly sorry. But sorry isn't a feeling, you understand. It's an action. A determination to make things right."

Rodriguez was still looking at the ground. I was cursing myself for fumbling the conversation.

"A lance corporal," Rodriguez said, "don't have the power to make anything right."

I tried to explain it wasn't about outcomes, which you can't control, but about the seriousness of intent. Rodriguez cut me off.

"If this is confession," he said, "that means you can't tell anybody what I said, right?"

"Yes."

"Then it's not confession. I'm not confessing shit. I ain't sorry for shit. You can tell anybody you want."

I spent that night thinking over what Rodriguez had told me, parsing the words until I wasn't sure he'd said anything at all. I kept thinking, They only shot when shot at. That seemed to be what he said. Maybe he was talking about a traffic stop where they killed a family that failed to brake in time. That sort of thing tore Marines up.

"Don't let this upset you," David had said about the death of Uriah, "the sword devours one as well as another." I built up a scenario where Rodriguez was talking about a bad judgment call, not a real violation of the ROE. That story ran through my mind enough to let me know I was avoiding the issue. By the next day, during morning prayers, I found my resolve. A coward, I thought, would tell himself it was all right. So I had to talk to someone or be a coward. Less than a priest. Less than a man.

But who to talk to? The obvious choice was to go to the company commander, who'd have the authority to step in. But Rodriguez's company commander was Captain Boden, and Boden was a lunatic. And if the rumors my RP told me were true, he was an alcoholic as well. Possibly self-medication for PTSD. Boden'd been in Ramadi in 2004, and his unit held the record for most casualties in the division. When you were in conversation with him, the first thing you'd notice was the abnormal eye contact — aggressive staring and then quick, paranoid looks around the room. His affect was off, too, alternating between quiet periods of deep sadness and barely suppressed rage. And he had vicious scars across his face — battle scars that gave him immediate credibility with his Marines. The man knew combat.

I wasn't the only one who thought there was something off with Boden. He'd seriously disturbed the trainers at Mojave Viper, the month-long predeployment workup in the California desert that the Marine Corps uses to prepare units for war. "These are a people who do not understand kindness," he'd told his company during a brief on Iraqi culture. "They see kindness as a weakness. And they will take advantage of it. And Marines will die." Charlie Company took his advice to heart, roughing up several role players during training. These were Iraqi Americans who dressed up and strolled through fake villages, playing either civilians or insurgents. If you followed Charlie on a practice cordon-and-search, you'd hear Marines screaming, "Put that bitch in the chair!" or, "Shut that motherfucker up!" to the civilians. When one of them lectured Charlie on how that style of counterinsurgency wasn't likely to win hearts and minds, Charlie found the complaints funny. Even funnier was the trainer from Civil Affairs who told the whole assembled battalion, "I'm very concerned that this battalion is overly focused on killing people."

You could see smirks everywhere. "I guess that pogue thinks he joined the fucking Peace Corps," I heard Boden stage-whisper to his first sergeant, loud enough for the Marines around him to hear. "Oh no," he continued in a mocking, high-pitched voice, "some real men might go out and kill some al-Qaeda. But I just wanna be friends."

That was his attitude before his company got dropped in the most violent sector of the most violent city in Iraq. I couldn't go to Captain Boden. He wouldn't care, and he wouldn't want me, a chaplain of all people, meddling.

Who else? The battalion commander wasn't much better. Lieutenant Colonel Fehr was universally loathed among the staff and paid attention to none of them. Before the deployment, before I'd even met him for the first time, our operations officer, Major Eklund, had felt the need to prepare me.

"He's gonna do this handshake," the major said. "It's called the dominance shake. He does it to everybody."

Eklund was a Catholic convert and had a tendency to tell me more than he should, inside the confessional and out.

"The dominance shake," I said, amused.

"That's what he calls it. He's going to take

your hand in his, grip it real hard, and then twist his wrist so his hand is on top of yours. That's the dominance position. And then, instead of shaking up and down, he'll pull you in and slap you on the shoulder and feel your bicep with his free hand. It's Fehr's little way of peeing on your personal tree."

"You think he'll do it to me? I'm a chaplain."

"He does it to everybody. I don't think he can help it. He did it to my nine-year-old son at the battalion Easter egg hunt."

Then I met the colonel, got dominance handshook, and received the vague introductory pleasantries that let me know this commander looked at chaplains as the pray-at-ceremonies guys, not as trusted advisers. Fehr was worlds more composed than Boden, but he didn't seem to care much for ROE either. Two months after our first meeting, I saw him interrupt a trainer at Mojave Viper going over escalation of force procedures.

"If a vehicle is coming toward you fast," the trainer said to the assembled Marines, "it might be a suicide bomber, or it might just be a frustrated, distracted Iraqi trying to get to work on time. If the first couple steps of EOF don't work, you can fire a round in front of the car, not trying to injure —"

Here's where the colonel jumped up and stopped the lesson. "When we shoot, we shoot to kill," he shouted. The Marines roared in response. "I'm not having any of my Marines die because they hesitated," the colonel continued. "Marines do not fire warning shots."

The trainer, a captain, was stunned. You can't contradict an O5, especially not in front of his men, so he didn't say anything, but the whole unit had just been taught to ignore MEF policy. The Marines got the message. Kill.

In the end, I went to Major Eklund. I figured he'd at least hear me out.

"I'm worried about Charlie Company."

"Yeah, we're all worried about Charlie Company." Major Eklund shrugged. "They're led by an idiot. What are you gonna do?"

I gave him a condensed, anonymous version of Rodriguez's story about doing naked jumping jacks to attract fire.

Major Eklund laughed. "That sounds like a lance corporal solution."

"You think this is funny."

"I'll bring it up with Captain Boden."

That hardly satisfied me. "The Marines don't seem to see much difference between civilians and combatants. Some Marines have been hinting at worse than stupid tactics."

Eklund sighed.

"Perhaps," I said, "some of their firefights could be looked into a little more. To make sure we're targeting actual enemy."

Eklund stiffened. "An investigation?" He shook his head. "Into what?"

"There are some questionable —"

"Only the commander can recommend an investigation." He shook his head. "And Chaps, all respect, but this is way the fuck out of your purview."

"Marines talk to me," I said, "and —"

"This is nothing," he said. "Last month Weapons Company shot two hajjis I know they didn't follow ROE on. And Colonel Fehr didn't think that was worth an investigation. You know what he told me? 'I don't want my Marines thinking I don't have their backs. And I really don't want them hesitating to shoot when they need to.' And that was the end of the story, Chaps."

He hadn't even paused to consider what I was suggesting. "You're saying this is weaker than that."

"Weak, strong, it doesn't matter," he said.

"You think Lieutenant Colonel Fehr will ever become Colonel Fehr if he tells higher, 'Hey, we think we did some war crimes'?"

It wasn't a question I wanted to answer. Eventually, looking at my feet, feeling childish, I said, "I suppose not."

"And he's the one who decides if there's something worth investigating. Look, you know how I feel about that man, but he's handling Charlie Company about as well as anybody could. They came to Iraq to kill people, so he gave them the kill people AO. And he's been shrinking their AO as Bravo gets better control of theirs."

What he was saying didn't really register. "Bravo?" I said.

"They're getting more responsibility while Charlie's getting less. And at the end of the deployment, Captain Boden will get a FITREP that makes sure he's never given a command again. Happy?"

He could see I wasn't.

"Look, Father," Eklund said. "In a war like this, there's no easy answer. Neighborhood gets roughed up, sometimes. Sometimes, by accident, there's civilian casualties. It's not our fault."

That was too much. "No?" I said. "It's never our fault?"

He leaned toward me and pointed his

finger in my face. "Look, Chaps, you have no idea what these guys are dealing with. On my last deployment I saw a couple insurgents literally hiding behind a group of Iraqi children and shooting at us. Do you know how hard it is to get shot at and not respond? And that's what my Marines did. They let themselves get shot at because they didn't want to risk hurting children."

"That's not what's happening now."

"Most Marines are good kids. Really good kids. But it's like they say, this is a morally bruising battlefield. My first deployment, some of those same Marines fired on a vehicle coming too fast at a TCP. They killed a family, but they followed EOF perfectly. The driver was drunk or crazy or whatever and kept coming, even after the warning shots. They fired on the car to save the lives of their fellow Marines. Which is noble, even if you then find out you didn't kill al-Qaeda — you killed a nine-year-old girl and her parents instead."

"Well," I said, "if Bravo's doing okay, and Charlie's —"

"Bravo's got good leaders and a calmer AO," he said. "They trained their Marines right. Captain Seiris is good. First Sergeant Nolan's a rock star. Their company gunny is retarded, but all of their lieutenants are good to go except maybe one, and he's got a stellar platoon sergeant. But not everybody can be competent. It's too late for Charlie to be anything other than what it is. Our Kill Company. But this is a war. A Kill Company's not the worst thing to have."

A few days later I voiced my concerns, in somewhat stronger language, to the JAG. I got the same response. What Rodriguez told me didn't warrant anything other than a discussion with the company commander, who would handle it as he thought appropriate. Nothing would happen. I felt I was letting Rodriguez down, but I had no power. And the war ground on.

Three weeks later we had our thirteenth casualty. Gerald Martin Vorencamp. IED. Two weeks after that, our fourteenth. Jean-Paul Sepion. Neither from Charlie Company, though they had a few more serious, nonfatal injuries during the same period.

Not long after Sepion's death, one of the Divine Office's morning prayers was Psalm 144: "Blessed be the Lord, my help, who trains my hands for battle, my fingers for war." Kneeling against my rack in my spare little trailer, I faltered. I turned back to the previous prayer, from Daniel: "Today there is no prince, no prophet, no leader, no holocaust, no sacrifice. No offering, no incense, no first-fruits offered to you — no way to obtain your mercy."

I stopped reading and tried to pray with my own words. I asked God to protect the battalion from further harm. I knew He would not. I asked Him to bring abuses to light. I knew He would not. I asked Him, finally, for grace.

When I turned back to the Divine Office, I read the words with empty disengagement.

That afternoon I met another Marine from Rodriguez's platoon, a lance corporal. He did little to calm my worries.

"This is fucking pointless," he told me.

The lance corporal wasn't Catholic, nor was he in need of religious counseling. He came to me when Combat Stress refused to give him what he needed — a ticket out of Iraq. I couldn't give it to him either, but I tried.

"What's pointless?"

"This whole fucking thing. What are we doing? We go down a street, get IED'd, the next day go down the same street and they've IED'd it again. It's like, just keep going till you all die."

He stared at me without breaking eye

contact. I thought of Captain Boden.

When I asked him why he felt the way he did, I got a long list. Since the deaths of two of his friends six weeks before, he'd been having mood swings, angry outbursts. He'd been punching walls, finding it impossible to sleep unless he quadrupled the maximum recommended dosage of sleeping pills, and when he did sleep he had nightmares about the deaths of his friends, about his own death, about violence. It was a pretty complete PTSD checklist — intense anxiety, sadness, shortness of breath, increased heart rate, and, most powerfully, an overwhelming feeling of utter helplessness.

"I know I won't make it out of combat alive," he said. "Every day, I have no choice. They send me to get myself killed. It's fucking pointless."

I tried to get him to talk about positive things, things that he liked, to determine if there was anything he was holding on to. Anything keeping him on the good side of sane.

"The only thing I want to do is kill Iraqis," he said. "That's it. Everything else is just, numb it until you can do something. Killing hajjis is the only thing that feels like doing something. Not just wasting time."

"Insurgents, you mean," I said.

"They're all insurgents," he said. He could see I didn't like that and got very agitated. "You," he said, hateful, "you want to see something?"

He pulled out a camera and started flipping through photos. When he got to the one he wanted, he turned it around so I could see.

I braced myself for something terrible, but the frame only showed a small Iraqi child bending over a box. "That kid's planting an IED," he said. "Caught in the fucking act. We blew it in place right after the kid left, because even Staff Sergeant Haupert didn't want to round up a kid."

"That boy can't be older than five or six," I said. "He couldn't know what he was doing."

"And that makes a difference to me?" he said. "I never know what I'm doing. Why we're going out. What the point of it is. This photo, this was early on when I took this. Now, I'd have shot that fucking kid. I'm mad I didn't. If I caught that kid today, I'd fucking hang him from the telephone wires outside his parents' house and have target practice till there's nothing left."

I didn't know what to say to that.

"Besides, some of the other guys . . ." He paused. "There's lots of reasons somebody's al-Qaeda. He's driving too slow. He's driving too fast. I don't like the look of the motherfucker."

After the meeting, I resolved that I'd do something. It wouldn't be like with Rodriguez. I would push.

First I spoke with his platoon commander, Staff Sergeant Haupert. He informed me that Combat Stress had diagnosed the lance corporal with combat and operational stress reaction, which was common and not a condition recognized as an ailment or a reason to remove a Marine from a combat zone. Furthermore, he said, while the lance corporal talked tough, he performed his duties fine and I shouldn't worry.

When I spoke to Boden and the first sergeant, I got the same. When I talked to Colonel Fehr, he asked me if I was a trained psychologist. When I talked to Combat Stress, they told me that if they sent home every Marine with COSR, there'd be nobody left to fight the war. "It's a normal reaction to abnormal events," they said. "Ramadi is full of abnormal events."

Finally I talked to the chaplain at Regiment, a Presbyterian minister with a good head on his shoulders. He told me that if I really wanted to piss people off, I should put my concerns in an e-mail and send it to the responsible parties so there was a clear record in case anything went wrong.

"They'll be more likely to play the CYA game if it's in an e-mail."

I sent an e-mail to the colonel, to Boden, to Haupert, and even to the docs at Combat Stress. Nobody responded.

In retrospect, it made sense. The lance corporal's breakdown — his lack of empathy, his anger, his hopelessness — was a natural reaction. He was an extreme case, but I could see it around me in plenty of Marines. I thought of Rodriguez. "They're all the same to me. They're all the enemy."

In seminary and after, I'd read plenty of St. Thomas Aquinas. "The sensitive appetite, though it obeys the reason, yet in a given case can resist by desiring what the reason forbids." Of course this would happen. Of course it was banal, and of course combat vets like Eklund and Boden wouldn't really care. The reaction is understandable, human, and so not a problem. If men inevitably act this way under stress, is it even a sin?

I found no answer that night in evening prayer, so I flipped through the books I'd brought with me to Iraq to cast about for some help. *"¿Cómo perseveras, ¡oh vida!, no viendo donde vives, y haciendo por que mueras las flechas que recibes de lo que del Amado en ti concibes?"*

There's always the saints to show us a way. St. John of the Cross, imprisoned in a tiny cell scarcely larger than his body, publicly lashed every week, and writing the *Spiritual Canticle.* But nobody expects sainthood, and it's offensive to demand it.

A journal entry from that time:

> I had at least thought there would be nobility in war. I know it exists. There are so many stories, and some of them have to be true. But I see mostly normal men, trying to do good, beaten down by horror, by their inability to quell their own rages, by their masculine posturing and their so-called hardness, their desire to be tougher, and therefore crueler, than their circumstance.
>
> And yet, I have this sense that this place is holier than back home. Gluttonous, fat, oversexed, overconsuming, materialist home, where we're too lazy to see our own faults. At least here, Rodriguez has the decency to worry about hell.
>
> The moon is unspeakably beautiful tonight. Ramadi is not. Strange that people live in such a place.

■ ■ ■ ■

Rodriguez spoke to me again about three weeks later. By this time, Charlie Company's AO had shrunk to less than half its original size. It was still dangerous, but they had far fewer incident reports than before. Rodriguez seemed calmer, though also strangely out of it. I thought of the little bag of Ambien.

"I don't believe in this war no more," Rodriguez told me. "People trying to kill you, everybody angry, everybody crazy all around you, smacking the shit out of people." He paused, eyes downcast. "I don't know what gets somebody killed, and what keeps them alive. Sometimes you can fuck up and it's all right. Sometimes you do the right thing and people get hurt."

"You're thinking you can control what happens," I said. "You can't. You can only control your own actions."

"No," he said. "You can't even do that all the time." He paused and looked down. "I been trying to do what I think Fuji might have wanted."

"That's good," I said, trying to encourage him.

"This city's an evil thing," he said. He

shrugged. "I do evil things. There's evil things all around me."

"Like what?" I said. "What evil things?"

"Acosta's gone," he said. "Acosta ain't Acosta no more. He's wild." He shook his head. "How can you say this place ain't evil? Have you been out there?" He gave me a cruel smile. "No. You haven't."

"I've been outside the wire," I said. "My vehicle was IED'd, once. But I'm not infantry."

Rodriguez shrugged. "If you were, you'd know."

I chose my words carefully. "This is a life you chose. Nobody forces you into the military, and certainly nobody forces you into the Marine infantry. What did you think you would find here?"

Rodriguez didn't seem to have heard me. "When Acosta says, I'm gonna do this one thing . . . And Acosta's got respect. Ditoro don't. Ditoro can't say shit because he's a pussy and everybody knows. But me, I got respect. I can slow Acosta down." He laughed.

"I used to think you could help me," he said. His face turned vicious. "But you're a priest, what can you do? You gotta keep your hands clean."

I tensed up. It was as though he had struck me.

"No one's hands are clean except Christ's," I said. "And I don't know what any of us can do except pray He gives us the strength to do what we must."

He smiled at that. I wasn't sure I believed the words I was saying to him or if there were any words I'd believe in. What do words matter in Ramadi?

"I don't think about God no more," he said. "I think about Fuji."

"It's like grace," I said. "God's grace, letting you hold on to Fujita."

Rodriguez sighed. "Look at my hands," he said. He put them out in front of me, calloused palms facing up, and then he turned them down and stretched out his fingers. "I look calm, right?"

"Yes."

"I don't sleep no more," he said. "Hardly ever. But see my hands — look at me. Look at my hands. It's like I'm calm."

The conversation stayed with me well after Rodriguez had gone. "You're a priest," he'd said, "what can you do?" I didn't know.

As a young priest, I'd had a father scream at me once. I was working in a hospital. He'd just lost his son. I thought my clerical collar gave me the right to speak, so right after the doctors called time of death, I went and assured him his infant son was in paradise. Stupid. And of all people, I should have known better. At age fourteen, I lost my mother to a rare form of cancer similar to what struck that father's son, and every empty condolence I received after my mother's death only deepened my angry teenage grief. But platitudes are most appealing when they're least appropriate.

This father had watched his healthy child waste away to nothing. It must have been maddening. The months of random emergency room visits. The brief rallies and the inevitable relapses. The inexorable course of the disease. The final night, his wife collapsed on the hospital floor in terror and grief, shrieking, "My baby!" over and over. Doctors repeatedly asked the father to authorize last-ditch attempts to keep his child breathing. Naturally, he did. So they proceeded to stab his son with needles, perform emergency surgery. Torture his child in front of him and at his request in a hopeless effort to continue a tiny, doomed life for a few minutes more. At the end, they were left with a very small and terribly battered corpse.

And then I came along, after the chemotherapy, after the bankrupting bills and the deterioration of his and his wife's careers, after the months of hoping and despair, after every possible medical violation had denied his child grace even in death. And I dared suggest some good had come of it? It was unbearable. It was disgusting. It was vile.

I didn't think hope of the life to come would provide comfort for Rodriguez, either. So many young people don't really believe in heaven, not in a serious way. If God is real, there must be some consolation on earth as well. Some grace. Some evidence of mercy.

That father had despaired, but at least he was looking at life head-on, stripped of the illusion that faith, or prayer, or goodness, or decency, or the divine order of the cosmos, would allow the cup to pass. It's a prerequisite, in my thinking, to any serious consideration of religion. What, like St. Augustine, can we say after Rome has been sacked? Except Augustine's answer, the City of God, is a comfort designed for the aftermath of a tragedy. Rodriguez, that lance corporal, Charlie Company, the whole battalion, they were a different matter. How do you spiritually minister to men who are still being assaulted?

■ ■ ■ ■

Having no answers myself, I reached out to an old mentor, Father Connelly, an elderly Jesuit who'd taught me Latin in high school and whom I'd had long conversations with when considering my own vocation. He didn't have e-mail, so it took weeks to get his response, written on a typewriter:

Dear Jeffery,

As always it is wonderful to hear from you, though of course I'm saddened to learn of your difficulties. When you return to the States you must visit. You could even come to a class. I've got the boys reading Caesar and Virgil, of course, and you might have something to say to them about war. Come in spring. The flowers in the quadrangle are more beautiful now than I ever remember, and we can talk about all this in greater depth. But until then, I have thought about what you wrote, and have a few comments.

First you must forgive me, though, an old priest who has spent his whole life in relative comfort, for pointing out that your problem is nothing new. I don't see why it qualifies as a "crisis of faith" to notice that formerly good men, under strain, experience a breakdown of virtue and become bitter, angry, and less inclined toward God. Suffering can indeed incline one to sin, but it can also be turned to good (think of Isaac Jogues, or any of the martyrs, or any of the mystics, or Christ Himself).

Your attempts to bring transgressions to command attention are salutory. But as for your religious duties, remember these suspected transgressions, if real, are but the eruptions of sin. Not sin itself. Never forget that, lest you be inclined to lose your pity for human weakness. Sin is a lonely thing, a worm wrapped around the soul, shielding it from love, from joy, from communion with fellow men and with God. The sense that I am alone, that none can hear me, none can understand, that no one answers my cries, it is a sickness over which, to borrow from Bernanos, "the vast tide of divine love, that sea of living, roaring flame which gave birth to all things, passes vainly." Your job, it seems, would be to find a crack through which some sort of communication can be made, one soul to another.

I kept the letter with me throughout the rest of the deployment — always in the breast pocket of my uniform, always in plastic to protect it from sweat. There was a human warmth to the paper. It was signed, "Your Brother in Christ."

■ ■ ■ ■

"Who here thinks," I asked the small group of Marines who'd gathered for Sunday Mass, "that when you get back to the States no civilians will be able to understand what you've gone through?"

A few hands went up.

"I had a parishioner whose six-month-old son developed a brain tumor. He watched his child go through intense suffering, chemotherapy, and finally a brutal, ungraceful death. Who would rather go through that than be in Ramadi?"

I could see confusion on the faces of the Marines in the audience. That was good. I didn't intend this to be a normal homily.

"I spoke to an Iraqi man the other day," I said. "A civilian, who lives out there in that city I've heard Marines say should be razed. Should be burned, with everyone in it perishing in the flames."

I had their attention.

"This Iraqi man's little daughter had been injured. A cooking accident. Hot oil spilled off the stove, all over the girl. And what did this man do? He ran, with her in his arms, to find help. And he found a Marine squad. At first, they thought he was carrying a bomb. He faced down the rifles aimed at his head, and he gave his desperately injured daughter, this tiny, tiny girl, to a very surprised, very burly corporal. And that corporal brought him to Charlie Medical, where the doctors saved his daughter's life.

"That's where I met this Iraqi man. This man of Ramadi. This father. I spoke to him there, and I asked him if he felt grateful to the Americans for what we'd done. Do you know what he told me?"

I held the question in the air for a moment.

" 'No.' That's what he said. 'No.' He had come to the Americans because they had the best doctors, the only safe doctors, not because he liked us. He'd already lost a son, he told me, to the violence that came after the invasion. He blamed us for that. He blames us for the fact that he can't walk down the street without fear of being killed for no reason. He blames us for his relatives in Baghdad who were tortured to death. And he particularly blames us for the time he was watching TV with his wife and a group of Americans kicked down his door, dragged his wife out by the hair, beat him in his own living room. They stuck rifles in his face. They kicked him in the side. They screamed at him in a language he did not understand. And they beat him when he could not answer their questions. Now, here's the question I have for you, Marines: Who would trade their seven-month deployment to Ramadi for that man's life, living here?"

No one raised a hand. Some Marines looked uncomfortable. Some looked angry. Some looked furious.

"Now, I wouldn't be surprised if this man supported the insurgency. The translator said the man was a bad guy. An 'ali baba.' But clearly, this man has suffered. And if this man, this father, does support the insurgency, it's because he thinks *his* suffering justifies making *you* suffer. If his story about his beating is true, it means the Marines who beat him think *their* suffering justifies making *him* suffer. But as Paul reminds us, 'There is none righteous, no, not one.' *All* of us suffer. We can either feel isolated, and alone, and lash out at others, or we can realize we're part of a community. A church. That father in my parish felt as if no one could understand him and it wasn't worth the effort to make them try. Maybe you don't think it's worth trying to understand the suffering of that Iraqi father. But being Christian means we can never look at another human being and say, 'He is not my brother.'

"I don't know if any of you know Wilfred Owen. He was a soldier who died in the First World War, a war that killed soldiers by the hundreds of thousands. Owen was a strange sort. A poet. A warrior. A homosexual. And as tough a man as any Marine I've ever met. In World War One, Owen was gassed. He was blown in the air by a mortar and lived. He spent days in one position, under fire, next to the scattered remains of a fellow officer. He received the Military Cross for killing enemy soldiers with a captured enemy machine gun and rallying his company after the death of his commander. And this is what he wrote about training soldiers for the trenches. These are, by the way, new soldiers. They hadn't seen combat yet. Not like he had.

"Owen writes: 'For 14 hours yesterday I was at work — teaching Christ to lift his cross by numbers, and how to adjust his crown; and not to imagine he thirsts until after the last halt. I attended his Supper to see that there were no complaints; and inspected his feet that they should be worthy of the nails. I see to it that he is dumb, and stands at attention before his accusers. With a piece of silver I buy him every day, and with maps I make him familiar with the topography of Golgotha.' "

I looked up from my sermon and looked hard at the audience, which was looking hard back at me.

"We are part of a long tradition of suffering. We can let it isolate us if we want, but we must realize that isolation is a lie. Consider Owen. Consider that Iraqi father and that American father. Consider their children. Do not suffer alone. Offer suffering up to God, respect your fellow man, and perhaps the sheer awfulness of this place will become a little more tolerable."

I felt flushed, triumphant, but my sermon hadn't gone over well. A number of Marines didn't come up for Communion. Afterward, as I was gathering the leftover Eucharist, my RP turned to me and said, "Whoa, Chaps. That got a bit real."

Our fifteenth casualty was from Charlie. Nikolai Levin. The Marines were enraged, not only because of the death, but because the sergeant major had told them it was Levin's fault.

"I'm not here to make friends, I'm here to keep Marines alive," the sergeant major said, haranguing the men only a few days afterward, "and the fact of the matter is, when a Marine comes in and he wasn't wearing his PPE when he was hit, because it's hot, and he doesn't want to wear it while he's at the OP, I'm the one who's got to say the thing nobody wants to say."

Levin had been hit in the neck. PPE wouldn't have helped. But I guess the sergeant major, like most people, needed death to be sensible. A reason for each casualty. I'd seen the same feeble theodicy at funerals in the civilian world. If lung disease, the deceased should be a smoker. If heart disease, a lover of red meat. Some sort of causality, no matter how tenuous, to sanitize it. As if mortality is a game with rules where the universe is rational and the God watching over maneuvers us like chess pieces, His fingers deep into the sides of the world.

By the end of the deployment, we had well over a hundred men injured. Sixteen total dead. George Dagal was the first. Then Roger Francis Ford. Johnny Ainsworth. Wayne Wallace Bailey. Edgardo Ramos. William James Hewitt. Hayward Toombs. Edward Victor Waits. Freddie Barca. Samuel Willis Sturdy. Sherman Dean Reynolds. Denton Tsakhia Fujita. Gerald Martin Vorencamp. Jean-Paul Sepion. Nikolai Levin. Then what we thought would be the last: Jeffrey Steven Lopinto.

I went through their names over and over on the flight back, a sort of prayer for the dead. We touched down and were processed. I watched the Marines hug their parents, kiss their wives or girlfriends, and hold their children. I wondered what they would tell them. How much would be told and how much could never be told.

My biggest duty stateside was planning the memorial service for all sixteen. I struggled to write out something satisfactory to say. How could I express what those deaths meant? I didn't know myself. In the end, yielding to exhaustion, I wrote an inoffensive little nothing, full of platitudes. The perfect speech for the occasion, actually. The ceremony wasn't about me. Better to serve my function and pass unnoticed.

Jason Peters succumbed to his injuries two months after the service, bringing the list of the dead to seventeen. Those who'd visited Peters generally agreed this was a good thing. He was missing both hands and one leg. The IED had burned off his eyelids, so he had goggles on that misted his eyes every few seconds. His body was in a mesh, his kidneys had failed, he couldn't breathe on his own, and he went through constant fevers. There was little indication Peters had much awareness of his surroundings, and those who'd seen him couldn't talk about it without going into a rage. His family had taken him off all life support, had the doctors give him an IV drip, and let him die with some measure of dignity.

Over the following months and years, there were other deaths. One car accident. One Marine who got into a fight on leave and was stabbed to death.

There were crimes and drug use, too. James Carter and Stanley Phillips, of Alpha Company, murdered Carter's wife and then mutilated her body trying to get it into the too-small hole they dug. Another Marine, high on cocaine, shot at a nightclub with an AR-15 and seriously injured one woman. Cocaine makes you feel invulnerable, which I suppose hypervigilant war vets must like. They don't like what comes after, though, when they get kicked out of the Corps and denied VA health services for their PTSD. That sort of thing happened to five or six Marines from the battalion, so the men started switching to substances that couldn't be easily picked up in a piss test.

Aiden Russo was the first of the suicides. He did it on leave, with his personal handgun. After Russo's death, the incoming chaplain, Reverend Brooks, gave a suicide prevention speech to the battalion. In his speech, he claimed America's suicide rates were a result of *Roe v. Wade.* Apparently, abortion was degrading our society's respect for the sanctity of life. Brooks was one of the hordes of born-again chaplains coming not from established churches, but from the loosely organized Independent Baptist Churches. My RP told me that after his talk, the Marines joked about how they thought I was going to punch him out midspeech.

Five months later, Albert Beilin killed himself with pills. Both Beilin and Russo were from Charlie Company.

A year later, José Ray, back in Iraq for the third time, shot himself in the head.

Two years later, Alexander Newberry, formerly of Charlie Company, appeared in an event called Winter Soldier, organized by the protest group Iraq Veterans Against the War. The event was supposed to prove the illegality of the war, and since a Marine from my old battalion was taking part, I watched most of it on YouTube. The panel of veterans was of varied quality. Many were vague and unconvincing, and what they complained about seemed more like the standard horror of war than any particular pattern of misconduct. Newberry, however, had brought a camera to Iraq and used photos and video to accompany his testimony. He claimed to have abused Iraqis and shot some just to take out aggression. He claimed Captain Boden congratulated every Marine on their first kill and told everyone that if a Marine got their first kill by stabbing someone to death, they'd get a ninety-six-hour pass when they got back. It sounded right.

Newberry had a series of slides he flipped through that were projected behind him, and he brought up pictures of two people he had killed, both of whom he claimed were innocent. He showed a video of Marines firing on mosques and talked about conducting "recon by fire," where he said they would shoot up a neighborhood in order to start a firefight.

The comments section beneath the video was a mess of antiwar and human rights folks either congratulating Newberry or calling him scum. A few posts seemed to be from Marines, and even Marines from the battalion. "I was there. Alex no telling the whole story." "This guy was the biggest shit bag ever." "boohoo they had to kill some people. what did he think was gonna happen when he became a MACHINE GUN-

NER IN THE MARINE INFANTRY." "It's the commanders fault don't feel bad Alex." "No one told him to kill innocent people he did it himself and blames the Corps he committed war crimes what a nut and its not true this happens often i know im a Marine."

At this time, I was still serving as a chaplain at Camp Lejeune. I'd done a stint at Base and then ended up transferred to a new battalion. While there, I'd occasionally run into Staff Sergeant Haupert, who'd been transferred to the same unit and whose Ramadi days were clearly still with him. He'd tattooed the name of every Marine from his company who'd died on his right arm. Combat deaths and suicides. He was widely respected in the unit.

The one time we discussed Winter Soldier, Haupert spoke of Newberry with intense hatred. "It's not whether it happened or not. You don't talk about some of the shit that happened. We lived in a place that was totally different from anything those hippies in that audience could possibly understand. All those jerks who think they're so good 'cause they've never had to go out on a street in Ramadi and weigh your life against the lives of the people in the building you're taking fire from. You can't describe it to someone who wasn't there, you can hardly remember how it was yourself because it makes so little sense. And to act like somebody could live and fight for months in that shit and not go insane, well, that's what's really crazy. And then Alex is gonna go and act like a big hero, telling everybody how bad we were. We weren't bad. I wanted to shoot every Iraqi I saw, every day. And I never did. Fuck him."

The next suicide was Rodriguez's old squad leader, Sergeant Ditoro. He did it around the time Lieutenant Colonel Fehr was promoted and made a regimental commander. Not long after, Rodriguez showed up at the base chapel. I didn't recognize him at first. He was pacing up and down the walkway to the chapel, and when I stepped outside to speak with him, he looked up, startled, looking lost and childlike. So different from before.

Haupert had already told me a little of Ditoro's story. In the last month of the deployment, an IED had blown Ditoro's arm off. Though he'd intended to be a career Marine, after a year in the Wounded Warrior Regiment he'd gotten out of the Corps and gone on to live in New Jersey for a few years. And then he'd shot himself, left-handed, in the head.

What I didn't know was that he'd e-mailed Rodriguez a suicide note right before he did it. That night, on the walkway outside the chapel, Rodriguez was holding it, a well-creased printout of Ditoro's last recorded words. When I walked up to him, he handed it to me without explanation, and I didn't even read it at first.

"It's Ramiro, right?" I said. "Ramiro Rodriguez. I haven't seen you in a long time."

He shrugged. His face was softer, more resigned than I'd ever seen it. I could smell alcohol on him. "I don't know if I did good or not," Rodriguez said. He rubbed his face with his hands. "They say Ramadi's quiet now. You can walk down the streets no problem."

I nodded. "Violence dropped in that city like ninety-something percent," I said. "That's where the Awakening started."

"You think we contributed to that?" he said. "You think what we did mattered?"

"Maybe. I'm not a tactics guy, I'm a chaplain."

"We killed a lot of hajjis," he said.

"Yes."

We stood in silence for a while. He looked down at the e-mail in my hands and I scanned it quickly.

i keep remembering where i was when i lost my arm. i wanted to die very fast because i was in ramadi and ramadi was the miserablest part of the world and i was in so much pain. did you see alex saying they were killing civilian? his platoon was fucked like ours but lets be honest that place was all war. remember that little kid planting ieds. i dont feel bad about shooting mosques and never will they were insurgent ratholes every fucking one. i hit sammie pretty bad and she left and could have threw me in jail if she wanted. i feel bad about that but most I feel bad about fuji who you said was my fault and there youre right. i was his squad leader and i sent him up there i dont think anything i can do would make up for that even if i got killed rescuing someone plus theres what you said about bicycle man. remember him. remember what acosta did after levin. i believe in god i believe in hell. id like to tell fujis family that the guy who got his son killed is facing judgment and hes scared but happy. judgement isnt hanging over his head anymore and now hell get what he deserves and maybe even mercy. maybe you could tell them. you were a good saw gunner and you did right. im glad you were in my squad.

When I finished I looked up at Rodriguez. My hands were shaking. His weren't.

"Do you blame yourself?" I said.

He looked out at the St. Francis Xavier Chapel, a small building ringed by trees.

"A bit," he said. He looked at me sidelong. "I blame you a bit, too. For not doing anything. But I blame myself more."

He rubbed his eyes.

"You didn't want forgiveness when we were over there," I said. "Do you want it now?"

"From you?"

I had to smile at that. "No," I said. "That I'm worthless is well established. God's forgiveness might be different."

He scowled. I think I wanted him to confess as much for my good as for his. It didn't really matter to me if he didn't think he believed anymore. Belief can come through process.

I grabbed hold of the small cross on my collar. "You know this was a torture device, right?"

At that he laughed. I didn't mind. I knew Rodriguez hadn't come here just to laugh at me.

"Twenty centuries of Christianity," I said. "You'd think we'd learn." I fingered the small cross. "In this world, He only promises we don't suffer alone."

Rodriguez turned and spat into the grass. "Great," he said.

Psychological Operations

I learned words from among the languages
of the earth
to seduce foreign women at night
and to capture tears!
— *Ahmed Abdel Mu'ti Hijazi*

Everything about Zara Davies forced you to take sides. Her attitude, her ideas, even her looks. She wasn't beautiful, exactly, but only because that's the wrong word. There were plenty of beautiful young people at Amherst. They blended with the scenery. Zara insisted on herself. She was aggressive, combative, and lovely.

I first saw her in Clark House at Punishment, Politics, and Culture. The course description read, "Other than war, punishment is the most dramatic manifestation of state power," and since thirteen months in Iraq had left me well acquainted with war, I figured I'd go learn about punishment.

Everybody in the class was white except for me and Zara.

The first day, she sat right across from the professor, wearing skintight jeans and a wide brass belt buckle, a thin yellow T-shirt, and brown suede boots. She had a dark caramel complexion and wore her hair natural, braided in the front with an Afro puff at the back. Though she was a freshman, she jumped into discussion right on the first day, setting the tone for the semester. She could be sharp and even a bit cutting when her classmates — the guys in khakis and polos, the girls either in sweatshirts or in expensively tasteful but boring clothes — said something she thought was stupid.

At the time, I tended to play the world-weary vet who'd seen something of life and could look at my fellow students' idealism with only the wistful sadness of a parent whose child is getting too old to believe in Santa Claus. It's amazing how well the veteran mystique plays, even at a school like Amherst, where I'd have thought the kids would be smart enough to know better. There's an old joke, "How many Vietnam vets does it take to screw in a lightbulb?" "You wouldn't know, you weren't there." And that's really the game. Everyone assumed I'd had some soul-scarring encounter with the Real: the harsh, unvarnished, violent world-as-it-actually-is, outside the bubble of America and academia, a sojourn to the Heart of Darkness that either destroys you or leaves you sadder and wiser.

It's bullshit, of course. Overseas I learned mainly that, yes, even tough men will piss themselves if things get scary enough, and no, it's not pleasant to be shot at, thank you very much; but other than that, the only thing I felt I really had on these kids was the knowledge of just how nasty and awful humans are. A not inconsiderable bit of wisdom, perhaps, but it gave me no added insight into, say, applying Althusserian interpellation to Gramsci's critique of ideological structures. Even the professor would yield authority when the discussions got to the social effects of rampant violence and criminality, like I'd tell them I'd seen "over there." Zara was the only one who saw through me.

She was running her own game. As a black girl from Baltimore, she had a fair share of street cred. That she was the daughter of a physics professor at Johns Hopkins and a real estate attorney and was thus a million times more privileged than 90 percent of the white guys I served with in the Army didn't particularly matter. Baltimore, everybody who'd seen an episode of *The Wire* could tell you, was a rough city.

My attitude was, she deserved the authority she took. The things you really deserve, no one gives to you, so take what you can get. And I liked having a sparring partner.

One time she cut me off right at the knees. I was midway through delivering an enjoyably self-righteous lecture to another student who'd made an offhand remark about the U.S. invading Iraq for oil.

"I was one of those people invading Iraq," I said, "and I didn't give a damn about oil. Neither did a single soldier I knew. And it's frankly a little —"

"Oh, come on," Zara snapped. "Who cares what the soldiers believe? It doesn't matter what the pawns on a chessboard think about how and why they're being played."

"Pawns?" I said, indignant. "You think I was a pawn?"

"Oh. Sorry." Zara smiled. "I'm sure you were a rook, at least. Same difference."

She wasn't scared to give offense, and I liked that.

When the class ended, though, so did my contact with her. Our social circles never intersected, and we'd only occasionally see each other on campus. Months after the class, though, she sought me out.

I was eating alone in Val when she sat down in front of me. I didn't recognize her at first. By this time the yellow T-shirt, which I had loved, which had hugged her rib cage and clung to her breasts in such an expressive way, was long gone. No more short skirts, no more jeans worn tight around muscular thighs. She had a long brown dress that went all the way down her legs to a rather disappointing pair of flats. Her hair was in a shawl. Everything was demure, and yet, perhaps because this was college in late springtime and every other girl was walking around with half her tits exposed, Zara stood out even more in a crowd than she had before. At least to me she did.

She was Muslim now, I guess. When I'd first met her, she'd been disillusioned. Then searching. And finally, somehow, Islam. I'd never pictured her as the sort to go for a religion about submission, even if that submission was to God.

She explained that since her recent conversion she'd been thinking more and more about Iraq. Specifically, about American imperialism and the fate of the *Ummah* and the unbelievable numbers of Iraqis getting killed, numbers too large to be conceptualized and that nobody seemed to care about. She sought me out for firsthand information. The real scoop on what was going on. Or what had been going on years ago when I'd been there.

"Be honest with me," she said.

It could only have ended badly. There's a perversity in me that, when I talk to conservatives, makes me want to bash the war and, when I talk to liberals, defend it. I'd lived through the Bush administration fucking up on a colossal scale, but I'd also gotten a very good look at the sort of state Zarqawi wanted to establish, and talking with anybody who thought they had a clear view of Iraq tended to make me want to rub shit in their eyes.

Besides, she didn't tiptoe around delicate subjects. "How could you kill your own people?" was, I believe, what she actually said to me.

"What?" I said, almost starting to laugh.

"How could you kill your own people?"

"They're not my people," I said.

"We're all one people," she said.

I supposed she meant some Malcolm-X-at-Mecca, "us Muslims are all one people" bullshit. I knew otherwise. The Sunni-Shi'a War had pretty clearly illustrated that the

Ummah wasn't a happy family. I snorted, took a pause, and, as I looked at her flat-heeled shoes, felt that old familiar vet-versus-civilian anger coming up.

"I'm not Muslim," I said.

Zara looked not so much surprised as concerned, as if she were witnessing me lose my mind. Her lips were pursed, perfectly formed, and beautiful, like every other part of her face. I couldn't tell if she was wearing makeup or not.

"I'm a Copt," I said, and since that never elicits any reaction, I added, "Coptic Orthodox Church. Egyptian Christians."

"Oh," she said. "Like Boutros Boutros-Ghali." Now she looked interested, head cocked, oval face looking straight at me.

"Muslims hate us," I said. "There are riots, sometimes. Like the pogroms in Russia against Jews." That's what my father always said. The time he saw his cousin die in one of those riots was a foundational myth for our family. Or, it was for him. Being Copt was not a major part of my life. Not if I could help it.

"So you don't pray," she said, "because . . ."

I laughed. "I pray," I said. "But not to Allah."

She frowned a little and gave me a look

that let me know I was never going to sleep with her.

"So you see, I can kill Muslims as much as I like," I said, smiling. "Shit, in my religion, that's how you help an angel get its wings."

I thought of it as a mild comment. In the Army it wouldn't have raised any eyebrows. And though Zara had stiffened up and ended the conversation a bit curtly, I hadn't thought her especially bothered. But two days later, I found myself face-to-face with the Special Assistant to the President for Diversity and Inclusion, a round little man with a potato head nestled on fat, fleshy shoulders. I'd met him before. As a veteran and a Copt, I was the most diverse thing Amherst had going.

At the time, I didn't even know what I'd done. The e-mail said I may have violated the provisions in the Amherst student honor code related to "respect for the rights, dignity, and integrity of others," with particular regard to harassment for reasons "that include but are not limited to race, color, religion, national origin, ethnic identification, age, political affiliation or belief, sexual orientation, gender, economic status, or physical or mental disability." That didn't help narrow things down for me.

The e-mail directed me to report to the Special Assistant's office the following morning, giving me all the time needed to work myself into a fervor. I was at the school on a combination of the G.I. Bill, the Yellow Ribbon Program, and various scholarship funds. If I was expelled or suspended, I didn't know what sort of jeopardy that money would be in. Everything was dependent on me remaining in "good standing with the school." I tried to call the VA but was put on hold so long I threw my phone at the wall. As I collected the pieces, I saw my father's face, his tired eyes and thick mustache, the mix of disappointment and, worse, resigned acceptance that this was my fate, to turn every opportunity into shame.

The next morning, I walked into the Special Assistant's office. He was seated at his desk, fat head sitting placidly on his shoulders, hands folded, his Salvation Army "Toy for Joy" posters and Ansel Adams prints framed on the wall behind him. All this was expected, even a little funny. But across from him, leaning forward and studiedly ignoring my entrance, sat Zara. That hurt. She wasn't a friend, but I'd thought we had a sort of respect. And I'd never picked her for another thin-skinned golden child, walking through campus like Humpty Dumpty on a tightrope, waiting for a scandalous word to unsteady her balance and shatter her precious identity. Worse, I knew what I'd said to her and how it would play.

The Special Assistant explained that this wasn't a "formal mediation" because Zara hadn't lodged a "formal complaint." He spoke in the soothing tones a mother would use to calm a frightened child, but he ruined it by explaining that, though no punishment was on the table, if our dispute "had to go to the dean of student conduct," the consequences could be "serious." He furrowed his brow theatrically to let me know he meant it.

I sat in my seat, across from the Special Assistant, next to Zara. If she ever got suspended, I thought, she'd be fine. She'd go back to Professor Mom and Daddy Esquire for a term, think about what she'd done, and then return to the school they were paying for. If I got suspended, my father would kick me out of the house. Again.

"Now, Waguih," the Special Assistant said. "Am I pronouncing that correctly? Wa-goo? Wah-geeh?"

"It's fine," I said.

The Special Assistant told me how seriously Amherst took threatening statements. Particularly against a group that had faced so much discrimination in recent years.

"You mean Muslims?" I said.

"Yes."

"She's been Muslim for like three days," I said. "I've been facing that shit for years."

He gave me a concerned face, and waved his hand at me to continue. I felt like I was in therapy.

"I'm Arab and I lived in North Carolina for four years," I said. "At least she gets to choose to be the terrorist."

"Muslims aren't terrorists," she said.

I turned to her, genuinely angry. "That's not what I'm saying. *Listen* to what I'm saying."

"We're listening," said the Special Assistant, "but you're not helping yourself out."

I looked down at my hands and took a breath. In the Army I'd been a 37F, a specialist in Psychological Operations. If I couldn't PsyOps my way out of this, I wasn't worth a damn.

I considered my options: grovel or bite back. My preference has always been the latter. In Iraq, we'd once broadcast the message "Brave terrorists, I am waiting here for the brave terrorists. Come and kill us." That stuff feels better than lying down and showing your belly.

"In the Army we had a saying," I said. "Perception is reality. In war, sometimes what matters isn't what's actually happening, but what people think is happening. The Southerners think Grant is winning Shiloh, so they break and run when he charges, and so he does, in fact, win. What you are doesn't always matter. After 9/11 my family got treated as potential terrorists. You get treated as you're seen. Perception is reality."

"*My* perception," said Zara, "is that you threatened me. And I talked to some of my friends at Noor, and they felt the same."

"Of course they feel threatened," I said to the Special Assistant, "I'm a crazy vet, right? But the only mention of violence came from her. When she accused me of murdering Muslims."

The Special Assistant's eyes shifted to Zara. She looked at me. In a way, I'd lied. She'd never used the word *murder.* I didn't want to give her time to respond.

"I got shot at," I said. "Kind of a lot. And I saw people, yes, gunned down. Blown up. Pieces of men. Women. Children." I was laying it on thick. "I helped as I could. I did what's right. Right by America, anyway. But those aren't pleasant memories. And for someone to get in your face . . ." I trailed off, glancing toward the ceiling with a look of anguish.

"I didn't —," she began.

"Accuse me of murder?" I said.

"I asked a reasonable question," she said. "There's hundreds of thousands dead and . . ."

The Special Assistant tried to calm us down. I gave him a tight smile.

"I understand why she said that," I said. "But . . . sometimes I can't sleep at night."

That wasn't true. Most nights I slept like a drunken baby. I noticed a slight look of panic on the Special Assistant's face and pushed forward, determined to get out of the corner they'd boxed me in.

"I see the dead," I said, letting my voice quaver. "I hear the explosions."

"No one is disrespecting what you've been through," said the Special Assistant, definitely panicked now. "I'm sure Zara had no intention of disrespecting you."

Zara, whose face had held a lively anger moments before, looked surprised and, I think, saddened. At first I thought it was because it disappointed her to see me playing the game. It didn't occur to me that she might simply be feeling sympathy for me. If

I'd known that, it would have made me angry.

"And I had no intention of threatening her," I said, feeling very clever. "But the damage was done."

The Special Assistant gave me a long stare. He seemed to be determining just how big a liar I was before deciding on a course of minimum liability. "Okay," he said, doing a Pontius Pilate–style washing motion with his hands. "So — a rational observer might conclude there was ample reason for both sides to be offended."

"I suppose that's fair," I said, allowing myself to appear calmer. We were in the realm of claim and counterclaim. I felt on firmer footing.

Then Zara explained her concerns in a slightly cowed voice. The "justifiable anxieties" of her fellow Muslims and the degree to which they felt they needed to band together and "move aggressively against intolerance." She explained herself not as though presenting her case, but as if apologizing for her overreaction. It surprised me, what my so-called sleepless nights had done to her sense of grievance. The spark she always had in class discussions was gone. When she finished, I graciously accepted her rationale for feeling threatened and said

I'd moderate my words in the future if she'd do the same. The Special Assistant was all approving nods. He told us, "You two have a lot in common," and we suffered through a little talk about how this was a teachable moment, how if we could get past our anger, we could learn so much from each other. We agreed to learn much from each other. And then he recommended, strongly, that I look into the health services that the college could offer regarding my sleepless nights. I said I would, and we were done. I'd escaped.

We walked out of the office and out of Converse Hall together, emerging into the sunlight. Zara had a dazed look about her. Around us were students heading to class or to breakfast. Since it was Amherst, there were even a few assholes playing Frisbee or, as they would call it, "throwing around the disk." The morning had a healthy, vibrant cast to it that played oddly against what had happened.

We stood there for a moment before Zara broke the silence.

"I didn't know," she said.

"Know what?"

"About what you've been through. I'm sorry."

And without another word she walked

away, swishing her legs under her dress and dissolving into the sunlight streaming in from the east.

As she faded, so did my relief at evading punishment, leaving me with what I'd done. She had, perhaps inartfully, asked me a genuine question. I'd given her nothing but lies. And now she had whatever guilt I'd dumped on her. To leave her with that, I thought, was cowardice.

I ran toward her, cutting a diagonal across the grass, pushing past other students, and planting myself directly in her path.

"What the fuck was that?" I said.

It clearly wasn't something she expected. The whole morning, perhaps, had been like that. Unsettling.

"What?" She shook her head. "What was what?"

"Why did you apologize to me?"

I could hear the anger in my voice and she stared back with amazement, perhaps with a little fear. But she said nothing.

"You think the big bad war broke me," I said, "and it made me an asshole. That's why you think I said those things. But what if I'm just an asshole?"

My breath was still coming quick — the aftermath of the run — and I was full of energy. My fists were balled tight. I wanted to pace back and forth. But she was still, sizing me up, colder every second. And then she spoke.

"Calling you a killer was out of line," she told me, "even if you are an asshole."

I smiled.

"You push my buttons," I said. "Good. You'd be boring if you didn't."

"And I care?" she said. "Whether you think I'm boring or not?"

"Did you believe that story in there?" I said. "Poor me and my hard little war?"

She gave me a blank look. "I guess," she said. "I don't know. I don't care. Whatever happened to you, I don't care."

"Sure you do," I said. "You asked."

"I'm not asking now," she said.

We stared at each other, each of us still.

"What if I want to tell you?" I said.

She shrugged. "Why?"

I took a breath. "Because I like you," I said. "Because you never give me any fucking respect. And because I want to level with you." I pointed back toward Potato Head's office in Converse Hall. "But without any of that lame bullshit."

"This isn't how you talk to people," she said. "Why do you talk to people like this?"

"I know how to talk to people," I said. "I can spin you some bullshit if you want. I'm good at that. But I don't want to lie. At least, not to you."

"I'm not your friend," she said.

I put up a hand to cut her off.

"I never killed anyone," I said. I let that hang for a moment, and once she nodded I said, "But I did see somebody die. Slowly."

That made her still. Then I said, "I'd like to tell you about it."

I wasn't PsyOpsing her into it, so I didn't know how she'd react. Or if I was PsyOpsing her, since you're always exerting some kind of pressure even when you're laying yourself bare, then it was the least conscious maneuvering I could do.

There was a long silence. "Why," she said, "do you think I would want to hear about it?"

"I don't know," I said. But I let her see, in my face, that it was important to me. PsyOps works best when you mean it.

There was another long silence. "Fine," she said, and motioned with her hands. "What happened?"

I looked around at the sunlight and the college students. Khakis and polos. Shorts and sandals. "Not here," I said. "This is a sit-down conversation. I don't just talk about this stuff to anyone."

"I've got to get breakfast," she said. "Then

I've got class."

I thought for a moment. "Have you ever smoked *shisha*?" I asked. "You know, hookah. Muslims love that shit, right?"

She rolled her eyes and let out a short laugh. "No," she said, and I knew she'd come.

After classes I went back to my apartment and brought the hookah to the porch. I sat down on my ratty couch, looked out at the street, and I waited.

When she arrived, ten minutes late, I already had the coals going. She'd had a full day to think it over and seemed restless and a little suspicious, settling herself in the chair with the rigid posture of someone who doesn't intend to stay long.

I asked her if she wanted rose- or apple-flavored tobacco, and when she said rose, I told her apple was better and she rolled her eyes and we went with that. I told her the rules of hookah — no pointing the mouthpiece at anyone, no left hand — and as I got out the tobacco she said, "So. You want to tell me a story."

I said, "Yes. And you want to hear it."

She smiled. "Possession of a hookah is against the student honor code," she said. "It's considered 'drug paraphernalia.' "

"Clearly," I said, "I don't follow the student honor code."

The hookah was ready. I pulled on it a couple times and held the smoke in my lungs before letting it out. It had a sweet, smooth flavor and feel, and it relaxed me.

I told her, "You know, technically I didn't even watch him die. It just felt that way," and she didn't say anything in response. She just looked at me, so I passed her the pipe and she took a pull.

"It's sweet," she said, breathing the smoke out with her words. She pulled again and let a slow curl ripple over her lips. Then she put the hose back down, pointed away from both of us.

I didn't know how to start, which was unusual. I'd told the story before. In bars, most times, and then it was all about the money shot, the death. But that was one death among hundreds of thousands. Meaningless to all but a few people. Me. That child's family. Perhaps, I thought, Zara.

I needed to ground myself. I began, as you do in the military, with geographic orientation. I told her about East Manhattan, which was a section of Fallujah north of Highway 10. A few weeks earlier, Marines from 3/4 had swept through the neighborhood, jumping roof to roof and clearing houses while thousands of civilians fled the city and the disorganized resistance tried to come up with some kind of plan. A lot of the fighting happened on Easter Sunday, which everybody thought was significant, even me. It was 2004, the third time in my life I could remember American Easter falling on the same day as Coptic Easter, and I spent that day watching a city explode.

But then the battle was called off and 3/4 wound up sitting in houses turned into defensive positions, sniping insurgents. Every fourth house had a sniper team. In the early part of the siege, they'd kill a dozen every day.

I tried to give Zara the feel of the city — not just the dust and the heat and the terror, but also the excitement. Everyone knew the ax was going to fall, it was only a question of when and how many would die.

"Each night," I said, "the mosques would blast the same messages over the *adhan* speakers. 'America is bringing in the Jews of Israel to steal Iraq's wealth and oil. Aid the holy warriors. Do not fear death. Protect Islam.' "

As PsyOps, I told her, part of our job was to counter those messages. Or at least to fuck with the insurgents and make them scared. Explaining that Islam was a religion of peace wasn't likely to work, but explaining that we would definitely kill you if you fucked with us might convince a few folks to chill out.

I told her how we used to go out in a Humvee strapped with speakers so we could spew our own propaganda. We'd dispense threats, promises, and a phone number for locals to call and report insurgent activity. We always got shot at. I didn't tell her what that felt like, hiding in a vehicle with nothing but your voice while you're taking fire, helpless and angry, depending on the grunts for safety. I just told her that I hated those missions.

The morning I saw someone die, we'd wanted to go out on the speakers again, so we staged behind a building held by 3/4. When we got there we realized the speakers weren't working. My sergeant, Sergeant Hernandez, fiddled with them as best he could.

When the shots rang out, the heavy burst of a Marine machine-gun section's 240G, I was in the building, standing in a doorway. The sound turned my head around, and through the corridor I could see the Marines who'd fired. They were stretched across the room in front of me, hiding in shadows toward the back and covering their sectors of fire through the broken windows to the front. They seemed so calm. Whoever got killed probably never even knew the Marines were there. I never heard any incoming AK fire.

"Gunfire was a part of daily life," I started — but that sounded too hard-guy. I wanted to be honest, so I said, "The truth is, it goosed me, hearing it that close and not being able to see anything, just the Marines."

I remember hearing a voice from a doorway on the other side of the room say, "Good to go," and then the response from a thin black Marine with corporal chevrons and a big enough wad of dip in his mouth to make him look deformed.

"Yeah," he said, "he's gonna fade for sure."

A little square-bodied Marine was the one actually manning the machine gun, and he kept saying, "I got him, I got him," like he couldn't believe it was true.

The thin black Marine spat and said, "Tell Gomez our section's a hundred percent now." That meant every man in his section had killed someone. Which meant the little square-bodied Marine had just done it for the first time.

"And Marines think that's a good thing," Zara said.

"Of course," I said, though I realized I

was simplifying. The corporal hadn't acted like it was a big deal, and it even seemed he found it distasteful, but there was also a lanky Marine in the far corner of the room who'd been nodding, giving the little Marine these small, approving grins.

I looked up from the porch. The daylight had turned soft. We were in that final hour of sun where everyone looks like the best version of themselves.

"And then that little Marine saw me," I said, "in my Army cammies. And he called out, 'Hey-o! PsyOps!' The kid was high off adrenaline. You could tell. His face was flushed. He was calling me out. And I didn't belong there, looking in on these Marines and their, I don't know . . . private moment."

"Private moment?" Zara said, curious.

"It was their last man finally doing it," I said.

"Finally doing it," she said, imitating my voice. "What? You mean he was a murder virgin?"

"Even you don't think it's murder," I said. "You're smarter than that."

She sighed and made no argument, so I told her how the little square-bodied Marine's eyes were wide, his face somewhere between terror and excitement, and he motioned to the scope as if to say, "Look into it." Somewhere between an offer and a plea.

The squad had been using thermal scopes because the heat signatures made it easier to tell the thin shadows of dogs from the bright white heat of humans. I told Zara how I walked into the room, where I didn't belong. And I told her how the corporal was staring at me, like he didn't want me there, and how I ignored him and looked out through the broken windows. The early morning was black. One or two shades of purple stretched across the landscape, but otherwise Fallujah was a dark, undifferentiated mass.

I knelt next to the little Marine, and I looked through the optic, and then the boxy skyline of Fallujah lay out before me in heat gradations of gray and black. Some buildings had a water cistern or fuel tank on the top, and I could tell how much fluid was in the cistern because the cooling line of the water across the metal was written in a light line of gray. A few days earlier, Marines clearing houses had hit a hard point at a building with a fuel cistern, just like that. They shot holes in it, waited until the fuel trickled down all through the house, and set it on fire with the muj inside. I wondered what that would have looked like, through that scope. A lot of white, I guess.

Closer in, immediately in front of me, was an open stretch of road and field and a bright jumble of limbs lying twenty feet out from the nearest building. A black strip alongside must have been the rifle, and I could see the poor bastard clearly hadn't gotten off a shot. A burst would have heated up the barrel, but all I saw was cold black next to the white heat of the body.

"Why'd you look?" Zara asked.

"Who wouldn't look?" I said.

"You wanted to see." Her voice was hard, accusing. "Why'd you look?"

"Why are you here, listening to this story?"

"You asked me to come here," she said. "You wanted me to hear."

It was difficult to explain to her how I'd both wanted and not wanted to see, and how the little Marine so clearly didn't. There was a mix of voyeurism and kindness in me stepping down and looking through the scope. And once I was on the scope, the thin black corporal told me to watch for the heat signature dying, the hot spot fading to the ambient temperature. He told me, "That's when we'll officially call in the kill."

A few kids on skateboards came rolling down the street in front of Zara and me.

They looked young. High school, probably. Townies, definitely. You forget not everybody in Amherst is in college. I had no idea where the kids could be going, and we waited until they rolled past and the sound of them disappeared. Then I continued.

"It happens slowly," I said. "I'd look up for a second and then back, to try to catch a change. The corporal kept looking at the doorways, as if he were worried some senior Marine would see me there and chew us all out. The little Marine kept saying, 'He's dead. He'll fade for sure,' but I couldn't tell, so I held my fingers out in front of the optic. They made this searing hot spot, glowing white against the grays of the background. There's no color in the scope, but it's not like a black-and-white movie. The scope tracks heat, not light, so everything, the shadings, the contrasts, they're off in this weird way. There are no shadows. It's all clearly outlined, but wrong, and I was waving these bright white fingers across the scope, my fingers — but looking so strange and disconnected. I was waving them in front of the body and trying to compare."

"And?" said Zara.

"And I thought I saw him twitch," I said. "I jumped back and that sent all the Marines into alert, the corporal screaming at me to tell them what I saw. When I told them the corpse twitched, they didn't believe me. The little Marine got back on the optic, saying, 'He's not moving, he's not moving,' repeating it over and over, and the lanky one asked if they had to go out and treat the hajji's wounds. But the corporal said the corpse was probably just settling. Gas escaping or something." I looked down at my hands. "The little Marine was angry now, they all were, and at me."

"Was he alive?" Zara asked.

"The corpse?" I said. "If he was, it wasn't for long. The little Marine put me back on the optic and it did look darker. That's what I told them. And the corporal told the little Marine he did good, while I stared into the scope and tried to see the life going out of him. Or the heat, I guess. It happens so slow. Sometimes I'd ask the little Marine if he wanted to look, but he never did. He was an unusual sort of Marine. The adrenaline was fading and he was just left with this thing he'd done, and he didn't want to watch."

We took in the late afternoon for a moment.

"So that's yours now," she said.

"What do you mean?"

"You watched him die."

"Just the heat signature," I said.

"That's yours now," she repeated. "You took it from him so he wouldn't have to watch."

I didn't say anything. Neither of us had used the hookah in a while, so I grabbed the hose and started pulling smoke into my lungs.

"And now you're telling me," she said.

I blew out smoke.

"Why are you telling me this?" she said.

"You asked me how I could kill my people," I said.

"And what?"

I put down the hose and she picked it up. I didn't have a real answer for her, and now that I'd told the story, I didn't feel I'd actually told her anything at all. I think she knew it, too, that the story hadn't been enough, that something was missing and neither of us knew how to find it.

"Who do you think he was?" she said.

"What do you mean?"

"The guy that Marine shot," she said.

I shrugged. "Some kid," I said. "A stupid death. That's what we were out there to prevent."

She let out smoke in a slow, sensual way, but her face looked concerned. Upset.

"What do you mean, 'prevent'?"

"I was PsyOps," I said. "Psychological Operations. I was supposed to tell the Iraqis how to not get themselves killed. And I actually spoke the language, so it was me on those loudspeakers, not a translator."

"Right," she said. "You spoke Arabic growing up."

I shook my head. "Egyptian Arabic," I said. "The soaps and the movies mean a lot of non-Egyptians understand it, but still, it's different."

She nodded. "I knew that."

"The Army didn't," I said. "My unit thought they'd hit the jackpot. They didn't even have to send me to language school. I tried to argue that they should, but then Sergeant Cortez came back from Monterrey speaking Modern Standard Arabic and I realized that U.S. Army mental retardation was a general problem."

"So what, you learned Iraqi on your own?"

"Yeah, I got books from an office friend of my father's," I said. "And I'd go out and tell the Iraqis what was what. These imams were up there getting everybody excited, telling them to fight us. And the teenagers ate that shit up. You'd have a bunch of kids with no military training who'd seen too many American action movies try to go

Rambo. It was crazy. An untrained kid against a Marine squad in camouflaged positions with marked fields of fire?"

"But of course that's gonna happen," she said, "when you send an army through a city."

"We tried to limit the damage. The generals had a bunch of meetings with the imams and sheikhs to tell them, 'Stop sending your stupid fucking kids against us, we're just going to kill them.' But it wouldn't change anything."

"In their eyes the problem wasn't the kids," she said.

"Things were crazy then. And we were fucking that city up."

"I've read there were hundreds, maybe thousands of civilians killed."

"There was propaganda on both sides. But I was trying to help people avoid getting killed. And not everybody was kids."

"But a good number were."

"Some," I said. "That one I saw fade, it was a small body. Hard to tell. But I always think, That was one I was supposed to save."

"Save?" she said. "By convincing him not to fight the soldiers invading his home?"

I laughed. "Yeah," I said. "It was such bullshit. The Marines would be sitting there waiting, hoping some dumb muj would make a suicide assault. Nobody wants to be the guy in the squad who hasn't killed anybody, and nobody joins the Marine Corps to avoid pulling triggers."

She nodded.

"That's not why I joined the Army," I said.

"So why did you?"

I laughed. " 'Be All That You Can Be'?" I said. "I don't know. That was the slogan for me, growing up. And then it was 'Army of One,' which I never understood, and then it was 'Army Strong,' which is about as good a slogan as 'Fire Hot' or 'Snickers Tasty' or 'Herpes Bad.' A better slogan would be, 'You Can't Afford College Without Us.' "

She seemed to be sizing me up, deciding how to take what I'd told her. I sat and smoked and didn't say anything. Eventually she leaned back into her chair and gave me the sort of straight look she'd use in class before tearing someone apart.

"So that's your story," she said. "The story you wanted to tell me. Now what?"

I shrugged.

"Do you tell this story to other girls?"

"I'm being honest," I said. "I'm not honest with other girls. It hurts my chances."

She shook her head. "You say you joined for college? I don't believe you." Then, imitating my voice, "Nobody joins the Army to avoid pulling triggers."

"You got no idea why anybody joins the military," I said, the words coming out angrier than I wanted. "No fucking clue."

She smiled and leaned in, enjoying my anger. It was her, the old Zara.

"I know what you think," I said. "I know your type."

"My type?" she said. "You mean Muslims?"

"Why's it always Muslims with you?"

"I know you don't like us."

"That's not true."

She shook her head. "We say things for a reason," she said.

I sighed. "I've been hated as a Muslim. The last time my father hit me was after a kid at school called me a 'sand nigger.' "

"What?" Zara said. "Your father hit *you*?"

"It's how I handled it. The fight . . ." I stopped for a moment, tried to figure how I'd explain it to her. "Look, I went to a nice high school in northern Virginia, in a town too expensive for us to live in. My father moved us there when I finished junior high. He wanted me to have the best education. Which was great, I guess, though I really didn't fit in.

"The fight turned out to be a big deal because a teacher overheard the kid using that word. The n-word. This was after 9/11, and it wasn't that kind of town, you know? They didn't see themselves that way. It became a big incident, and there was a lot of sympathy for me, because I was Arab, and because of 9/11, and because of what he said. I hated all of it. I don't like pity."

"What did you do to the kid?"

"Yelled back a few names."

"That's not really enough, is it?"

"My dad didn't think so. It's why he hit me. Because I hadn't fought the kid who was insulting me and, by implication, our whole family. Or maybe he was just pissed the school principal seemed to think we were Muslim, too."

Zara looked down and fiddled with her head scarf. "My father thinks Islam is the religion of poor blacks," she said. "He says people will think I picked it up in prison."

"Is that why you joined?" I said. "To piss off Daddy?"

She sighed and shook her head.

"So why?" I said.

"I'm learning why," she said. "The practice of it teaches me."

"And the clothes?" I said. "The whole . . ." I waved my hands at her.

She touched her head wrap. "It's part of the commitment," she said quietly. "What was it you said to the Special Assistant? Perception is reality?"

"Yeah."

"Wearing this, people treat me like I've made a change in my life. Which I have." She smiled. "That matters," she said.

"In the military," I said, "that's part of why they give you the uniform."

She nodded and we were quiet again. I could feel her slipping away. Her mind, perhaps, wandering off to other subjects. I knew I'd failed to communicate. Of course I had. I didn't know what I wanted to tell her, just that I'd tell her anything to keep her listening.

Silence became awkward, then agonizing. She looked at me, her body relaxed but her eyes fixed on mine. Words, I thought, any words will do. If I were seducing her, I'd know what to say.

She broke the silence first. "You told the Special Assistant things turned ugly," she said, "for you and your family, around 9/11. Is that true?"

"Yes," I said, relieved we were talking. "If you saw my mother, you'd think she was white, but my dad's different. He's darker than me and he's got that Arab dictator mustache thing going on. He looks exactly like Saddam Hussein."

"Exactly?" she said. "Like he could be a body double?" She leaned in toward me. That simple movement, the physical expression of interest, excited me. "What I mean is, would you think that if your family still lived in Egypt?"

I laughed. "They look alike, especially with the mustache. And he won't shave it. It's a manhood thing."

"And that caused problems," she said.

"Some," I said. "He's so stubborn. And he became Mister Über-America. He had flags flying at our house, and 'Support Our Troops' magnets all over the bumper of his car. Not that that changed anything, the way he looked. Or the way we all looked, and with our Arab-sounding names, going through airport security."

"I can imagine."

"No, you can't. Because when they'd pull him aside to pat him down by hand, he'd tell them, loud so everybody could hear, 'I know you get a lot of flak, but I want you guys to know I support what you're doing. You are protecting our American freedoms.' "

Zara shook her head sadly.

"And my mother, Jesus. She came from a totally different universe than my dad. Copt, yeah, but not the type to have family in

Garbage City. Growing up, her friends were all Muslim, even one Jew, rich kids who read Fanon and talked radical politics before getting real and marrying each other. But my mom was more radical than all of them. More radical than my grandmom, even, who was a straight-up Communist before the June War. She married my dad. And then he pulled his American freedoms act? I thought she was gonna kill him the first time he did it. That shit nearly broke their marriage."

"Why didn't it?"

"She's religious," I said.

Zara smiled. "What did you think?"

"I was seventeen," I said. "You've got to understand — my father was there when his cousin died. He was badly beaten himself. And then the people my father had told me were bad all my life had finally got my country really pissed. And those stories he'd told me weren't bullshit anymore. My father, I mean, the man has never given two shits about me. He's not a cuddly guy."

"The Army was a way to make him proud?"

I winced. It didn't sound so good coming from her mouth. "Make myself proud. But part of that would be in his eyes."

"I imagine the Arab stuff got worse in the Army."

"No," I said. "Not at all. It was more direct, though." I laughed. "One drill instructor, during inspection, he asked what I'd do if my brother joined al-Qaeda. Would I shoot him in the face? My own brother?"

"That's awful."

"I'm an only child," I said. "I told him yes. Basic isn't a place for subtleties."

"What about the other recruits?"

"There was one guy, Travis. He had an uncle who worked construction, and after Travis joined the Army his uncle started refusing to work with this family of Muslim electricians. It was in Travis' honor."

"I've heard stories like that," said Zara. "Actually, I've heard a lot worse."

"Travis told it to me and then was like, 'What you gonna do about it, faggot?' "

"What'd you do?"

"I told him I wasn't Muslim. Or gay. It's a nice card to have in your back pocket when you run into that stuff."

"I don't know if I could fight for an organization that treated me like that."

"You're thinking about it the wrong way," I said. "That shit is just people. It wasn't alienating. This" — I waved my hand toward the college — "this is alienating. All these special little children and their bright futures. Look, if Travis was the type to die for his buddies, and he might have been, I think he'd do it for me just as soon as for anyone else wearing Army cammies. That he hated me, and that I hated the ignorant fuck right back, well, there are circumstances that trump personal feelings."

"The circumstances," she said, "being a war. Where the Army was going to go kill all those people you've been mistaken for. And you get to watch."

I rolled my eyes, though I was angrier than I let on. So I took the hookah and smoked for a while in silence. The benefit of hookah is that those moments aren't dead space. You can blow smoke rings. You can perform and not say anything. You can think.

She didn't seem to realize how this conversation was different from class, where we bullshitted over political theory. This mattered. And every time she contradicted me with her smug little assumptions about who I was and why I did what I'd done, it grated. It made me want to shut my mouth and hate her. Hate her for her ignorance when she was wrong, and hate her for her arrogance when she was right. But if you're going to be understood, you have to keep talking. And that was the mission. Make her understand me.

"When I graduated from basic," I said, "my father was prouder of me than he'd ever been. By this point, he was listening to Limbaugh and O'Reilly and Hannity non-stop, and my mother had a standing rule that he wasn't allowed to talk politics in the house. Afghanistan, back then, felt like it'd been a complete success, and Bush was making the case for Iraq."

Zara said, "I remember." I put down the pipe and she picked it up.

"I'd been at Fort Benning," I said, "getting the shit beat out of me. It'd been hot and awful and I'd been screamed at and PT'd half to death. I hadn't seen my dad in months. But images of Saddam were everywhere. TV. Newspapers." I took a breath. "And then there he was. The same face. The same build. He even walked with that cocky fucking strut. And there was that mustache."

"So you saw him," she said.

"And I saw Saddam." I took a breath. "I mean, my dad, too. But everybody, my platoon, the DIs, they all knew what he looked like."

Zara blew smoke. "You saw him through their eyes."

"Through my own."

"But how they saw him," she said. "Maybe

part of how they saw you, too?"

"I wonder if he knew," I said. "We don't really talk, but, I wonder. I mean, the man is an asshole. It's just who he is. But I wonder if deep down, beyond the politics, if the mustache was a giant 'fuck you.' Maybe not to America, but to Americans, you know? All those God-fearing assholes who talk Jesus but don't know that true Christianity is the Coptic Church."

"My father's a deacon," she said. "But he's not a very good man. It took me a long time to realize that. . . ."

"And I . . . I was there because of him. When he hugged me and told me how proud he was of me — which he didn't even do at my high school graduation — I took it in. Graduation from basic's a big deal. All this pageantry. Uniforms and flags and everybody telling everybody over and over how brave we were, how patriotic, and what great Americans we were. You can't resist hundreds of people feeling proud of you. You can't. And then my dad, like it was just an offhand comment, he asks me, 'So, when you signed up, why didn't you pick infantry?' and the feeling popped like a bubble."

"What'd you do?"

"Nothing. I was in the Army now. I went

to training. I got care packages from my mom and patriotic e-mails from my dad. He'd send me PowerPoints with pictures of soldiers, or jokes and speeches about 'the troops' that talked about them like they shat gold. I was eighteen, I ate it up. But I was also learning how to do propaganda in our classes, and it felt pretty fucking weird.

"We had one instructor," I said, "who spent a class telling us about all the advertisement that went into us joining the Army and how dumb we were to fall for it. He'd say, 'I love the Army. But how bullshit are those commercials?' He was all about getting us to recognize the propaganda in civilian life so we could use the same techniques in war. He'd say, 'Real life doesn't fit on bumper stickers, so remember: If you tell too much truth, nobody will believe you.' "

"I don't think that's a good way to think about it."

"Yeah, well, he's right. In Iraq, we told a lot of truth and a lot of bullshit to the Iraqis. Some of the bullshit worked really well."

"It's strange to think of somebody doing that for a living," she said. "You hear the word *propaganda,* it makes you think of those World War Two posters. Or Stalinist Russia. Something from another time, before we got sophisticated."

"Propaganda is sophisticated," I said. "It's not just pamphlets and posters. As a Psy-Ops specialist, as anything in the Army, you're part of a weapons system. Language is a technology. They trained me to use it to increase my unit's lethality. After all, the Army's an organization built around killing people. But you're not like an infantryman. You can't think about the enemy as nothing but an enemy. A hajji. A gook. A bad guy needing a bullet. You've got to get inside their heads."

The night had come in force while we talked, and there was a full moon lying low in the sky. The streets were quiet. I felt close to her because she'd listened, and I'd told everything straight, pretty much, with a minimum of artifice. It made me want to go further, but that would require careful packaging.

"You know," I said, "I lied to you before. A little."

"How?"

"I did kill people."

She was very still.

"I didn't shoot anybody, but I was definitely responsible."

The two of us let that hang in the air for a while.

"The last person I told this to was my

dad," I said. "It got me kicked out of the house."

Zara looked down at her hands, folded in front of her, then up at me. She gave a little smile. "Well, I couldn't get you kicked out of here if I tried."

"And you sure have," I said.

She shook her head. "It wasn't a formal complaint," she said. "My friends wanted me to make a formal complaint, but all I wanted was for you to have to listen. You're not very good at that."

"I'm sorry," I said. "Truly."

She shrugged. "Tell your story."

"I was in the Battle of Fallujah," I said. "We did a lot of crazy stuff there. We'd play shit just to fuck with the muj. Real loud Eminem and AC/DC and Metallica. Especially when they'd try to coordinate over their own loudspeakers. We'd play shit to drown them out, hurt their command and control. Sometimes we'd roll up to a position and play the Predator chuckle. You ever see that movie?"

"No."

"It's this deep, creepy, evil laugh. Even the Marines didn't like it. We'd have something going on all the time. And the muj would play shit, too. Prayers and songs. There was one that cracked me up. It was like, 'We fight under the slogan Allahu Akbar. We have a date with death, and we're going to get our heads chopped off.' "

"Very poetic," she said.

"It was horrible. There was gunfire and explosions and the mosques blaring messages and Arabic music and we were blaring Drowning Pool and Eminem. The Marines started calling it Lalafallujah. A music festival from hell."

"In a city," she said, "filled with people."

"But it wasn't just music," I said. "The Marines, they'd compete to find the dirtiest insults they could think of. And then we'd go scream over the loudspeakers, taunting holed-up insurgents until they'd come running out of the mosques, all mad, and we'd mow them down."

"Out of the mosques?" she said.

"You're in this crazy city, death everywhere, and you see a lieutenant go to his men, as if it was the most serious thing in the world, and ask, 'Do we go with, "You suck your mothers' cocks," or, "You fuck dogs and eat the shit of children"?' "

"Really? Out of the mosques?" she said again.

"Sure," I said. "What? Are you kidding me?"

She shook her head. "So how did you kill

people?" she said.

"The insults," I said. "And of everything we did, that got the most satisfying feedback. I mean, the muj would charge and we'd listen as the Marines mowed them down. Sergeant Hernandez called it 'Jedi mind trick shit.' "

"Okay," she said.

"It's brilliant," I said.

"Unless your average schoolyard bully is brilliant," she said, "it's not. But I get why it worked."

"Worked almost too well. We spent the next couple months trying to get the same fucks we'd riled up to stop charging because a lot of them were just teenagers. Marines don't like killing children. It fucks them up in the head."

"What'd it do to you?" she said.

"I feel good about what I've done," I said.

"No, you don't," she said. "Or why are you telling these stories?"

"What are you?" I said, grinning. "My therapist?"

"Maybe," she said. "That's how this feels."

"Fucking with insurgents saved lives at Fallujah. And then I probably saved lives afterwards, telling the truth about what would happen if you fucked with us."

"So is that what got you kicked out of

your father's house? Saving lives?"

"No. Not saving lives." I stopped, then started again. "It was over Laith al-Tawhid. If there's one guy I killed, that's the guy."

Zara didn't say anything. I picked up the hookah and pulled on it and got nothing. The coals were dead. I felt nervous, even though she'd been good to me. Patient. But if I kept going and told her the story, I didn't know if she'd understand. Or rather, I didn't know if she'd understand it the way I did, which is what I really wanted. Not to share something, but to unload it.

"When I got back," I said, "there was no big ceremony. If you're not part of a battalion, you come back on a plane with other cats and dogs, soldiers from different shops. I did my redeployment stuff, and then I went home."

I looked down at my hands, then back up at Zara. I didn't know how to tell her what coming home meant. The weird thing with being a veteran, at least for me, is that you do feel better than most people. You risked your life for something bigger than yourself. How many people can say that? You chose to serve. Maybe you didn't understand American foreign policy or why we were at war. Maybe you never will. But it doesn't matter. You held up your hand and said,

"I'm willing to die for these worthless civilians."

At the same time, though, you feel somehow less. What happened, what I was a part of, maybe it was the right thing. We were fighting very bad people. But it was an ugly thing.

"When I'd left for the Army," I said, "the living room had just three paintings on the wall — two icons, and one Matisse print of fish in a bowl. They're my mother's. Now alongside them there's a framed American flag, and one of those 9/11 medallions that supposedly had steel from the World Trade Center but later turned out to be a scam. It was home, but . . ."

"You didn't belong there anymore?" said Zara.

"Maybe not," I said, "I don't know. My dad was standing there in a suit. My mom had a little cross hanging from her neck. She got more religious when I went over. She prayed every day. And she told me if I wanted, she'd make me some kosheri, this lentil-tomato dish I love. And she put her hand on my back and started rubbing my shoulders, and I felt if I didn't do something, I'd start crying."

I kept my eyes on my hands, telling Zara the story. Looking at her would be too much, though maybe I could have let her see how I was feeling. Maybe she'd have pitied me. It wouldn't have been entirely manipulative. I felt sad and lost. Somehow it felt the same as that day in my parents' house, with my mom rubbing my shoulders and me thinking about what I'd been through and how much I would never tell her because it would only break her heart.

"But my dad," I said, "he wouldn't have it. 'The boy's back from war,' he told my mom, 'we should take him out for a real American meal. Outback Steakhouse!' He thought that was a real funny joke. I didn't know how to take it. Serious Copts are supposed to eat vegetarian about two hundred days out of the year — no food with a soul — and it was close to Christmas. But my mom didn't say anything and so we went. My dad ordered a steak to show me it'd be all right. My mom and I had salads.

"We got through dinner with small talk, but when we got home my mom went off to work — she's a nurse — and that left me and my dad alone. He sat me down in the living room and said he'd make me coffee. Then he handed me a few sheets of paper with a rubber band around them. He said, 'I sent an e-mail out to the guys in the office, and they all wanted to thank you.' He looked so happy and proud. It didn't feel like basic. I wasn't a disappointment. I'd been to war. And I'd missed him."

I looked up at Zara and her eyes met mine. The darkness gave her a softer look than she had in the daytime.

"The paper," I said, "it was printouts of e-mails from his Muslim friends at work."

"He had Muslim friends?" she said.

"Colleagues," I said. "Some friends. Sort of. He'd say he was keeping an eye on them. That was his joke. He works for a company that does translation services, mostly for NGOs and government agencies, and he's in the Arabic department. So there's a lot of Muslims. And they wrote me letters. Mostly short e-mails like, 'Good job, thank you for your service,' or, 'Whether this war is right or wrong, you have done an honorable thing.' But some were more involved. One talked about how the war was terrible, but he hoped having a 'sensitive young man' like me over there would make the suffering less."

"A sensitive young man?" she said. I saw a hint of a smile.

"I've changed," I said. "Another was from a guy who'd been in the Yemeni civil war. He told me, 'Whatever you go through, it is the responsibility of those who sent you.'

And a bunch of the other e-mails were real pro-war."

"I guess there was a lot of anger among American Muslims toward Saddam."

"Well, one was so pro-war not even my father could have written it. That guy told me I was going to write a new chapter in history. My dad underlined the sentence."

"And what'd you think," she said, "when you saw that?"

"It made me angry," I said.

My voice was soft, speaking to Zara. It was as though I were saying loving words.

"I didn't tell him exactly what I told you," I said. "I wanted to hurt him. I was angry. I'd gotten a lot of Thank You For Your Service handshakes, but nobody really knew what that service meant, you know?"

"You're angry with your father because people thanked you for your service?" she said. "Or is he why you're angry with those people?"

"He's a part of it," I said. "That sentiment."

"So should I thank vets for their service?" she said. "Or spit on them, like Vietnam?"

I thought for a moment and then gave her a crooked smile. "I reserve the right to be angry at you whatever you do."

"Why?"

"It's all phony," I said. "When the war started, almost three hundred congressmen voted for it. And seventy-seven senators. But now, everybody's washed their hands of it."

"There was bad information," Zara said. "You know, 'Bush lied, people died.' "

"Oh, my God!" I clapped my hands to my cheeks and put on a shocked face. "A politician lied! Then it's not your fault!"

"You used to kill people with playground insults," Zara said, "and you think it doesn't matter what the president says? Or here's a better question. Did you believe it? Did you support the war?"

"I still support the war," I said. "Just not the guy who ran it."

"Is that what you told your dad that made him so angry?"

"No." I hunched over, with my elbows resting on my knees. "No. He knew the war was poorly run. He's a smart guy."

I considered how I could frame what I was going to tell her.

"This is not the sort of thing you'll like," I said. "It's not the sort of thing my father could deal with."

"I'm not fragile," she said.

"Now you've got to understand," I said. "In my family, I wasn't even allowed to curse."

I paused. After a second, Zara reached over and took my hand, and I let her. She shouldn't have done that. It made me want to stop. It made me want to say something cruel, to let her know that what I'd been through had made me stronger, not weaker. From down the street I heard laughter. Frat kids from Psi U, maybe. Drunk, maybe, or just walking over to get a calzone at Bruno's.

"I guess your dad wasn't too big on you using dirty words to kill terrorists," Zara said.

Her hand pressed into mine. "My dad thought the idea of the insults was funny," I said. "He thought it was brilliant. Tribal culture is honor and shame. Like the rural South. Or inner-city America. But eventually we played that trick too much. We'd shouted too many insults, killed all the insurgents dumb enough to fall for it. And I'm telling this to my dad in our living room in their house in Virginia. It's not the house I grew up in. They'd moved to a cheaper area once I was out of high school, and we're in this tiny little room with an icon of Saint Moses the Black, who was a thief and a slave, and Saint Mary of Egypt, who was a prostitute, and Matisse's stupid fish and that goddamn flag and the fake 9/11 steel coin. And he's leaning forward, he's listening. It's the first man-to-man we've ever had."

"And it's about war," she said. "That's what gets him to listen."

"So I tell him how there's this one area where intel knows who the enemy is. This little band of Islamists called the al-Tawhid Martyrs Brigade. And my dad's like, 'Okay. Al-Qaeda.' And I'm like, 'No. Just desert fuckers who didn't like having Americans roaming around in their country.' It was the first time I'd cursed in front of my dad."

"What'd he do?"

"Nothing. He just said, 'Okay. So basically al-Qaeda.' I wanted to smack him." I took a breath. "Anyway, we knew the name of these guys' leader. Laith al-Tawhid. Intel had him on the BOLO list and so I had his name."

I squeezed Zara's hand, hard. "I had his name," I said. "In all the confusion, I could call him by name. I could talk to him and he would know it. And so would all his men."

"That gave you an advantage."

"Yes," I said. "And I had a plan. Normally, this sort of thing wouldn't start with a SPC, but they trusted me. They thought I had the magic knowledge, because, you know, I'm an Arab Muslim."

Zara was leaning forward, the same posture as my father. Her eyes were on me now.

"Now, Laith al-Tawhid was no idiot. He was fundamentalist, not dumb. He wasn't going to come running because I called him names. But I knew how to get him. Women."

"Women?"

"His women were at home," I said. "Outside of Fallujah. And the old-school guys, guys like Laith al-Tawhid, they treat women like dogs. Like dogs who can destroy all your family's honor if they act up or show an ounce of free will."

She nodded.

"There was a Marine company holding an office building in front of Laith's position," I said. "I told the Marines what we wanted to do and they loved it."

"What did you say?"

"Laith al-Tawhid, we have your women," I said, "your wife and your daughters."

She frowned. "So he had to come and fight you," she said.

"I told him we found them whoring themselves out to American soldiers, and we were bringing them to the office building."

She nodded. "You told this to your father."

"I told him everything. How I screamed out, in the Iraqi Arabic I'd learned in my private time, that we'd fuck his daughters on the roof and put their mouths to the loudspeaker so he could hear their screams."

Zara pulled back her hand. I'd expected that. "So that's how you fought," she said. There was a touch of contempt in her voice, and I smiled. I'm not sure why, I wasn't happy.

"I didn't send it up the flagpole. But the platoon loved it. I stayed on those speakers for an hour. Telling him how when his daughters bent down to pray, we'd put our shoes on their heads and rape them in the ass. Rub our foreskins on their faces. A thousand dicks in your religion, I told him, and in forty minutes, a thousand American dicks in your daughters."

"That's disgusting," she said.

"Everybody laughed as we came up with what we'd tell them. All the Marines had suggestions, but I turned them down. Americans think the best insults are all 'cunt' and 'pussy,' but in Arabic it's all 'shoes' and 'foreskins' and 'putting a dick in your mother's rib cage.' "

"I get the idea," she said.

"Well, this worked," I said. "They didn't charge out of the mosques like idiots, but they still assaulted, and they got mowed down."

"I don't care if it worked."

"I mean, all this guy's men were hearing him being disrespected. Humiliated. For an hour. This was a violent time. There were a hundred little insurgent groups, a hundred little local chiefs trying to grab power. And I was shaming him in front of everybody. I told him, 'You think fighting us will win you honor, but we have your daughters. You've fucked with us, so you've fucked your children. There is no honor.' He didn't have a choice. And I never saw him die. I never saw him at all. I just heard the Marines shooting him down. They told me he led his little suicide charge."

"I get it," she said.

"But you don't like it," I said. "My dad didn't either. He'd rather I shot them in the face. In his mind, that's so much nicer. So much more honorable. He'd have been proud of me, if I'd done that. You'd like me better, too."

"I'd rather you hadn't done anything," she said.

"And I told my father everything. Insult by insult. What I said. All the things I'd learned in America, all the things I'd learned from him, all the things that'd been said to me, all the things I could think of, and I could think of a lot."

"I get it," she said again, this time in the

same tone of voice that my father had used when I told him and he'd said, "Enough." But with my father I'd kept going, described every sexual act, every foul Arabic word. I'd cursed for him and at him in English, in Egyptian, in Iraqi, in MSA, in Koranic Arabic, in Bedouin slang, and he'd said, "Enough, enough," his voice shaking with rage and then terror, because I was standing over him, shouting insults in his face, and he couldn't see his son any more than I — standing over him and letting my rage wash out — could see my father.

"You think I'm ashamed of it?" I said to Zara, and I saw my father, heard the words he couldn't even get out of his mouth because the shock of it was too much. His hands had trembled, his eyes were downcast. There was gray in his mustache. He looked old. Beaten. I'd never seen him that way before.

Zara asked, "What happened to his daughters?"

I didn't know.

"When I think about killing that man," I said, "I think of that kid with the heat fading out."

I slumped down into the couch. We were quiet again. I thought about firing up more coals but I lacked the energy. After cursing my father I'd spent the night in a Motel 6, where my mother found me and brought me home. My father and I didn't talk for the rest of my leave.

"Okay," Zara said. She paused, looked out at the street. "So . . . what am I supposed to do? Am I supposed to forgive you?"

"Forgive me?" I said. "How? For what?"

"And even if I did," she said, "would it matter? Because I'm Muslim? You think that matters to the kid you watched die?"

I smiled at her. How far from the point, I thought, was that kid's death. It was at best the point of somebody else's story, though I guess Zara knew that.

"I tell vets the scope story," I said. "They usually laugh."

Zara stood up slowly, anger lighting her face. I didn't move from my seat. I looked up at her and waited for a response. Even covered up, her body was still lovely under her clothes. I kept smiling, enjoying her in front of me and enjoying the superiority I knew I'd feel when her outburst came. No one can really cut you when they're angry. It clouds their mind too much. Better to be like me in Fallujah, lying through your teeth and shouting hateful things with calm intelligence, every word calibrated for maximum harm.

But Zara's outburst didn't come. She just stood there. And then some emotion I couldn't identify moved through her, and she didn't seem angry anymore. She stepped back and looked at me, considering. She reached up and adjusted her shawl.

"Okay," she said at last. "It's okay."

For the first time since that morning, walking into the Special Assistant's office and seeing her there, I was the unsettled one. She wasn't playing any of the moves I'd envisioned for her.

"What do you mean?" I said.

She reached over and put her hand on my shoulder, her touch light and warm. Even though her face was calm, my heart was beating and I looked up at her as though she were passing down a sentence. There was an unearthly quality to her then.

"It's okay," she said. "I'm glad you can talk about it." Then she walked down the steps of the porch and stopped at the bottom. Behind her were the elm trees and the shoddy clapboard houses of South Whitney Street, housing for the off-campus frats and the few Amherst students who didn't live in dorms. She didn't quite belong here, I thought, and neither did I.

Zara stood in the yard, not moving. After a moment, she turned back and looked up the stairs to where I was still sitting by the hookah.

"Maybe we'll talk another time," she said. Then she gave a slight wave with her hand, turned, and walked back to campus.

War Stories

"I'm tired of telling war stories," I say, not so much to Jenks as to the empty bar behind him. We're at a table in the corner, with a view of the entrance.

Jenks shrugs and makes a face. Hard to tell what it means. There's so much scar tissue and wrinkled skin, I never know if he's happy or sad or pissed or what. He's got no hair and no ears either, so even though it's been three years after he got hit, I still feel like his head is something I shouldn't stare at. But you look a man in the eye when you talk to him, so for Jenks I force my eyes in line with his.

"I don't tell war stories," he says, and takes a sip of his glass of water.

"Well, you're gonna have to when Jessie and Sarah get here."

He gives a nervous laugh and points to his face. "What's to say?"

I take a sip of my beer and look him up

and down. "Not a lot."

Jenks's story is pretty obvious, and that's another weird thing because Jenks used to be me, basically. We're the same height, grew up in the same kind of shitty suburban towns, joined the Marine Corps at the same time, and had the same plan to move to New York when we got out. Everybody always said we could be brothers. Now, looking at him is like looking at what I would have been if my vehicle had hit that pressure plate. He's me, but less lucky.

Jenks sighs and sits back in his chair. "At least for you, it gets you laid," he says.

"What does?"

"Telling war stories."

"Sure." I take a sip of beer. "I don't know. Depends."

"On what?"

"Circumstances."

Jenks nods. "Remember that little reunion we had with all the ESB guys?"

"Hell, yeah," I say. "Way we were talking, you would have thought we were some Delta Force, Jedi ninja motherfuckers."

"The girls ate it up."

"We did pretty well," I say, "for a bunch of dumbass Marines hitting on city girls."

Jenks gives me a look. Right around his eyes is the only place where his skin looks halfway normal; the eyes themselves are pale powder blue. They never really struck me before he got hit, but they've got a sort of intensity now in contrast with the boiled-pork-pink smoothness of his skin grafts. "Of course, that shit only worked because I was there," he says.

Now I'm laughing, and after a second Jenks starts laughing, too. "Damn straight," I say. "Who's gonna call bullshit when you're sitting there in the corner looking all *Nightmare on Elm Street*?"

He chuckles. "Happy to help," he says.

"It does help. I mean, you tell a chick, 'Yeah, I went to war, but I never fired my rifle. . . .' "

"Or 'Hey, I spent most of the deployment paving roads. Building force pro. Repairing potholes.' "

"Exactly," I say. "Even the antiwar chicks — which in this city is all of them — want to hear you were in some shit."

Jenks points to his face. "Some shit."

"Right. Don't have to say anything. They'll start imagining all sorts of stuff."

"Black Hawk Down."

"The Hurt Locker."

He laughs again. "Or like you said, *Nightmare on Elm Street.*"

I lean forward, elbows on the table. "You

remember what it was like, going to a bar in dress blues?"

Jenks gets quiet for a second. "Fuck, man. Yeah. Automatic panty dropper."

"No matter how ugly you are."

He grunts. "Well, there's a limit."

We sit in silence for a bit, and then I let out a sigh. "I'm just fucking tired of chicks getting off on it."

"On what? The war?"

"I don't know," I say. "I had a girl start crying when I told her some shit."

"About what?"

"I don't know. Some bullshit."

"About me?"

"Yeah, about you, motherfucker." Now he's definitely smiling. The left side of his face is twisted up, the wrinkled skin over the cheeks bunched and his thin-lipped slit of a mouth straining toward where his ear should be. The right side stays still, but that's standard for him, given the nerve damage.

"That's nice," he says.

"I wanted to choke her."

"Why?"

I don't have an exact answer for that, and while I'm trying to find a way to put it into words, the door swings open and two girls walk in, though they're not the girls we're waiting for. Jenks turns and looks. Without even thinking about it, I size them up — one pretty girl, maybe a seven or an eight, with her less attractive friend, who isn't really worth giving a number to. Jenks turns away from them and looks back at me.

"I don't know," I continue. "I was playing her. You know. 'Oh, baby, I'm hurting and I need your soft woman touch.' "

"You were playing her," he said. "And it worked. So you wanted to choke her?"

"Yeah." I laugh. "That's kind of fucked up."

"At least you're getting some."

"I'd rather go to Nevada, fuck a prostitute." I almost believe what I'm saying. Using money would be better. But I'd probably just end up telling the hooker about Jenks anyway.

Jenks looks down at his glass, his eyes tight.

"You ever thought of getting a hooker?" I ask. "We could check the ads at the back of the *Village Voice,* see if anybody catches your eye. Why not?"

Jenks takes a sip of water. "You think I can't get some?" His voice sounds playful, like he's making a joke, but I can't tell.

"No," I say.

"Not even a pity fuck?"

"You don't want that."

"No, I don't."

I look at the girls down at the other end of the bar. Pretty girl's got dark hair slashing down the side of her face and a lip piercing. Her friend is in a bright green coat.

"Think of all those other burn victims out there." I look back at Jenks and give him a big grin. "And really fat chicks."

"And chicks with AIDS," he says.

"Nah, that's not enough. Maybe, like, AIDS and herpes combined."

"Yeah, that sounds awesome," he says. "I'll put an ad on Craigslist."

Now he's laughing for sure. Even before he got hit, when things got shitty he'd start laughing. I keep a smile plastered on my face, but for some reason now I start feeling it, the same feeling I get when I talk about Jenks and I get into it for real. Sometimes, when I'm drunk and I'm with a chick who seems like she cares, I let it out. Problem is, if I do, I can't sleep with her. Or I shouldn't, because then I feel like shit afterward and I walk around the city wanting to kill someone.

"There's plenty other guys like me," Jenks says. "I know one guy, got married, he's having a kid."

"Anything can happen," I say.

"It's bullshit anyway." There's a bit of hardness in his voice.

"What?"

"Finding somebody."

I'm not sure if he's serious.

"I was okay at it before," he says. "And in dress blues I was a fucking player. Now, it'd be insulting for me to even roll up on a chick."

"Like, 'Hey, I think you're ugly enough you might fuck me.' " I put a stupid smile on my face, but Jenks doesn't seem to notice.

"Nobody wants this," he says. "Nobody even wants to have to look past this. It's too much."

There's a little silence where I'm trying to come up with something to say to that, and then Jenks puts his hand on my arm.

"But it's okay," he says. "I've given up."

"Yeah? That's okay?"

"You see that girl over there?"

Jenks points to the pair of girls, and though he doesn't specify, he's obviously talking about the hot one.

"Before, I'd see her, and I'd feel like I had to come up with a plan, get her to talk to me. But now, with Jessie and Sarah" — he checks his watch — "whenever they get here, I can just have a conversation." He looks briefly back at the girls. "Used to be, I could never just sit in a bar with a woman." He looks at me, then back to the girls. "Now, knowing I got no chance, it's relaxing. I don't have to bother. Nobody's gonna think I'm less of a man if I can't pick up some girl. I only talk to people I actually give a shit about."

He raises his glass and I clink mine with his. Someone told me toasting with water was bad luck, but there's got to be an exception for guys like Jenks.

"As for kids," Jenks says, "I'm gonna give my shit to a sperm bank."

"Serious?"

"Hell yeah. The Jenks line ain't gonna die with me. My sperm isn't disfigured."

I have nothing to say to that.

"I'll have some baby out there," Jenks continues. "Some little Jenks running around. Won't be called Jenks, but I can't have everything, can I?"

"No," I say. "You can't."

"You should go ahead with it," he says. He jerks his head in the direction of the girls. "Go tell your war stories. I'll tell mine to Jessie and Sarah, whenever they get here."

"Fuck that," I say.

"Seriously, I don't mind."

"Seriously. Fuck you."

Jenks shrugs, and I stare him down for a while, but then the door opens again and there's Jessie and Sarah, who's Jessie's actor friend. I look up and so does Jenks.

The two of them are like the first pair that walked in the door, one a beauty and one not, though here the difference is starker. Sarah, the pretty girl, is a stunner. Jenks raises a mangled hand to wave them over, and Jessie, the not beautiful girl, waves a four-fingered hand back.

"Hey, Jessie," I say, and turn to the beautiful one. "You must be Sarah."

Sarah is tall and thin and bored. Jessie is all smiles. She hugs Jenks, then looks me over and laughs.

"You're wearing combat boots," she says. "That to give you extra cred with Sarah?"

I look down at my feet, like a dumbass. "They're comfortable," I mumble.

"Sure," she says, and gives me a wink.

Jessie's an interesting case. Aside from a missing finger, she doesn't have any major problems I can see, but I know the Army's got her on 100 percent disability. Plus, a missing finger is a good indication of something more. She's not bad-looking, though. And I don't mean that to say she's good-looking — I mean that she's a hair on the good side of ugly. She's got a fleshy oval face, but a trim, compact body. A softball player's body. The sort of girl you look at and say, "You'll do." The sort of girl you pick up in a club in the last hour before it closes. But also the sort of girl you'd never want to date because you'd never be able to bring her around your friends without them thinking, Why her?

Except when Jenks first met Jessie at some disabled veterans function, he fell for her hard. He'd never admit it, of course, but why else would he be here, with no one but me to back him up, ready to talk Iraq to a total stranger? This Sarah. This pretty, pretty girl.

"Let me get you guys a drink," says Jessie.

Jessie always gets us the first round. She says engineers reinforced her ECP two days before an SVBIED attack, so she owes engineers big-time. Doesn't matter if we mostly did pothole repair. She gets me drinks, the only woman I know who makes a point of it.

I point to my glass. "I'm drinking Brooklyn."

"Water," Jenks says.

"Yeah?" Jessie says, smiling. "Cheap date, you."

"Hey, Jess," says Sarah, cutting in, "can you get me a gin and diet tonic? With lime."

Jessie rolls her eyes and heads to the bar. Jenks's eyes are full of her as she goes. I wonder what the fuck she thinks she's doing. I wonder what Jenks thinks she's doing.

Jenks turns back to Sarah. "So you're an actress," he says.

"Yeah," she says, "and I bartend to make rent."

Sarah's holding it together well. Apart from the occasional quick sidelong glance at Jenks, you'd think everybody at the table had a normal face.

"A bartender," I say. "Where? Can we come by, get free drinks?"

"You're getting free drinks," she says, pointing toward Jessie at the bar.

I smile a little "fuck you" smile. This Sarah is way too hot not to hate. Straight brown hair, sharp features, undetectable makeup, long pretty face, long thin legs, and a starvation zone body. Her getup is all vintage clothes, the carefully careless look worn by half of white Brooklyn. If you pick this girl up at a bar, other guys will respect you. Take her home, you win. And I can already tell she's way too smart to ever give a guy like me a chance.

"So you want to talk some war shit," I say.

"Sort of," she says, feigning disinterest. "A couple of the people in the project are doing interviews with vets."

"You got Jessie," I say. "When she was a Lioness she was in some real war shit. Hanging with the grunts, doing female engagement, getting in firefights. Her war dick is this big —" I throw my hands out in the lying fisherman pose. "Ours is tiny."

"Speak for yourself," Jenks says.

"It's better than no war dick at all," I say.

"Did Jessie explain the project?" asks Sarah.

"You want me to tell you about the IED," Jenks says. "For a play."

"We're working with a group of writers from the Iraq Veterans Against the War," she says. "They've been doing workshops, a sort of healing through writing thing."

Jenks and I trade a look.

"But this is different," Sarah says quickly. "It's not political."

"You're writing a play," I say.

"It's a collaboration with the New York veterans community."

I want to ask what percentage the "vet community" is getting, but Jessie comes back, precariously holding two pints of beer, one diet G&T, and a glass of water, her left hand on the bottom and the other on top, a finger or thumb in each glass. She smiles at Jenks as she puts them down on the table, and I can see him visibly relax.

Sarah starts explaining that the point of the thing isn't to be pro- or antiwar, but to give people a better understanding of "what's really going on."

"Whatever that means." Jessie laughs.

"So you're with the IVAW now?" I say.

"Oh, no," Jessie says. "I've known Sarah since kindergarten."

That makes more sense. I always picked her for the bleeds-green type. I'd bet my left nut she voted McCain, and I'd bet my right nut this Sarah girl voted Obama. I didn't vote at all.

"IEDs cause the signature wounds of this war," Sarah says.

"Wars," I say.

"Wars," Sarah says.

"Burns and TBIs, you mean?" says Jenks. "I don't have a TBI."

"There's PTSD, too," I say, "if you believe *The New York Times.*"

"We've got some PTSD vets," Sarah says, making it sound like she's keeping them in jars somewhere.

"No bad burns?" I ask.

"Not like Jenks," she says to me, then quickly turns to Jenks. "No offense."

Jenks makes one of those maybe-a-smile faces and nods.

She leans forward. "I just want you to go through what it was like, in your own words."

"The attack?" says Jenks. "Or after?"

"Both."

Most people, when they try to draw Jenks out, talk to him in a "here, kitty-kitty" voice, but Sarah's all business — clipped, polite.

"At your pace," she says. "Whatever you think people should know." She puts a concerned face on. I've seen that face on women at bars when I open up. When I'm sober, it makes me angry. When I'm drunk, it's what I'm looking for.

"It's like a lot of pain for a long, long time," Jenks says. Sarah puts one hand up, a delicate, pale hand with long fingers, and with the other she reaches into her bag and pulls out her smartphone, fiddles with some app for recording.

Jenks is tense again, which is why I'm here. For backup of some kind. Or protection. Jessie flashes him a smile and puts her fucked-up hand on his, and Jenks reaches his free hand into his pocket and pulls out a wad of folded-up notebook paper. I look away, toward the other table with the other two girls. They're drinking beer. I read a study somewhere that people who drink beer are more likely to sleep with someone on the first date.

"He'd remember the IED better than I would," Jenks says, looking at me. I look at Sarah and know for a certified fact I'm not telling this girl shit. "I can't even tell you that much after," he goes on. "Scraps and pieces, at best. I've been working for a long time to put them together." He taps the paper but doesn't unfold it. I know what's in there. I've read it. I've read the draft before and the draft before that.

"I know I was in a lot of pain," Jenks says. "Pain like you can't imagine. But pain like I can't imagine either, because" — he reaches up and rubs a hand over his fucked-up scalp — "a lot of the memories are gone. Nothing. Like, system overload. Which is okay. I don't need the memories. Plus, they had me on a cycle of morphine, an epidural drip, IV Dilaudid, Versed."

"What's the first thing you remember?" Sarah asks. She's talking about the attack, but Jenks is already sliding away from that.

"My family," Jenks says. He stops and opens the paper, flipping through the first few pages, the pages she's here for. "They didn't act like anything was wrong with me. And I couldn't talk to them. I had a tube in my throat." He looks down at the paper and starts reading. "It must have been worse for my family than for me —"

"Do you want me to maybe just read that?" she says, pointing at the papers. "Then ask you questions afterwards? I mean, if you've already got it written down . . ."

Jenks pulls the papers away from her. He looks at me.

"Or okay," she says. "You read it. That's best."

Jenks takes a breath. He sips water and I sip beer. Jessie's scowling at her friend and squeezing Jenks's hand. After a moment, Jenks clears his throat and holds the papers out again.

"It must have been worse for my family than for me," he starts again. "People look at me now and think, God, how terrible. But it was so much worse then. They didn't know if I'd survive, and I didn't look like myself. When a body loses as much blood as I did, weird things happen. I was holding an extra forty pounds of fluid in my body, puffing up my neck and face like a bloated fish. I was bandaged and oiled wherever I was burned and —"

"Do you remember the explosion itself?" Sarah cuts in. Jenks gives her a flat look. The day before, when he'd asked me to come, I'd told him that if he gave this girl his story, it wouldn't be his anymore. Like, if you take a photograph of someone, you're stealing their soul, except this would be deeper than a picture. Your story *is* you. Jenks had disagreed. He never argues with me, he just goes his own way. I told him I'd come with him whatever he chose to do.

"I've worked hard to remember it," he tells Sarah, flipping back through his pages but not looking at them. "The problem is I'm not sure what's real memory and what's my brain filling in details, like a guy whose heart stops and he thinks he sees a bright light. Except I'm sure of my bright light. There was a flash, definitely. There was a sulfur smell, like the Fourth of July, but real close."

I don't remember sulfur. I remember meat. Grilled meat. So, yeah, Fourth of July. Barbecue. It's why I'm vegetarian now, and why the hippie chicks in Billyburg sometimes think I'm like them, which I'm not.

"And black hitting so hard," Jenks says.

"Black?"

"Everything black and quick, a knockout. You ever been knocked out?"

"Actually, yes."

I let out a loud snort. There's no way Sarah's ever been knocked out. I bet her parents had put her in Bubble Wrap all the way to the Ivy Leagues.

"Then yeah. Black hitting you, like a knockout punch to the head, no gloves, but the knuckle is bigger than you are, it hits your whole body all at once, and it's on fire. It killed the two other guys in the vehicle, Chuck Lavel and Victor Roiche, who were amazing Marines and the best friends I've ever had, though I didn't know they'd died until later. And then there are scraps of memories and then waking up in another country, wondering where my battle buddies are, and at the same time knowing they're dead, but not being able to ask because I couldn't move or talk and had a tube in my throat."

Chuck and Victor were my friends too, and good friends of Jenks's, but never his best friends. That was always me.

"So the scraps," Sarah says.

"I remember screaming," Jenks says, "I don't know — from the explosion, from later, in the hospital, screaming. Though I couldn't have screamed in the hospital."

"Because of the tube."

"I feel like there were times I was screaming, or maybe times when I dreamed how things should have been."

"What do you remember?" Sarah turns to me. So does Jessie. "Do you remember screaming?"

Jenks is looking down at his hands. He sips water.

"Maybe," I say. "Who cares? My A-driver didn't hear shit. No sounds at all. A thing like that, if you got ten people there, then you'll have ten different stories. And they don't match."

I don't trust my memories. I trust the vehicle, burnt and twisted and torn. Like Jenks. No stories. Things. Bodies. People lie. Memories lie.

"It helps to put things in order," Jenks says, one palm resting on his paper.

"Helps with what?" Sarah says.

Jenks shrugs. He's been doing that a lot. "Nightmares," he says. "Weird reactions when you hear something, smell something."

"PTSD," she says.

"No," Jenks says matter-of-factly. "Explosions don't startle me. I'm all good. Fireworks, light and sound, it's all fine. Everybody thought the Fourth of July would freak me out, but it doesn't unless there are too many smells. And I don't lose it or anything. Just . . . weird reactions."

"So you try to remember —"

"This way, it's me remembering what happened," Jenks says. "I'd rather that than be walking down the street and I smell something and the day remembers itself for me."

"PTSD," she says.

"No," he says, his voice sharp, "I'm fine. Who wouldn't have a few weird reactions? It doesn't mess with my life."

He taps his paper. "I've written this twenty times," he says. "I always start with the explosions, the smells."

I want to smoke a cigarette. I've got a pack in my pocket, my last from a carton I picked up visiting friends in the Carolinas. In this city, smoking'll kill your bank account way before it kills your lungs.

"So you got knocked out . . . ," Sarah tries again.

"No," I say. "He was awake."

"I was frozen," Jenks says. "My eardrums had burst. I couldn't hear."

"But you heard screaming?"

Jenks shrugs again.

"Sorry," Sarah says. Jessie's eyes are on Sarah. She looks unhappy.

Jenks goes back to reading from the papers. "I kept thinking, I can't move, why can't I move? And I couldn't see, either. The only reason I can see today is I was wearing Eye Pro. I had shrapnel in my head, face, neck, shoulders, arms, the sides of my torso, my legs. I couldn't see, but my eyes worked. I went black. I woke up, still on the road. The smells were the same."

Your smells are off, I think.

"There was burning inside my body. The shrapnel in my skin and organs was still red hot and burning me from the inside while I burned from the outside. Ammo was cooking off inside the vehicle and one round struck my leg, but I didn't know it at the time. Honestly, I was so out of it. I feel more sorry for the guys who had to rush in and treat me than for myself."

This is Jenks's standard line. It's utter bullshit.

He turns to me. So do the girls. "It was what it was," I say. "Not the greatest day."

Jessie laughs. Sarah looks at her like she's crazy.

"Memory gets really spotty after that," Jenks says. "There's this drug, Versed, it kills your recall. I guess that's good. So this is all stuff they told me after the fact." He looks down at his papers and starts flipping through while we all wait. I sip beer. Then he starts reading. "They pumped blood into me using a power infuser. At one point I lost pulse and went into PEA, pulseless electrical activity. My heart had electrical activity going on but not in an organized fashion, so it couldn't form an effective contraction of the ventricle. It's not a flatline, but it's not good. They were pushing blood and epinephrine into me as quickly as they could. I was on a respirator. Earlier, Doc Sampson had put tourniquets on both my arms and everybody I talked to was very clear: Those tourniquets saved my life."

"So —"

Jenks holds up a hand to shut her up. "What they are not clear about but what is very clear to me is that it was not just Doc Sampson who saved my life. It was the first guys who got to my vehicle" — he looks up at me — "the Marines who called in a nine-line. The pilots who flew out. The flight nurse who kept me alive on my flight. The docs at TQ who stabilized me. The docs at Landstuhl. All the docs at all the places I've been to stateside."

Jenks sounds a bit choked up and he's looking at his paper, though I know he doesn't need it there. This bit hasn't changed from the first draft. I've never heard him read it aloud.

"I am alive because of so many people. My life was saved not once, but repeatedly, by more people than I will ever know. They tell me I fought, kicking and screaming, before they drugged me. And some of the techniques that saved my life didn't even exist until Iraq, like giving patients fresh plasma along with packed red blood cells to help clotting. I needed to clot, and I couldn't do it with just my blood. I needed the blood that the soldiers and airmen who I will never know lined up to give me, and I needed the docs to have the knowledge to give it to me. So I owe my life to the doc who figured out the best way to push trauma victims' blood, and I owe it to all the Marines that doc watched die before he figured it out."

Jenks takes a pause and Jessie nods, saying, "Yeah, yeah."

There's a bit more to read, but Jenks very slowly slides the paper over to me. Sarah looks at Jessie with a cocked eyebrow, but Jessie isn't looking at her.

"Yeah?" I say to Jenks, who doesn't make a sound. I can't read anything on his face. I look down at the paper, though I've probably got it by heart.

"Whether I'm a poor, disfigured vet who got exactly what he volunteered for," I read, "or the luckiest man on earth, surrounded by love and care at what is unquestionably the worst period of my life, is really a matter of perspective. There's no upside to bitterness, so why be bitter? Perhaps I've sacrificed more for my country than most, but I've sacrificed far, far less than some. I have good friends. I have all my limbs. I have my brain and my soul and hope for the future. What sort of fool would I have to be, to not accept these gifts with the joy they deserve?"

Sarah gives a quick nod. "Okay, great," she says, not even stopping to dwell on Jenks's little personal statement of recovery and hope. "So you get back, your family is there. You can't talk. You're happy to be alive. But you've got fifty-four surgeries ahead of you, right? Can you take me through those?"

And Jenks, who has always separated the pain that came before and the pain that came after, takes a breath. Sarah still looks concerned, but also unyielding. I think, Jenks blew his story of triumph too early in the conversation. Especially since he ultimately gave up, told them he'd rather look like this for the rest of his life than go through more surgeries.

"They had to reconstruct me," Jenks begins.

Sarah checks her phone, to make sure it's still recording.

"Some stuff," he says, "the way they do it, the orthopedics, it's like building a table. Other stuff . . ."

He sips water. One of the other girls in the bar, the ugly one, goes out for a smoke. Her hot friend starts checking her phone.

"They had to move muscles around and sew them together to cover exposed bone, clean out dead tissue, and seal it with grafts. They take, well, what's basically a cheese grater to some of your healthy skin and re-attach it where it's needed and grow skin from a single layer." He takes another swig of water. "That wasn't like the other pain. Drugs didn't help. And there were the infections. That's how I lost my ears. And there was physical therapy. There still is physical therapy. Sometimes the pain was so bad, I'd count to thirty in my head over and over again. I'd tell myself, I can do this. I can make it to thirty. If I can survive to thirty, it's okay."

"Good," Sarah says. "But let's slow down. What happened first?"

She's got a sliver of ice in her, I think. I look down at my glass. It's empty. I don't remember drinking from it that much. I want more beer. I want a cigarette. I want to go outside and smoke with the ugly girl and get her phone number, just because.

"First thing," Jenks says, "is the pain every time they changed my bandages. Every day, for hours."

I get up, not yet sure why. They all look at me. "Smoke," I say.

"I'll join you," says Jessie.

"Let's take a break," I say, "all of us. Don't say anything until I get back."

That amuses Sarah. "Are you his lawyer?" she says.

"I need a break," I say.

And then I'm outside with Jessie and the ugly girl, who stands apart from us, while I'm lighting my cigarette and Sarah's inside probably grilling Jenks on his torture. The setup has me on edge — one goddamn cigarette's not gonna help, and with Jessie here I've got no shot with the ugly girl. No distractions, no hope to break off the evening with the potential for something new.

"You ever gonna fuck Jenks?" I ask.

Jessie smiles at me. She spent part of Iraq as one of the only females in with a bunch of grunts, so there's pretty much nothing you could say that'd faze her. "Are you?" she shoots back.

"It's your patriotic duty," I say, and she just grins like an indulgent mother looking at a naughty child. Then she gives me the finger, which looks weird on her fucked-up hand, but I don't gawk, I look her in the eye.

"Don't let her get to you," Jessie says, "she's been like that since high school."

"A bitch?"

"She's better than she seems."

"Is Sarah gonna fuck Jenks?" I say. " 'Cause that'd be acceptable, too."

"She'll listen to him."

"Yeah, and then she'll write her play. Great."

The ugly girl finishes her cigarette and goes inside — opportunity fully blown. I throw mine to the ground and stomp it out. Jessie's looking at me with this half-amused, half-concerned face. I pull out my pack and offer her a smoke, firing up another one for myself. Jessie takes it and examines the end, blowing on it gently, and the cherry briefly burns a brighter red.

"You shouldn't worry about Jenks so much," Jessie says. "This'll be good. He'll get out and do something. Be engaged with other humans, not just you and me sitting around going, 'Hey, remember the time?' "

"So send him to hang with a bunch of IVAW pussies?"

"One of those pussies was a scout sniper. What'd you do in Iraq again?"

"IVAW and artists, great. To pick over his bones for a fucking play, feeding off him like a bunch of maggots."

"They used maggots on me," she says. "Maggots clean out dead skin."

That's new information for me. Not an image I needed. I look through the window of the bar to where Jenks and Sarah are talking. If that IED had hit my vehicle, maybe I'd be in there, talking to Sarah about how all the support I'd got in my recovery had given me a newfound respect for life and love and friendship. And Sarah'd be bored and drilling me to find out how long it was before I could take a shit on my own.

"Artists," I say, putting all the contempt I can into the word. "I bet they'll find what happened to him *interesting.* Oh, so *interesting.* What fun."

"This isn't for fun," she says. "Fun is video games. Or movies and TV."

"Or blow jobs and strip clubs. An eight ball of coke, I bet, and a shot of heroin. I wouldn't know."

We smoke for a bit, with Jessie looking at me through those soft brown eyes of hers.

"What's the point of a play?" I say.

"What do you mean?"

"It's not fun, so what is it?"

Jessie taps her cigarette and a dusting of ash floats down to the ground.

"My dad was in Vietnam," she says. "My granddad, Korea. But when my dad went in, he didn't think of the guys stuck in the Frozen Chosin after that asshole MacArthur thought it'd be a good idea to go rogue and poke China with a stick. My dad thought — flag raising at Iwo Jima. D-Day and Audie Murphy. And when I went in —"

"Platoon and *Full Metal Jacket."*

"Yeah. Definitely not my dad in an admin shop."

"I bet more Marines have joined the Corps because of *Full Metal Jacket* than because of any fucking recruiting commercial."

"And that's an antiwar film."

"Nothing's an antiwar film," I say. "There's no such thing."

"Growing up," Jessie says, "Sarah spent a lot of time at our house, and she still spends some holidays with us. Her family is a mess. And last Thanksgiving we were talking with my grandpa about how nobody remembers Korea, and he said the only way to do it right wasn't to do a film about the war. Do a film about a kid, growing up. About the girl he falls in love with and breaks his heart and how he joins the Army after World War Two. Then he starts a family and his first kid is born and it teaches him what it means to value life and to have something to live for and how to care for other people. And then Korea happens and he's sent over there and he's excited and scared and he wonders if he'll be courageous and he's kind of proud and then in the last sixty seconds of the film they put them in boats to go to Inchon and he's shot in the water and drowns in three feet of surf and the movie doesn't even give him a close-up, it just ends. That'd be a war film."

"So, what? That's the Jenks story? Getting blown up first thing?"

"And then fifty-four surgeries. Make the war the least little thing."

"Jenks isn't telling Sarah about growing up and the girl who broke his heart," I say. "And even if he were, she wouldn't give a shit."

Jessie grounds out her cigarette. Mine's burning down to the filter, but I keep it in my hand, squeezed between the tips of my fingers.

"Want to teach people about war?" I say, tossing the cigarette butt down right as it starts to burn my fingers. "Start shooting motherfuckers. Set bombs in the streets. Get some retarded kids to walk into crowds and blow themselves up. Snipe the NYPD."

"I don't want to teach people anything," she says.

"Or maybe have them fix potholes for

seven months. That'd teach them. Shit. There's the title for your play — *Fixin' Potholes with Wilson and Jenks.* The people'll come by the fucking thousands."

Jessie looks through the window of the bar. "I thought it might be good for him," she says, "to tell his story to a civilian who'd really listen."

I think about lighting another cigarette, but I've already left Jenks too long.

"You think we should get out of Afghanistan?" I say.

Jessie laughs. "You know me," she says. "I'd like a national draft. Do it serious."

We both start laughing. Then we head back inside. Jenks looks okay, and he waves to me as I enter.

"Hey," Sarah says before I can sit back down, "Jenks has been telling me you and him are like the same person."

"I don't have Jenks's style," I say. But that's not enough, so I add, "He's who I should have been."

Sarah gives a polite smile. "So what was he like, when you first met him?"

He was like me, I think. But that's not what I tell her. "He was a bit of an asshole," I say, and I smile at Jenks, who stares back with one of those looks I can't interpret. "To be perfectly honest, he was a worthless piece of shit. No subject for a play, that's for sure." I smile. "Good thing he caught on fire, right?"

Unless It's a Sucking Chest Wound

When the call wakes me and I see the name "Kevin Boylan" glowing in the middle of my phone, I don't want to answer. I'm still in that half-dream state, and I've got this sense that if I pick up it won't be Boylan on the other end of the line, but Vockler, which is impossible because Vockler is dead. And when I do pick up and hear Boylan's voice telling me he's coming into town, it throws me even further. With a guy like Kevin Boylan, captain in the USMC, it's not just an old friend calling. It's my old gods.

"I'm coming to New York to get blacked the fuck out," he slurs into the phone. "Prepare yourself."

I should mention that Boylan has a Bronze Star with a combat distinguishing device for valor. My old gods have their idiosyncrasies.

"When?" I say.

"All I know is I'm coming," Boylan proclaims. "I just got back."

He means from Afghanistan.

"I just got a job offer," I say.

"Sweet!" he says. "How much they gonna pay?"

Not the sort of question I'm expecting, but it's Boylan, so I answer. "A hundred and sixty thousand dollars," I say. "Plus bonuses." Before he called, I'd been depressed about the job. As soon as I name the figure, though, I'm suddenly delirious, saying it, but also feeling like a schmuck because anybody with an Internet connection can find out exactly how much Boylan — an O3 with no dependents and six years in — is making. Hint: Less.

"Dude!" he says. And I'm smiling, because it's a big deal to him and because my fellow law students at NYU couldn't give two shits. Most of them are heading to the same sorts of firms, most of them knowing how much they'll hate it because they've already done the summer associate thing.

There's a pause and then he says, "One hundred sixty . . . whoa. I guess you made the right choice getting out, huh?" And there it is — the least hint of approval from a real Marine and I'm swelling with pride. Though I'm not even sure he actually approves. There was a German zoologist, Jakob von Uexküll, who claimed a tick would try to feed off any liquid at the temperature of mammalian blood. Law school has left me starving, and I'll take what I'm offered.

I ask Boylan how he's been and he tells me, "Afghanistan's not Iraq, dude," which makes sense but probably needed to be said, because Iraq's what I'm thinking — the sound of his voice sending me nostalgic, as if I'm missing Iraq. I'm not. What I'm missing is the idea of Iraq all my civilian friends imagine when they say the word, an Iraq filled with honor and violence, an Iraq I can't help feeling I should have experienced but didn't through my own stupid fault, because I went for an MOS that wouldn't put me in harm's way. My Iraq was a stack of papers. Excel spreadsheets. A window full of sandbags behind a cheap desk.

"They kept changing the mission on us," he's telling me. "War's end is a weird, weird time to be at war."

We talk a little more, and when we hang up I stay motionless for a while, sitting in my bed in my dark room with the curtains drawn against New York, still huffing that same old glory in the air, the taste like that first time I got popped one good in the face during training and didn't back down while my inner lip bled past my gums. That time.

So I get up and go to my computer, where I've got my whole life in pictures and files, and I pull up Deme's citation. "For extraordinary heroism while serving as a Rifle Squad Leader, Company K . . ." I tear up a little, like I always do. It was when I got choked up the first time that I knew I'd nailed writing the thing.

See, our unit had one no-shit hero. Hero like you read about, like you see in the movies, and that hero was Sergeant Julien Deme, and that sergeant was good, and that sergeant was brave, and that sergeant is dead, but most important, that sergeant was Boylan's, and he's the whole reason Boylan and me are tight, and why at two in the morning, drunk off his ass but full of plans to continue to drink away his deployment money and his demons, Boylan is calling me.

That's Boylan's motivation. I never knew Deme, so Deme is not why I'm answering the phone. James Vockler is why I'm answering the phone.

I'd been 3/6's adjutant, on my second deployment to Fallujah. Of all the lieutenants in that unit, Boylan was my favorite. Not the greatest at writing FITREPs or awards or doing any of the things that would bring him to my office — on a purely professional basis, he was a pain in the ass — but still, he was sweet. Sweet in that way that gentle giants sometimes are. Boylan had wide ears, a round, expressive face, and a stooped posture that seemed to be perpetually apologizing for the sheer monstrous size of him — arms thicker than my thighs, thighs thicker than my torso, a neck thicker than my head. Also, thicker than his own head. Boylan's pride at the time was being able to do a quick six faster than any other officer in the battalion, sucking down beer quicker than I can drink water. He belonged more to the frat house than the battlefield, the ideal dudebro and the sort of guy who made girls feel comfortable because he'd always give the skeezy ones a good talking-to. He was also the only officer who never seemed to think that, because he was in the infantry and I was an adjutant, there was some huge penis differential between the two of us.

So when Deme died, Boylan came to me with the hopelessly shitty citation he'd written, begging for help. Deme had been shot trying to pull injured Marines out of an ambush, the sort of thing that, if he'd survived, would have certainly been Silver Star worthy. With Deme dead, the unit as a whole was talking Medal of Honor. More important, so was the battalion commander.

"I know it's no good," Boylan told me, clutching the citation. The two of us were alone in my office in Camp Blue Diamond, right outside of Fallujah but effectively in another universe from the violence Boylan lived and breathed every day. "I'm no good at these."

It had been only a few days. There still wasn't a clear account of exactly what had happened, and I had a distraught Boylan looking ready to go to pieces with only a thin plywood door separating us from the junior Marines who worked for me. It wouldn't do to let them overhear an officer breaking down and weeping in my arms. That happened later, stateside, and it wasn't pretty.

"You're better than most," I said, skimming the pathetic write-up. "You care."

Therapist is not part of the adjutant's responsibilities. I was supposed to handle the battalion's paperwork: casualty reports, correspondence, awards, FITREPs, legal issues, et cetera. Difficult work, even if you don't take into account that most infantry guys didn't join the Corps to do paperwork and tend to suck at it. But mental issues — guilt, terror, helpless anxiety, inability to sleep, suicidal thoughts — that was all for Combat Stress.

"Most lieutenants," I said, "when they get into their first firefight, they write themselves up for the Combat Action Ribbon immediately. I get it before the dust has settled from the IED."

Boylan nodded his huge head with its large, childlike eyes.

"Their men," I said, "that comes later. When they get around to it. But you're the only guy, in either of my deployments, who ever put in all your men and forgot to write up yourself."

"Deme has two kids," Boylan said. He paused. "They're too young to remember him."

We were getting far afield. "The citation . . . ," I said, looking it over again. "A lot of what you write here . . . it's beside the point."

Boylan put his head in his hands.

"Look, Kevin," I said, "I've edited a million citations. Some of them for valor. And the point is not what a wonderful guy Deme was. I'm sure there's plenty of wonderful guys in your unit. I think you're a wonderful guy. Should we give all of you the Medal of Honor?"

Boylan shook his head.

I turned to my computer and clicked through my folders. At random, I pulled up a citation from my last deployment. It was for a Corpsman who'd treated Marines injured in an IED despite having a ballpoint pen–sized piece of shrapnel stuck a centimeter below his groin, barely missing his balls and a hair away from his femoral artery. "Displaying the utmost courage . . . ," I read, "with complete disregard for his own injuries." I closed the file and opened another. "Decisive leadership," I read, "fearlessly exposing himself to enemy fire . . . great personal risk . . . with complete disregard for his own safety." I opened another one. "Displaying the utmost courage . . . bold leadership . . . wise judgment . . . his courageous actions enabled . . ." I looked up. "You get the idea."

Boylan's face let me know he didn't.

"We don't give awards for being a great guy," I said.

"He was a great guy," Boylan said.

"No shit. That's pretty fucking clear. But you don't use a citation to describe the richness of all his humanity and blah blah blah. He's got to measure up to every other Marine who did ridiculously brave shit. And there's a lot of ridiculously brave Marines. Really. It's ridiculous. So it's not about

Deme. Or rather, what it's about is how Marine he was, not how Deme he was. You've got to fit him into all the right categories."

Boylan didn't seem to be listening.

"Hey," I said. He looked up. "There's good news. Decisive leadership, check. Rapidly organized his unit to provide suppressive fire, check. Complete disregard for his own safety, check. Utmost courage, check. I could go on. I don't know the full details, but there's a lot to work with here."

Boylan smiled. "It's good talking to you," he said. "There's no chicks here. But I can talk to you."

I sighed. "Great," I said. "How about I write the damn thing?"

Boylan nodded happily, one small weight among many lifting off his shoulders.

The colonel let me track down the details and I ended up getting the story in bits and pieces. The Marines I talked to tended to ramble in little grief-stricken monologues, so I learned not only what Deme did that day, but also that he and his wife rescued pit bulls, that he wrote terrible rap songs and sang them over oddly soothing homemade beats, that his wife was "crazy hot, wanna-lick-her-ass-like-an-ice-cream-cone hot," and that his daughters were "crazy fuckin' retardedly cute." But I also got, "There was a ceiling of small-arms fire," and, "When I saw Vockler's head snap back like a broken fucking doll," and, in a hollow monotone from James Vockler himself, "I should be dead, not him." Everything I needed, and I took those phrases and turned them into the flat, regimented prose the Corps requires for its medals.

Here's what you won't get from Vockler, who quickly became known in the battalion as "the guy Deme died saving." The highlights:

After the (unidentified) enemy opened up on his squad in a narrow alley, Sergeant Deme rushed to the front of the squad, realized he had three helplessly wounded men, organized suppressive fire, and ran into the kill zone to rescue his guys. I don't have any experience with combat, and I certainly don't have any experience with organizing suppressive fire, running into kill zones, or rescuing people, but I'm reliably informed by Marines who know about those things that it takes huge fucking balls.

With bullets flying everywhere, ricocheting off the narrow walls of the alley like some pinball machine of death on tilt, Sergeant Deme ran up and grabbed the unconscious Vockler by his flak and pulled him out of danger. Then he ran back and was pretty much immediately shot in the face. So it's more accurate to say that Sergeant Deme died while trying unsuccessfully to save the lives of the other two Marines in Vockler's fire team than it is to say he died saving Vockler.

As an added bit of irony, Vockler might not have even died if Sergeant Deme had left him there. Unlike the other two Marines, who were bleeding out in an exposed position, Vockler was neither in any immediate danger nor in need of immediate medical care. An AK round had smacked into the top left side of his helmet, true, but it hadn't penetrated. The force of the glancing shot knocked Vockler out and sent him sprawling backward into a relatively safe position behind a marginal bit of cover in the trash-filled alley. So it's possible Deme could have left Vockler there.

Nobody ever told this to Vockler. As far as he knew, he went through a second of gunfire and terror, got shot (sort of) in the head, and woke up to his squad telling him that Sergeant Deme, whom he revered, had proven once and for all how goddamn Marine he was by dying in the most heroic way a Marine can — saving your stupid, worthless, not-even-badly-injured-enough-to-need-a-MEDEVAC ass.

None of this discounts Deme's heroism, but if Vockler knew the full truth, it'd weigh on him even heavier than it already did. Unlike your average American citizen, Vockler could locate who had died for him in a particular human being. A particular human being he'd known and loved with the sort of passion Marines have for good combat leaders. Even most marriages can't compare with that, because most partners in a marriage aren't routinely aware that they'd be way more likely to get killed every day if their partner wasn't such a hell-of-a-baller spouse. So to add to that the notion that, hey, maybe Deme could have left you where you were and possibly saved one of your fire-team buddies before getting himself killed . . . that wouldn't help.

Rough, even to get it secondhand. The experience of talking to Deme's squad put life into all the phrases I'd seen trotted out in all the awards I'd ever processed. And this wasn't just any write-up. It was for the Medal of fucking Honor, which a part of me knew wasn't going to happen, but still, it didn't matter. Deme would get something, maybe even the Navy Cross, and he'd at least be considered for the big one. Just writing the words was exciting.

Medal of Honor recipients are the saints of the Corps. You've got Dan Daly in Belleau Wood and Smedley Butler in the Banana Wars and close to three hundred others in American conflicts stretching from the Civil War to the present day.

So I wrote the citation with my every frustration melting away in the excitement of the thing. Like reaching out with my fingers and touching a god through the keyboard of my computer. My job, I felt, meant something.

I even wrote about Deme in the personal statement I submitted, midway through the deployment, as part of my application to law school.

"Even the best adjutants aren't saving lives, like Sergeant Deme, or risking their life on daily patrols, like your average grunt. But the best of us make sure those sacrifices are honored by providing them the administrative support they need, whether it be getting them absentee ballots or in assisting them with their wills. There isn't any glory in this kind of work. The adjutant's job is generally only noticed when it goes wrong. Both of my deployments have been spent at a desk, relieving Marines of burdens they will never know could have existed. That's enough for me. It's more than enough. And it's what has led me to desire a public interest career in law."

What I didn't mention was that the death toll for our battalion by the end of the deployment was five, meaning that alley had been responsible for more than half of our total casualties. I also didn't mention that that alley was in an area where the previous commander had warned our battalion to avoid aggressive patrolling. "We're not going to see success here until we develop better relationships with the local population," he'd said.

The reaction of the unit had been unanimous: "Those guys are idiots! We're Marine infantry! We don't avoid the enemy, we close with and destroy the enemy!" Lieutenant Colonel Motes, our CO, had an aggressive style, and the battalion didn't really get on the COIN train until afterward.

That he'd sent his platoon into a death zone was not lost on Boylan, who had spent every moment since second-guessing every decision he made, convinced better leadership could have saved those Marines' lives. His instincts about that were probably right. Boylan came back to the States thirty pounds lighter than when he'd left — skeletal, with bruise-purple skin underlining eyes that looked out from the bottom of an ocean. I'd never had a personal relationship with any of the five fallen Marines, so I tended to think of their deaths with a solemn, patriotic pride rather than the self-loathing and self-doubt so clearly tearing Boylan to shreds.

When we got back from Iraq he was a mess, embarrassing himself at the Marine Ball, blacking out every weekend and probably weekdays, too. I remember him one time walking into the admin office, eight in the morning, hung over, with a huge dip of chewing tobacco in his lip, asking, "Anybody got a dip cup?" Nobody wanted to let him spit into anything they owned, so he shrugged, said, "Ahhhh, fuck it," and then grabbed the collar of his cammie blouse and spit into his shirt. The Marines talked about it for weeks.

That was one approach. Vockler had another. Pretty much as soon as we got back, he'd started angling to get on a deployment to Afghanistan. Iraq was running down; that much was already clear by the tail end of our deployment. So he stalked a company commander from 1/9 until he got them to reserve a line number for him. Which led him to the admin office, my office, and instead of having my Marines handle his shit, I had them send him in to me. I wanted to see him again, face-to-face.

"So you want to go to Afghanistan?" I said.

"Yes, sir, that's where the fighting is."

"1/9," I said. "The Walking Dead." As battalion mottos go, they've probably got the best. Thanks to Vietnam, 1/9 boasts the highest killed in action rate in Marine Corps history. Marines, who like to think of themselves as suicidally aggressive rabid dogs and who sometimes even live up to that self-image, consider this "cool."

"Yes, sir."

"You know," I said, "they set minimum dwell time for a reason. Just because you think you're ready to deploy again doesn't mean you are."

"There's a lot of Marines from 1/9 who've never deployed, sir."

"And you've got the experience they need?"

"Yes, sir. They'll need good NCOs."

Marines often speak to officers in platitudes, so it's sometimes hard to tell how much of what they're saying they actually believe.

"1/9's got a lot of Marines who've been over three, four, five times," I said.

He nodded. "Sir, I know what it's like to

have really bad things happen."

Impossible to argue with that.

"It's very hard," he said, his voice calm, as though he were describing weather patterns. "Chances are, these guys are gonna have to deal with the same thing."

"Some probably will."

"I'm good with people," he said. "I'd be good with that." He spoke with absolute composure. It made the room around him feel cold and still.

"Good to go," I said. "I'm glad you'll be over there. They'll need good NCOs."

I went through some of the steps he'd need to take as he checked out, then sent him on his way. The last thing he asked me was, "Sir, do you think they'll give Sergeant Deme the Medal of Honor?" It was the only point where a little of his composure seemed to crack to let some emotion through.

"I don't know," I said. "I hope so." It hardly seemed a decent answer.

I saw Vockler only two more times after that day in my office. First was at the ceremony where they awarded Sergeant Deme the Navy Cross, where he and Boylan both tried and failed to avoid crying. That was the week I got my acceptance letter from NYU. I was certain I wouldn't have gotten in without my Marine Corps résumé. To NYU, I was a veteran. Two deployments. That meant something to them.

The last time was the day Vockler left for Afghanistan. I was doing a three-mile run during my lunch break and his company was staged up off McHugh Boulevard, waiting for the buses. The families had enough U.S. flags that if you'd draped yourself in the Stars and Stripes it'd have constituted camouflage, and it was hot enough that every fat uncle there had pit stains big enough to meet in the middle of their chest.

Vockler was in a circle of Marines, all of them smoking and joking like they were about to go on a camping trip, which from a certain perspective was true.

I stopped my run and dropped by. Vockler saw me and grinned. "Sir!" he said. He didn't salute, but it didn't seem disrespectful.

"Corporal," I said. I put my hand out and he shook it vigorously. "Good luck over there."

"Thank you, sir."

"You'll do great," I told him. "Handling your transfer, that's one of the things in my job I get to feel proud of."

"Oo-rah, sir."

I thought about making some sort of joke,

like, "Stay off the opium," but I didn't want to force anything. So I continued on my run, and three weeks later I was out of the Corps.

There's a month after my discharge I can't really account for. I traveled. I moved to New York, and then I think I spent a lot of time in my underwear, watching TV. My mom says I was "decompressing."

At the time, most of my college friends were in corporate law or investment banking or were reevaluating life after dropping out of Teach for America.

Strangely, I started feeling more like a Marine out of the Corps than I'd felt while in it. You don't run into a lot of Marines in New York. All of my friends thought of me as "the Marine," and to everyone I met, I was "the Marine." If they didn't know, I'd make sure to slip it into conversations first chance I got. I kept my hair short and worked out just as hard as before. And when I started at NYU and I met all those kids right out of undergrad, I thought, Hell, yeah, I'm a fucking Marine.

Some of them, highly educated kids at a top five law school, didn't even know what the Marine Corps did. ("It's like a stronger Army, right?") Few of them followed the wars at all, and most subscribed to a "It's a terrible mess, so let's not think about it too much" way of thinking. Then there were the political kids, who had definite opinions and were my least favorite to talk to. A lot of these overlapped with the insufferable public interest crowd, who hated the war, couldn't see why anybody'd ever do corporate law, didn't understand why anyone would ever join the military, didn't understand why anyone would ever want to own a gun, let alone fire one, but who still paid lip service to the idea that I deserved some sort of respect and that I was, in an imprecise way that was clearly related to action movies and recruiting commercials, far more "hard-core" than your average civilian. So sure, I was a Marine. At the very least, I wasn't them.

NYU prides itself on sending a high number of law students into public interest, "high" meaning 10 to 15 percent. If an NYU student gets a public interest job that pays under a certain amount, they get partial or full debt forgiveness, saving them more money than the average American makes in three years. Like everybody else without a Root Scholarship or wealthy parents or a fiancée at a hedge fund, I'd sat through

NYU's presentation on the program and thought, Oh, they want me to work my ass off and live in Bed-Stuy for six years. With incentives like that, four out of five NYU students take a good look at public interest jobs, hem and haw, consider the trajectories of all the fire starters they admire, and then go to the same huge law firms as everybody else.

Joe-the-corporate-lawyer told me, "Do Legal Aid. Do the Public Defender's Office."

We were having drinks at a rooftop bar with a stunning view of the Chrysler Building. The drink Joe had bought me was made with a cardamom-infused liquor. I'd never had anything quite like it.

"I'm not really an idealist anymore," I said.

"You don't have to be," he said. "You just have to be a guy who doesn't want their life crushed doing shit that isn't even mentally challenging. Sometimes I hate my clients and want them to lose, but that's actually a rare improvement over most cases, which involve huge corporations where I can't even bring myself to care. Aside from bonuses, which get smaller every year, I'm on a set salary. But I bill by the hour, which means the equity partners make more money the more I work. And nobody works their ass off for ten years to become partner because they've got a burning ambition to improve the lifestyles of first-year associates. They do it for money. And so do I."

"You're paying off law school and college debt," I said.

"Which you won't be," he said, "thanks to the G.I. Bill and the Yellow Ribbon Program and your savings from the Corps. If you go my route, you'll be stuck doing doc review every day and every night and every goddamn weekend and you'll want to blow your brains out."

Joe was right about the debt, but I already had some experience as a true believer, and if the Marine Corps was any indication, idealism-based jobs didn't save you from wanting to shoot yourself in the head.

Paul-the-Teach-for-America-dropout told me, "If you go public interest, be careful where you go."

We'd met up in Morningside Heights at the railroad apartment he shared with his two roommates. The place was schizophrenically decorated with old "Rage Against the Machine" posters, framed *New Yorker* covers, and Tibetan prayer flags.

"America is broken, man." Paul took a

swig of beer. "Trust me, you don't want to be the guy bailing water out of a sinking ship."

"Iraq vet," I said, pointing at my chest. "Been there, done that."

"Me too," he said. "I'll throw my middle school tour against your deployment any day."

"They shoot at you?"

"One day a student stabbed another kid."

That wouldn't have trumped Vockler or Boylan, and it sure as hell didn't trump dead, heroic Deme, but it trumped the shit out of me. Closest I ever came to violence was watching the injured and dying come into the base hospital.

"Saddest thing in that school," he said, "was the kids who gave a shit. Because, honestly, that school was so fucked the smart option would have been to check the fuck out."

"So what's the solution? Charter schools? No Child Left Behind? Standardized testing?"

"Yo, I got no idea. Why you think I went to get a master's in education leadership?" He laughed. "So if you go public interest —"

"I need to make sure I'm not the Band-Aid on a giant sucking chest wound."

■ ■ ■ ■

"You're not doing public interest," Ed-the-investment-banker told me while the two of us smoked cigars at a James Bond–themed bar that required khakis and nice shoes to get in.

"But I think —"

"How long have I known you? You're going to a firm. It's the easy option. Let me break it down for you."

"Joe says —"

"Joe's a lawyer. I hire lawyers." Not strictly true. His bank hired lawyers, though I suppose it doesn't really make a difference, because a guy like him can make a guy like Joe work until five A.M. if he wants.

"Listen to me," he said, spreading his hands. "There are fourteen top law schools. Not thirteen. Not fifteen. There's fourteen that matter. And guess what, congrats, you're in one of them."

"NYU is top five."

"Top six, but who's counting," he said. "The top firms, they hire pretty much from those schools. Maybe a handful from schools a bit lower down, a few kids from Fordham or someplace who did amazing and are so shit-hot they learned to shoot fireworks out of their dicks. But for the most part, if you're not from one of those schools, it's a hard life trying to get a job in this city."

"You mean getting a job like Joe's. And Joe hates his job."

"Of course he does. He's at a law firm, not a brewery. He works longer hours than you did in the Corps, and I guarantee that at no point in his life will a complete stranger walk up to him and say, 'Thank you for your service.' But here's how it works. All the top firms pay the same, except for one, which is the top, which you're not getting into unless you too learn to shoot fireworks out your dick —"

"I didn't know that was an important legal skill."

"In this city, it is. There's a million lawyers and only so many really good jobs. Even the top public interest jobs, like the U.S. Attorney's Office or Federal Defender, tend to hire people from top firms. So everything matters. What school you go to determines what clerkship you get, what firm you work at. If you don't have the right credentials from the right sorts of places, you're fucked."

"So what are you telling me?"

"Don't screw around like you did in college. Welcome to adult life. What you do matters."

I found out about Vockler a month later, alone in my empty apartment, bare walls and one lone chair next to the windowsill where I put my computer. The Corps had accustomed me to spartan living, though I figured if I ever brought a woman home, it'd probably give off a serial killer vibe.

The one thing the place had going for it was the view. Facing midtown from a side street off York Avenue, I had the city from Central Park to the Empire State. Late evenings when I came in drunk, I'd stop and gape at the constellations of apartments. And then, sometimes, I'd open my computer and check DefenseLink. The idea was to go through the Web site to see if anybody I knew had died. On their "Releases" section, there's a mass of links running down the Web page, and I generally click on the ones that read either "DoD Identifies Marine Casualty" or, if it's a bad day, "DoD Identifies Marine Casualties." Then it takes you to a page with the names.

Earlier that night, I'd had a few drinks with Joe-the-lawyer and Ed-the-banker. With them I'd reverted back to college, cracking dirty jokes and telling drunk stories, so when I sat down at my computer,

I think I wanted to recover whatever it is that I am when I look at the names of the dead.

I sat in my chair and clicked on one of the bad ones, snapping my night in half. Joe and Ed drifted off, insubstantial.

> The Department of Defense announced today the death of two Marines who were supporting Operation Enduring Freedom. Lance Cpl. Shield S. Mason, 27, of Oneida, N.Y., and Cpl. James R. Vockler, 21, of Fairhope, Ala., died October 3 of wounds suffered while supporting combat operations in Helmand province, Afghanistan. They were assigned to the 1st Battalion, 9th Marine Regiment, 2nd Marine Division, II Marine Expeditionary Force, Camp Lejeune, N.C.
>
> For additional background information on this Marine, news media representatives may contact the II Marine Expeditionary Force public affairs office at (910) 451-7200.

The date on the release, October 3, was more than a week and a half before. I typed his name into Google to see what might come up, and a slew of news articles appeared. "Baldwin County Marine Killed in

Afghanistan." "Fallen Marine Returns Home." And, bizarrely, an older article entitled "Home for Christmas!" I clicked on it.

A page opened with a photo of Vockler, his arms outstretched to the sky, while his two younger sisters give him a hug, one on each side. The girls only came up to his shoulders, and the photo looked as though it had been taken the day he left. Below was a block of text.

> Today my wife and I watched our son, our Marine, Corporal James Robert Vockler, go off to war. Though it is hard for us to see our son embark on such a dangerous mission, we are tremendously proud of him and his brother Marines.
>
> We drove down earlier this week with James and can report that he and his brother Marines are in high spirits. Despite the dangers, they are excited at the opportunity to do their mission, which will be to clear the enemy out of strongholds in southern Afghanistan. This is an important task they have been training months to do.
>
> James is a 21-year-old Class of 2006 graduate of Fairhope High School. He fought in Iraq last year and returned home

safe for Thanksgiving. He joins his Fairhope High School classmates Cpl. John Coburn and Lance Cpl. Andrew Roussos, who also fought in Iraq with him.

We look forward to the Marines accomplishing their mission and their safe return this Christmas.

— George, Anna, Jonathan,
Ashley, and Lauren Vockler

I clicked away, back to the search results, and I looked around the room. Empty corners, a twin mattress lying pathetically on the floor. Quiet. I looked back to the computer. There were video results as well. I clicked on a YouTube link.

On the screen, a line curled around a school building — Fairhope High School, I guess. It looked like the images of Iraqis queuing to vote during those first elections, everyone patient and serious. This was Vockler's wake. The whole community had come out to mourn. I thought I caught a glimpse of Boylan in his Alphas, but the video quality was too poor to tell. I closed the computer.

There was no alcohol in the apartment, and I didn't want to go out. I didn't know any vets in the city. I didn't want to talk to any civilians. As I lay on my mattress, struggling with a violence you might as well call grief, I realized why no one had thought to inform me of Vockler's death. I was in New York. I was out of the Corps. I wasn't a Marine anymore.

That Saturday I went to a documentary with Ed-the-banker. It was Ed's idea. The film was about veterans dealing with civilian life, the four main characters ranging from a congressional candidate to a complete train wreck of a human being. One, a mixed martial arts fighter with PTSD, described an incident overseas where he'd shot up a civilian vehicle and killed a small girl about the age of his daughter.

After the film, the couple who made the documentary stood up, answered questions, and then chatted with the audience at a small reception. I walked over and thanked them for making it. I told them that the difficulties of transitioning to civilian life weren't covered enough and that I especially appreciated how they avoided taking political positions that would have interfered with telling the men's stories. I had a sense I was the only veteran in the room and thus better equipped to talk than anybody else. If I'd seen just one single guy rocking one of those OIF combat veteran ball caps, I would have kept my fucking mouth shut.

"Very powerful," I told Ed-the-banker as we walked out.

He mentioned the scene where the MMA fighter described killing the little girl.

"Yeah," I said, feeling this was another area I could speak with confidence. "You know, I saw a lot of injured kids in Iraq . . ."

There I stalled. My throat constricted. This was unexpected. I wanted to tell him the suicide truck bomb story, a story I'd told so often that I sometimes had to fake emotions so I wouldn't seem heartless. But I couldn't get it out. I forced out, "Excuse me," and ran upstairs to the bathroom, where I found a stall and cried until I got myself under control.

The incident surprised and humiliated me. When I walked out, neither Ed nor I said a word about what happened.

When I got back to my room, I checked DefenseLink and scanned past the newest names — all of them meaningless to me. So I started Googling "1st Battalion, 9th Marines," Vockler's battalion, and then I started reading the articles and watching the YouTube clips that came up.

With the Internet you can do nothing but watch war all day if you want. Footage of firefights, mortar attacks, IEDs, it's all there. There's Marines explaining what the desert heat is like, what the desert cold is like, what it feels like to shoot a man, what it feels like to lose a Marine, what it feels like to kill a civilian, what it feels like to be shot.

I listened to the clips, sitting in my apartment. There was no answer to how I felt, but there were exams to study for, books to read, papers to write. Contracts, Procedure, Torts, and Lawyering. An insane amount of work floating in the back of my consciousness. I brought it to the front.

Over the following weeks, I stopped thinking about the Marines in Afghanistan. I did my work. Days spent busy don't feel like time.

I didn't form friendships easily at NYU, and for the first year I didn't date anyone. I'd started the year with contempt for my fellow students, but you spend enough time alone and you end up feeling somehow defective. And the girl who finally got to me, another student who was handling law school the same way a high-functioning alcoholic drives, she sniffed that out pretty early.

One day she pulled me aside to tell me the sorts of things you don't tell people you don't know that well, the sorts of things you tell only close friends or your psychiatrist. "I thought I could trust you," she said after going through her whole history of child abuse, "because, you know, you've got PTSD, too." I don't have PTSD, but I guess her thinking that I did is part of the weird pedestal vets are on now. Either way, I didn't contradict her.

"Look," she said, "I'm tall, I'm blond. I can do the girl thing. But eventually I have to tell people. And they're gonna think, This one is damaged."

I nodded. That was absolutely what I was thinking.

"And I'm not comparing what I've been through to what you have." That surprised me. "Mine is just, whatever, and I'm sure you've gone through stuff . . ."

"I haven't," I said.

"Well, I'm not saying mine's as bad."

It didn't seem appropriate to tell her she'd been through infinitely worse.

We had sex a week later, when we were both drunk and lonely and after I'd told her about Vockler — partially as a way of getting it out and partially as a way of reciprocating for all the things she'd told me.

The first few months we had a lot of sex,

and I went on a lot of runs. You run fast enough, it gets better, all the pent-up emotions expressed in the swing of your arms, the burn in your chest, the slow, heavy weight of exhaustion in your legs, and you can just think. You can think in a rage, in sorrow, in anything at all, and it doesn't tear you up because you're doing something, something hard enough to feel like an appropriate response to the turmoil in your head. Emotions need some kind of physical outlet. And if you're lucky, the physical takes over completely. When I used to do mixed martial arts, that would happen. You exhaust yourself to the point where only pain and euphoria remain. When you're in that state, you don't miss everything else, all the little feelings you have.

When I was in Iraq, I saw Marines come in injured and I'd go visit them with Lieutenant Colonel Motes, the incompetent asshole whose poor grasp of COIN was getting them hurt. A lot of them, they wouldn't ask about themselves or about the terrible injuries they had. They'd ask about their buddies, the Marines with them, even the ones not hurt as bad. Inspiring stuff. Except when I saw those guys, they'd already been given anesthetics of some kind. Plus, all the really bad ones were unconscious. After the suicide bombing, though, some of the Iraqis we saw were in so much pain, they were just writhings. If their eyes were open, they weren't seeing, and those whose ears hadn't burst weren't hearing, and I'm sure if they could have thought anything, they'd have thought about their sons, daughters, fathers, mothers, friends, but their mouths were just screaming. A human being in enough pain is just a screaming animal.

You can't get there with pleasure. You can try, but you can't.

"Think termites," I told Ed-the-banker two weeks after the breakup. We were in his apartment in the West Village, drinking his Scotch. It felt very grown-up.

"There was a medical researcher named Lewis Thomas," I said. "Thomas had something of a poet's mind."

"I'm sure that's a useful trait in a doctor," Ed-the-banker said, since he wasn't the sort to let you complete a thought.

"Thomas says if you put two termites in a patch of dirt, they'll roll it into little balls, move it from place to place. But they don't accomplish anything."

"Like poets," he said.

"Thomas was the poet," I said. "Not the termites."

He was smiling broadly now. He finds all my problems amusing, which I guess they are if you've got the right perspective.

"They're little Sisyphuses," I said, "with their little balls of dirt. I'm sure for a termite, it's a regular old existential crisis."

"Maybe they need a termitess." This is Ed-the-banker's solution to most problems, and it's generally not a bad solution.

"They need more termites," I said. "Two won't cut it. If they had enough brain cells to feel, they'd feel lost, awash in the loneliness in the heart of the universe or whatever. Nothing to depend on. Just dirt and each other. Two won't cut it."

"So what? Ménage à trois?"

"It doesn't help to add only a few more termites. You might get piles of dirt, but the behavior is still purposeless."

"To you," Ed-the-banker said. "Maybe pushing around little balls of dirt is like, the termite version of watching Internet porn."

"No," I said, "they're not excited until you start adding more and more termites. Eventually you reach critical mass, though, enough of the little fuckers to really do something. The termites get excited, and they get to work. Thomas says they work like artists. Bits of earth stacked on bits of earth, forming columns, arches, termites on both sides building toward one another. It's all perfect, Thomas says, symmetrical. As though there's a blueprint. Or an architect. And the columns reach each other, touching, forming chambers, and the termites connect chamber to chamber, form a hive, a home."

"Which would be the Marine Corps," Ed-the-banker said.

"Two hundred thousand workers all yoked to the same goal. Two hundred thousand workers risking their lives for that goal."

"Which would make the civilian world —"

"A bunch of lone little animals, pushing their balls of dirt around."

Ed-the-banker laughed. "The civilian world," he said, "or corporate law?"

"Either," I said. "Basically, I'm not sure which little group of confused, hopeless animals I should join, and how I can possibly bring myself to care about what they think they're building."

"I told you," he said. "You should have gone into finance."

That was last fall. And now, two weeks after the phone call from Boylan that woke me up in the middle of the night, he's here, trundling into Grand Central like an oversize toddler dressed in a hand-me-down suit he's already outgrown. The breast pulls, the pant cuffs show too much of the socks, and his grin indicates a blissful lack of awareness of how absurdly his body has been crammed into the clothes of a lesser man. I've seen Boylan ripped, a hulking giant. And at the end of our shared deployment, I'd seen him a gaunt, enormous skeleton. But I've never seen him looking so soft — pudgy in the middle and fleshy in his face. He had a staff job in Afghanistan, and it shows.

"I got this at a thrift store for twenty-five bucks," he says, grabbing his lapel and spinning to show off his sartorial splendor.

"Why are you in a suit?" I say, and his face registers a moment of confusion.

"You said you'd take me to the Yale Club."

It takes me a moment, but I realize I had indeed said that, three years ago. Funny what people remember.

"You don't want to go there," I say. "You don't want to be anywhere around here." I raise my arms to indicate Grand Central, the teeming masses, the cathedral beauty of it, with its constellation map gilt backward on the ceiling and its tasteful Apple store discreetly occupying the top of the east staircase. "Midtown's got no life to it. Just seventeen-dollar drinks and the assholes that can pay for them."

"That'll be you soon, Mister Hundred Sixty Thousand."

"Not yet," I say. "And since I'm buying all drinks tonight — no, I am — we're getting the fuck out of here."

We take the 6 train to Astor and head to a dive bar with an all-night special of $5 for a can of PBR and a shot of what they call "Jameson." I figure we won't be able to spend more than $80 before going into comas. We head in and sit at the bar, and I order the first round as Boylan untucks his shirt and loosens his tie.

"I'm glad . . . ," I start to tell him, and I want to say I'm glad he's alive, but that's too maudlin even if it's true, so I finish with, "To see you," and he grins. Once the drinks arrive, he clinks his whiskey to mine and we shoot them back.

"Why didn't you stay in the Corps, man?" he says.

It's becoming increasingly apparent Boylan is already a bit drunk, and I wonder who, if anyone, he could have been drinking with. Near most stations they sell plastic bottles for the commuters to get hammered on the train. If that's what he was doing, he wouldn't be the only one.

"Why not, man?" he says. "You were good.

Everybody says you were good."

"Because I'm a pussy," I say. "When you getting promoted to major?"

"Never. I got a DUI." He gives a sheepish grin and before I can respond says, "I know, I know, I'm an idiot. No more drunk driving for me." And then he starts asking me about law school, about if I'm dating anybody, about all sorts of shit, and I realize that as much as I want to hear about his war shit, he wants to hear some civilian shit.

So we talk civilian shit. I tell him about my girl and how the sex was good and the rest was bad but I wish her the best. And I tell him I'm going to go corporate and then figure shit out, because it's impossible to figure out now. "A lot of people, their careers ping-pong back and forth between government and Big-law. Do something to feel good about yourself for a while, then go back and make money. Then feel good about yourself again. Then go back to Big-law and make some money. It's like a karmic binge-and-purge."

We get drunker, and eventually Boylan says, "You want to see a trick?" He doesn't wait for an answer. Instead, he crams the edge of the PBR can against his incisors, cutting into the aluminum. He rotates the can quickly, spinning it against his teeth until he slices it in a perfect circle, mouthfuls of beer spilling out the sides and onto his suit.

"Ha!" he says, holding the two halves out to me. "Whaddaya think?"

"Impressive," I say. I notice he's missing his tie, and I wonder if he knows where it is.

The bartender walks over and says, "Don't do that," and Boylan tells him to fuck himself. Then he looks at me like, "You gonna back me up on this?"

Long story short, we head to my apartment and start in on some whiskey, and when we get drunk enough, we finally get to war.

I bring up the videos of air strikes they'd show us at the Basic School, grainy videos of some hajji hot spot and then, boom, dead hajjis. Though the explosions are never as big as you think they should be. Hollywood fucks that up for you.

I tell Boylan, "It was like video games," and he gets animated.

"Yeah, yeah," he says. "You see any of the helmet cams?"

I haven't, so he gets on my computer, standing by my desk and swaying back and forth while he tries to type into the YouTube search engine, his meaty hands spilling over and hitting multiple keys at once..

"Dude, this is cool," he says.

Eventually he finds it, POV-style footage taken with a camera strapped to a Marine's head during a firefight in Afghanistan.

"Now this is like a video game," he says, and as the video plays, I realize he's right. The Marine ducks behind a wall and I see the barrel of his rifle cutting across the screen in the exact same way it does in *Call of Duty.* And then he pops up and lets off a few rounds, just like *Call of Duty.* No wonder Marines like that game so much.

There's a lot of yelling going on as well, and I catch a few commands but nothing clear. At the end of the video, one soldier has been shot, but not seriously.

"So this is what it's like," I say.

"Huh?"

"You've been in combat. This is what it's like?"

Boylan looks at the screen for a second. "Nah," he says.

I wait for more, but nothing's coming.

"Well then," I say, "that's what it looks like. At least, to shoot a bad guy."

He looks at the screen again. "Nah."

"But that's an actual firefight."

"Fuck, dude," he says. "Whatever."

"That's a fucking video camera shooting

an actual fucking firefight."

He looks at the screen for a long time. "Camera's not the same," he says, and he taps his head and smiles at me crooked.

I look back at the screen, which has recommendations for other videos, mostly war related, though for whatever reason one of them is a screenshot of some Japanese writing and a cartoon squid.

"I'd never let them put a camera on me," he says.

His skin is waxy, sallow. I want to ask if Vockler had an open casket or if his body was too damaged, though of course I can't.

"Iraq," I say instead. "What do you think? Did we win?"

"Uhh . . . we did okay," he says, looking at the screen of combat videos and one cartoon squid.

The first time I met Boylan, he was in his Alphas and the Bronze Star with the V was right there on his chest for anybody to see. I'd gone and looked it up immediately, but now I can't remember exactly what it had been for. Boylan hadn't meant much to me then, and the citation wasn't as exciting or clear as Deme's, since for Boylan it'd been a slow accumulation of minor heroic actions taken over the course of a long and hellish day, rather than the sort of intense crucible that makes for great drama. At least he got it, though. Vockler died in an IED, like the majority of combat casualties in these wars, a death that doesn't offer a story younger Marines can read and get inspired by. IEDs don't let you be a hero. That's what makes Deme so important. The cold, hard courage that sends veterans like Vockler back to war is not what makes teenagers join the Corps in the first place. Without the rare stories like Deme's, who'd sign up?

Eventually, Boylan is sleeping on my floor and I'm sitting by his side, drinking whiskey slow and envying him from the depths of my noncombat heart. I don't know why. He's not proud of his Bronze Star. He refuses to tell the story. "It was a bad day," is the most I've ever heard from him. I don't even know what it is he has that I want. I just know I want it. And he's right here in front of me, close enough that I've spilled whiskey on him twice.

Agamben speaks of the difference between men and animals being that animals are in thrall to stimuli. Think a deer in the headlights. He describes experiments where scientists give a worker bee a source of nectar. As it imbibes, they cut away its abdomen, so that instead of filling the bee up, the nectar falls out through the wound in a trickle that pours as fast as the bee drinks. You'd think the bee might change its behavior in response, but it doesn't. It keeps happily sucking away at the nectar and will continue indefinitely, enthralled by one stimulus — the presence of nectar — until released by another — the sensation of satiety. But that second stimulus never comes — the wound keeps the bee drinking until it finally starves.

I splash a little more whiskey on Boylan, halfway hoping he'll wake up.

Ten Kliks South

This morning our gun dropped about 270 pounds of ICM on a smuggler's checkpoint ten kliks south of us. We took out a group of insurgents and then we went to the Fallujah chow hall for lunch. I got fish and lima beans. I try to eat healthy.

At the table, all nine of us are smiling and laughing. I'm still jittery with nervous excitement over it, and I keep grinning and wringing my hands, twisting my wedding band about my finger. I'm sitting next to Voorstadt, our number one guy, and Jewett, who's on the ammo team with me and Bolander. Voorstadt's got a big plate of ravioli and Pop-Tarts, and before digging in, he looks up and down the table and says, "I can't believe we finally had an arty mission."

Sanchez says, "It's about time we killed someone," and Sergeant Deetz laughs. Even I chuckle, a little. We've been in Iraq two months, one of the few artillery units actually doing artillery, except so far we've only shot illumination missions. The grunts usually don't want to risk the collateral damage. Some of the other guns in the battery had shot bad guys, but not us. Not until today. Today, the whole damn battery fired. And we know we hit our target. The lieutenant told us so.

Jewett, who's been pretty quiet, asks, "How many insurgents do you think we killed?"

"Platoon-sized element," says Sergeant Deetz.

"What?" says Bolander. He's a rat-faced professional cynic, and he starts laughing. "Platoon-sized? Sergeant, AQI don't have platoons."

"Why you think we needed the whole damn battery?" says Sergeant Deetz, grunting out the words.

"We didn't," says Bolander. "Each gun only fired two rounds. I figure they just wanted us all to have gun time on an actual target. Besides, even one round of ICM would be enough to take out a platoon in open desert. No way we needed the whole battery. But it was fun."

Sergeant Deetz shakes his head slowly, his heavy shoulders hunched over the table. "Platoon-sized element," he says again.

"That's what it was. And two rounds a gun was what we needed to take it out."

"But," says Jewett in a small voice, "I didn't mean the whole battery. I meant, our gun. How many did our gun, just our gun, kill?"

"How am I supposed to know?" says Sergeant Deetz.

"Platoon-sized is like, forty," I say. "Figure, six guns, so divide and you got, six, I don't know, six point six people per gun."

"Yeah," says Bolander. "We killed exactly 6.6 people."

Sanchez takes out a notebook and starts doing the math, scratching out the numbers in his mechanically precise handwriting. "Divide it by nine Marines on the gun, and you, personally, you've killed zero point seven something people today. That's like, a torso and a head. Or maybe a torso and a leg."

"That's not funny," says Jewett.

"We definitely got more," says Sergeant Deetz. "We're the best shots in the battery."

Bolander snorts. "We're just firing on the quadrant and deflection the FDC gives us, Sergeant. I mean . . ."

"We're better shots," says Sergeant Deetz. "Put a round down a rabbit hole at eighteen miles."

"But even if we were on target . . . ," says Jewett.

"We were on target," says Sergeant Deetz.

"Okay, Sergeant, we were on target," says Jewett. "But the other guns, their rounds could have hit first. Maybe everybody was already dead."

I can see that, the shrapnel thudding into shattered corpses, the force of it jerking the limbs this way and that.

"Look," says Bolander, "even if their rounds hit first, it doesn't mean everybody was dead, necessarily. Maybe some insurgent had shrapnel in his chest, right, and he's like —" Bolander sticks his tongue out and clutches his chest dramatically, as if he were dying in an old black-and-white movie. "Then our round comes down, boom, blows his fucking head off. He was dying already, but the cause of death would be 'blown the hell up,' not 'shrapnel to the chest.' "

"Yeah, sure," says Jewett, "I guess. But I don't *feel* like I killed anybody. I think I'd know if I killed somebody."

"Naw," says Sergeant Deetz, "you wouldn't know. Not until you'd seen the bodies." The table quiets for a second. Sergeant Deetz shrugs. "It's better this way."

"Doesn't it feel weird to you," says Jewett, "after our first real mission, to just be eating lunch?"

Sergeant Deetz scowls at him, then takes a big bite of his Salisbury steak and grins. "Gotta eat," he says with his mouth full of food.

"It feels good," Voorstadt says. "We just killed some bad guys."

Sanchez gives a quick nod. "It *is* good."

"I don't think I killed anybody," says Jewett.

"Technically, I'm the one that pulled the lanyard," says Voorstadt. "I fired the thing. You just loaded."

"Like I couldn't pull a lanyard," says Jewett.

"Yeah, but you didn't," says Voorstadt.

"Drop it," says Sergeant Deetz. "It's a crew-served weapon. It takes a crew."

"If we used a howitzer to kill somebody back in the States," I say, "I wonder what crime they'd charge us with."

"Murder," says Sergeant Deetz. "What are you, an idiot?"

"Yeah, murder, sure," I say, "but for each of us? In what degree? I mean, me and Bolander and Jewett loaded, right? If I loaded an M16 and handed it to Voorstadt and he shot somebody, I wouldn't say I'd killed anyone."

"It's a crew-served weapon," says Sergeant

Deetz. "Crew. Served. Weapon. It's different."

"And I loaded, but we got the ammo from the ASP," I say. "Shouldn't they be responsible, too, the ASP Marines?"

"Yeah," says Jewett. "Why not the ASP?"

"Why not the factory workers who made the ammo?" says Sergeant Deetz. "Or the taxpayers who paid for it? You know why not? Because that's retarded."

"The lieutenant gave the order," I say. "He'd get it in court, right?"

"Oh, you believe that? You think officers would take the hit?" Voorstadt laughs. "How long you been in the military?"

Sergeant Deetz thumps his fist on the table. "Listen to me. We're Gun Six. We're responsible for that gun. We just killed some bad guys. With our gun. All of us. And that's a good day's work."

"I still don't feel like I killed anybody, Sergeant," says Jewett.

Sergeant Deetz lets out a long breath. It's quiet for a second. Then he shakes his head and starts laughing. "Yeah, well, all of us except you," he says.

When we get out of the chow hall, I don't know what to do with myself. We don't have anything planned until evening, when we have another illum mission, so most of the guys want to hit the racks. But I don't want to sleep. I feel like I'm finally fully awake. This morning I'd gotten up boot-camp-style, off two hours of sleep, dressed and ready to kill before my brain had time to start working. But now, even though my body is tired, my mind is up and I want to keep it that way.

"Head back to the can?" I say to Jewett.

He nods and we start walking the perimeter of the Battle Square, shaded by the palm trees that grow along the road.

"I kind of wish we had some weed," says Jewett.

"Okay," I say.

"Just saying."

I shake my head. We get to the corner of the Battle Square, Fallujah Surgical straight ahead of us, and turn right.

Jewett says, "Well, it's something to tell my mom about, finally."

"Yeah," I say. "Something to tell Jessie about."

"When's the last time you talked to her?"

"Week and a half."

Jewett doesn't say anything to that. I look down at my wedding band. Jessie and I'd gotten a courthouse wedding a week before I deployed so that if I died, Jessie'd get benefits. It doesn't feel like I'm married.

"What am I supposed to tell her?" I say.

Jewett shrugs.

"She thinks I'm a badass. She thinks I'm in danger."

"We get mortared from time to time."

I give Jewett a flat look.

"It's something," he says. "Anyway, now you can say you got some bad guys."

"Maybe." I look at my watch. "It's zero four, her time. I'll have to wait before I can tell her what a hero I am."

"That's what I tell my mom every day."

When we get near the cans, I tell Jewett I left something at the gun line and peel off.

The gun line's a two-minute walk. As I get closer, the palm trees thin out into desert, and I can see the Camp Fallujah post office. Here the sky expands to the edge of the horizon. It's perfectly blue and cloudless, as it has been every day for the last two months. I can see the guns pointing up into the air. Only Guns Two and Three are manned, and their Marines are just sitting around. When I got here this morning, all the guns were manned and everybody was frantic. The sky was black, with just a touch of red bleeding in from the rim of the horizon. In the half-light, you could see the outline of the massive, forty-feet-long, dark steel barrels pointed into the dark morning sky and below them the shapes of Marines hustling about, checking the guns, the rounds, the powder.

In the daylight, the guns shine crisp in the sun, but earlier this morning was dark and dirty. Me and Bolander and Jewett stood in the back right, waiting by the ammo, while Sanchez called out the quadrant and deflection they were giving to Gun Three.

I had put my hands on one of our rounds, the first one we sent out. Also the first I'd ever fired at human targets. I'd wanted to lift it up right then and there, feel the heft of it tug on my shoulders. I had trained to load those rounds. Trained so much that I had scars on my hands from when they had slammed on my fingers or torn my skin.

Then Gun Three had fired two targeting rounds. Then: "Fire mission. Battery. Two rounds." Then Sanchez had called out the quadrant and deflection and Sergeant Deetz had repeated it and Dupont and Coleman, our gunner and A-gunner, had repeated it and set it and checked it and had Sergeant Deetz check it and Sanchez verify, and we got round and time and Jackson had gotten powder and we moved smooth, like we trained to, me and Jewett on either side of the stretcher holding the round, Bolander behind with the ramming rod. Sergeant

Deetz checked the powder and read, "Three, four, five, white bag." Then, to Sanchez: "Charge five, white bag." Verified.

We moved in with the round, up to the open hatch, and Bolander shoved it in with the ramming rod until we heard it ring, and Voorstadt closed the hatch.

Sanchez said, "Hook up."

Deetz said, "Hook up."

Voorstadt hooked the lanyard to the trigger. I'd seen him do it a thousand times.

Sanchez said, "Stand by."

Deetz said, "Stand by."

Voorstadt pulled out the slack in the lanyard, holding it against his waist.

Sanchez said, "Fire."

Deetz said, "Fire."

Voorstadt did a left face and our gun was alive.

The sound of it hit us, vibrating through our bodies, down deep in our chests and in our guts and in the back of our teeth. I could taste the gunpowder in the air. As the guns fired, the barrels shot back like pistons and reseated, the force of each round going off kicking up smoke and dust into the air. When I looked down the line, I couldn't see six guns. I just saw fires through the haze, or not even fires, just flashes of red in the dust and the cordite. And I could feel the roar of each gun, not just ours, as it fired. And I thought, God, this is why I'm glad I'm an artilleryman.

Because what's a grunt with an M16 shooting? 5.56? Even the .50-cal., what can you really do with that? Or the main gun of a tank. Your range is what? A mile or two? And you can kill what? A small house? An armored vehicle? Wherever we were dropping these rounds, somewhere six miles south of us, those rounds were striking harder than anything else in ground warfare. Each shell weighs 130 pounds, a casing filled with eighty-eight bomblets that scatter over the target area. Each bomblet has a shaped explosive charge that can penetrate two inches of solid steel and send shrapnel flying over the battlefield. Putting those rounds downrange takes nine men moving in perfect unison. It takes an FDC, and a good spotter, and math and physics and art and skill and experience. And though I only loaded, maybe I was only one-third of the ammo team, but I moved perfectly, and the round went in with that satisfying ring, and the round went off with that incredible roar, and it shot out into the sky and hit six miles south of us. The target area. And wherever we hit, everything within a hundred yards, everything within a circle with a radius as long as a football field, everything died.

Voorstadt had the lanyard unhooked and the breech open before the gun had fully reseated, and he washed the bore with the chamber swab and we loaded another round, the second I had fired at a human target that day, although by this point, surely, there were no more living targets. And we fired again, and we felt it in our bones, and we saw the fireball burst from the barrel, and more dust and cordite went into the air, choking us with the sand of the Iraqi desert.

And then it was done.

Smoke surrounded us. We couldn't see beyond our position. I was breathing hard, taking in the smell and taste of gunpowder. And I'd looked at our gun, standing above us, quiet, massive, and felt a kind of love for it.

But the dust began to settle. And a wind came and started picking at the smoke, tugging it and lifting it over us, then higher, into the sky, the only cloud I'd seen in two months. And then the cloud thinned, disappearing into the air, blending with the soft red Iraqi sunrise.

Now, standing before the guns with the sky a perfect blue and the barrels piercing up into the air, it doesn't seem as though any of it could have happened. No speck of this morning remains in our gun. Sergeant Deetz made us clean it after the mission was over. A ritual, of sorts, for our first kill as Gun Six. We'd taken apart the ramming rod and the cleaning swab, attached the two poles together, along with a bore brush, and drenched the brush in CLP. Then we'd all stood in line behind the gun, holding the pole, and in unison had rammed it through the bore. And then we'd repeated the process, and black streaks of CLP and carbon snaked down the pole, staining our hands. We'd kept at it until our gun was clean.

So there's no indication here of what happened, though I know ten kliks south of us is a cratered area riddled with shrapnel and ruined buildings, burned-out vehicles and twisted corpses. The bodies. Sergeant Deetz had seen them on his first deployment, during the initial invasion. None of the rest of us have.

I turn sharply away from the gun line. It's too pristine. And maybe this is the wrong way to think about it. Somewhere, there's a corpse lying out, bleaching in the sun. Before it was a corpse, it was a man who lived and breathed and maybe murdered and maybe tortured, the kind of man I'd always wanted to kill. Whatever the case, a man definitely dead.

So I walk back to our battery area, never turning around. It's a short walk, and when I get back I find a couple of the guys playing Texas hold 'em by a smoke pit. There's Sergeant Deetz, Bolander, Voorstadt, and Sanchez. Deetz has fewer chips than the others and is leaning his bulk over the table, scowling at the pot.

"Oo-rah, motivator," he says when he sees me.

"Oo-rah, Sergeant." I watch them play. Sanchez flips the turn card and everybody checks.

"Sergeant?" I say.

"What?"

I'm not sure where to start. "Don't you think, maybe, we should have a patrol out, to see if there were any survivors?"

"What?" Sergeant Deetz is focused on the game. As soon as Sanchez flips the river, he throws his cards in.

"I mean, the mission we had. Shouldn't we go out, like, in a patrol, to see if there are any survivors?"

Sergeant Deetz looks up at me. "You are an idiot, aren't you?"

"No, Sergeant."

"There weren't any survivors," says Voorstadt, tossing his cards in as well.

"You see al-Qaeda rolling around in tanks?" says Sergeant Deetz.

"No, Sergeant."

"You see al-Qaeda building crazy bunkers and trenches?"

"No, Sergeant."

"You think al-Qaeda's got some magic, ICM-doesn't-kill-my-ass ninja powers?"

"No, Sergeant."

"No, you're goddamn right, no."

"Yes, Sergeant."

The betting is now between Sanchez and Bolander. Sanchez, looking at the pot, says to no one in particular, "I think the 2nd and 136th does patrols out there."

"But, Sergeant," I say, "what about the bodies? Doesn't somebody have to clean up the bodies?"

"Jesus, Lance Corporal. Do I look like a PRP Marine to you?"

"No, Sergeant."

"What do I look like?"

"Like an artilleryman, Sergeant."

"You're goddamn right, killer. I'm an artilleryman. We *provide* the bodies. We don't clean 'em up. You hear me?"

"Yes, Sergeant."

He looks up at me. "And what are you, Lance Corporal?"

"An artilleryman, Sergeant."

"And what do you do?"

"Provide the bodies, Sergeant."

"You're goddamn right, killer. You're goddamn right."

Sergeant Deetz turns back to the game. I use the opportunity to slip away. It was stupid to ask Deetz, but what he said has me thinking. PRP: personnel retrieval and processing, aka Mortuary Affairs. I'd forgotten about them. They must have collected the bodies from this morning.

The thought of PRP works and worms through my brain. The bodies could be sitting here, on base. But I don't know where PRP is. I'd never wanted to know, and I don't want to ask anyone the way, either. Why would anyone go there? But I leave the battery area and walk around the perimeter of the Battle Square, over to the CLB buildings, dodging officers and staff NCOs. It takes a good half hour, sneaking around, reading the signs outside of buildings, until I find it, a long, low, rectangular building surrounded by palm trees. It's offset from the rest of the CLB complex, but otherwise just like every other building. That feels wrong — if they cleaned up from today, severed limbs should be spilling out the door.

I stand outside, looking at the entrance.

It's a simple wooden door. One I shouldn't be in front of, one I shouldn't open, one I shouldn't step through. I'm in a combat arms unit, and I don't belong here. It's bad voodoo. But I came all this way, I found it, and I'm not a coward. So I open the door.

Inside is cool air, a long hallway full of closed doors, and a Marine at a desk facing away from me. He has headphones on. They're plugged into a computer that's playing some sort of TV show. On the screen, a woman in a poofy dress is hailing a cab. She looks pretty at first, but then the screen cuts to a close-up and it's clear she's not.

The Marine at the desk turns around and takes off his headphones, looking up at me, confused. I look for chevrons on his collar and see he's a gunnery sergeant, but he seems far older than most gunnys. A trim white mustache sits on his lip and he has a white fuzz of hair over the ears, but the rest of his head is shiny and bald. As he squints up to look at me, the skin around his eyes scrunches into wrinkles. He's fat, too. Even through the uniform, I can tell. They say PRP is all reservists, no active duty undertakers in the Marine Corps, and he looks like a reservist for sure.

"Can I help you, Lance Corporal?" he

says. There's a soft, southern drawl in his voice.

I stand there looking at him, my mouth open, and the seconds tick by.

Then the old gunny's face softens and he leans forward and says, "Did you lose someone, son?"

It takes me a second to figure it out. "No," I say. "No. No no no. No."

He looks at me, confused, and arches an eyebrow.

"I'm an artilleryman," I say.

"Okay," he says.

We look at each other.

"We had a mission today. Target was ten kliks south of here?" I look at him, hoping he'll get it. I feel constricted by the narrow hallway, with the desk squeezed in and the fat old gunny looking at me quizzically.

"Okay?" he says.

"It was my first mission like that. . . ."

"Okay?" he says again. He leans forward and squints up at me, like if he gets a better look, he'll know what the hell I'm talking about.

"I mean, I'm from Nebraska. From Ord, Nebraska. We don't do anything in Ord." I'm fully aware I sound like an idiot.

"You all right, Lance Corporal?" The old gunny looks at me intently, waiting. Any gunny in an arty unit would have chewed my ass by now. Any gunny in an arty unit would have chewed my ass as soon as I walked through the door, waltzing into someplace I didn't belong. But this gunny, maybe because he's a reservist, maybe because he's old, maybe because he's fat, just looks up and waits for me to get out what I need to say.

"I just never killed anybody before."

"Neither have I," he says.

"But I did. I think. I mean, we just shot the rounds off."

"Okay," he says. "So why'd you come here?"

I look at him helplessly. "I thought, maybe, you'd been out there. And seen what we'd done."

The old gunny leans back in his chair and purses his lips tight. "No," he says.

He takes a breath and lets it out slow.

"We handle U.S. casualties. Iraqis take care of their own. Only time I see enemy dead is when they pass in a U.S. med facility. Like Fallujah Surgical." He waves his hand in the general direction of the base hospital. "Besides, TQ's got a PRP section. They'd probably have handled anything in that AO."

"Oh," I say. "Okay."

"We didn't have anything like that today."
"Okay," I say.
"You'll be all right," he says.
"Yeah," I say. "Thanks, Gunny."
I stand there, looking at him for a second. Then I look down at all the closed doors in the hallway, doors with nothing behind them. On the computer screen behind the gunny, a group of women drink pink martinis.
"You married, Lance Corporal?" The gunny is looking at my hands, at my wedding band.
"Yeah," I say. "About two months now."
"How old are you?" he asks.
"Nineteen."
He nods, then sits there as though turning some hard thing over in his mind. Right when I'm about to take my leave, he says, "Here's something you could do for me. Can you do me a favor?"
"Sure, Gunny."
He points at my wedding band. "Take that off and put it on the chain with your dog tags." He scoops at the chain around his own neck with two fingers and pulls out his dog tags to show me. There, hanging next to the two metal tabs with his kill data, is a gold ring. "Okay? . . .
"We need to collect personal effects," he

says, putting his dog tags back in his shirt. "For me, the hardest thing is taking off the wedding rings."

"Oh." I take a step back.

"Can you do that?" he says.

"Yeah," I say, "I can do that."

"Thanks," he says.

"I should go," I say.

"You should," he says.

I turn quickly, open the door, and step out into the oven air. I walk away slow, back straight, controlling my steps, and I walk with my right hand over my left, worrying at my wedding band, twisting it around my finger.

I'd told the gunny I would do it, so as I walk I work at my ring, getting it off my finger. It feels like bad voodoo, to put it with my dog tags. But I take them from around my neck, undo the snap clasp, slip the ring onto the chain, redo the clasp, and put the dog tags back around my neck. I can feel the metal of the ring against my chest.

I walk away, not paying attention to where my steps are leading me, passing under the palm trees lining the road around the Battle Square. I'm hungry, and it should be time for chow, but I don't go that way. I go to the road by Fallujah Surgical and I stop.

It's a squat, dull building, beige and

beaten down by the brightness of the sun like everything else. There's a smoke pit nearby and two Corpsmen are sitting there, talking and dragging on cigarettes, sending faint puffs of smoke into the air. I wait, looking at the building as if something incredible might emerge.

Nothing happens, of course. But there in the heat, standing before Fallujah Surgical, I remember the cooler air of the morning two days before. We'd been going to chow, all of Gun Six, laughing and joking until Sergeant Deetz, who was yelling something about the Spartans being gay, stopped midsentence. He froze, then shifted, straightened to his full height, and whispered, "Ahhh-ten-HUT."

We all snapped to attention, not knowing why. Sergeant Deetz raised his right hand in a salute, and so did we. Then I saw, off in the distance, well down the road, four Corpsmen coming out of Fallujah Surgical carrying a stretcher draped with the American flag. Everything was silent, still. All down the road, Marines and sailors had snapped to.

I could barely see it in the early morning light. I strained my eyes looking at the outline of the body under the thick fabric of the flag. And then the stretcher passed from view.

Now, standing there in the daytime, looking at the two Corpsmen in the smoke pit, I wonder if they'd been the ones carrying that body. They must have carried some.

Everyone standing on the road as the body went past had been so utterly silent, so still. There was no sound or movement except for the slow steps of the Corpsmen and the steady progress of the corpse. It'd been an image of death from another world. But now I know where that corpse was headed, to the old gunny at PRP. And if there was a wedding ring, the gunny would have slowly worked it off the stiff, dead fingers. He would have gathered all the personal effects and prepared the body for transport. Then it would have gone by air to TQ. And as it was unloaded off the bird, the Marines would have stood silent and still, just as we had in Fallujah. And they would have put it on a C-130 to Kuwait. And they would have stood silent and still in Kuwait. And they would have stood silent and still in Germany, and silent and still at Dover Air Force Base. Everywhere it went, Marines and sailors and soldiers and airmen would have stood at attention as it traveled to the family of the fallen, where the silence, the stillness, would end.

ACKNOWLEDGMENTS

This book could not exist without the work of a large group of people who have been incredibly generous with their time. Foremost are the people who read and gave me extensive feedback on every story and as such have had a tremendous influence on the shape of this book. I generally gave early drafts to Christopher Robinson, then to Lauren Holmes and Roy Scranton. After they'd finished, I'd send newer versions to Patrick Blanchfield and my wife, Jessica Alvarez. And then finally it went to my incredible editor at The Penguin Press, Andrea Walker, who had a fine-tuned sense for what I wanted to accomplish. These stories would not be worth reading without all of their intelligence and insight.

I also received intensely valuable input, be it through editing stories or helping with technical details or simply through sharing war stories, from Ellah Allfrey, Carmiel Banasky, Vincent Biagi, SJ, Anna Bierhaus, Peter Carey, Kevin Carmody, Bill Cheng, Scott Cheshire, John Davis, Alex Derichemont, Wayne Edmiston, Nathan Englander, Eric Fair, Matt Gallagher, Michael Green, Thomas Griffith, Jonathan Gurfein, Jason Hansman, Josh Hauser, Ryan-Daniel Healy, David Imbert, Mariette Kalinowski, Andrew Kalwitz, Gavin Kovite, Molly Wallace Kovite, Jess Lacher, Christopher Lindahl, Matt Mellina, Colum McCann, Patrick McGrath, Perry O'Brien, Evan Pettyjohn, Virginia Ramadan, Adam Schein, Carl Schillhammer, Jacob Siegel, Jeremy Warneke, Matt Weiss, and others.

I am deeply indebted to the Hunter MFA program, without which I would be a much weaker writer. Thanks to everyone I met there, students and faculty, and to Susan Hertog, whose Hertog Fellowship provided funds while I was working on this book.

The other major influence on this book was the NYU Veterans Writing Workshop, which was created by Ambassador Jean Kennedy Smith and NYU, and which provided an invaluable space for me to interact with other veteran writers. Thanks to everyone involved, especially Deborah Landau, Zachary Sussman, Sativa January, Brian Trimboli, Emily Brandt, Craig Moreau, and the Disabled American Veterans Charitable Service Trust.

I'd like to thank John Freeman, who gave me my first opportunity to publish a short story.

Thanks to my agent, Eric Simonoff, and to everybody at WME — Claudia Ballard, Cathryn Summerhayes, Laura Bonner, and others.

Thanks to Tom Sleigh, who has helped guide my writing life since I first met him ten years ago at Dartmouth College.

Thanks to my parents and to my brothers — Byrne, Ben, Jon, and Dave. And of course, thanks to the aunties — Aunt Mimi, Aunt Pixie, and the late and dearly missed Aunt Boo.

The writing of this book required a lot of research, and below are some of the books I consulted:

David Abrams's *Fobbit,* Giorgio Agamben's *The Open,* Omnia Amin and Rick London's translations of Ahmed Abdel Muti Hijazi's poetry, Peter Van Buren's *We Meant Well,* Donovan Campbell's *Joker One,* C. J. Chivers's *The Gun,* Seth Connor's *Boredom by Day, Death by Night,* Daniel Danelo's *Blood Stripes,* Kimberly Dozier's *Breathing the Fire,* Nathan Englander's *What We Talk About When We Talk About Anne*

Frank, Siobhan Fallon's *You Know When the Men Are Gone,* Nathaniel Fick's *One Bullet Away,* Dexter Filkins's *The Forever War,* David Finkel's *The Good Soldiers,* Jim Frederick's *Black Hearts,* Matt Gallagher's *Kaboom,* Jessica Goodell's *Shade It Black,* J. Glenn Gray's *The Warriors,* Dave Grossman's *On Killing* and *On Combat,* Judith Herman's *Trauma and Recovery,* Kirsten Holmstedt's *Band of Sisters,* Karl Marlantes's *Matterhorn,* Colum McCann's *Dancer,* Patrick McGrath's *Trauma,* Jonathan Shay's *Odysseus in America* and *Achilles in Vietnam,* Roy Scranton's essays and fiction, the Special Inspector for Iraq Reconstruction Report *Hard Lessons,* Bing West's *The Strongest Tribe* and *No True Glory,* Kayla Williams's *Love My Rifle More Than You.*

ABOUT THE AUTHOR

Phil Klay is a Dartmouth graduate and a veteran of the U.S. Marine Corps. He served in Iraq during the surge and subsequently received an MFA from Hunter College. His first published story, "Redeployment," appeared in *Granta*'s Summer 2011 issue. His writing has also appeared in the *New York Times,* the *New York Daily News, Tin House,* and in *The Best American Nonrequired Reading 2012.*

The employees of Thorndike Press hope you have enjoyed this Large Print book. All our Thorndike, Wheeler, and Kennebec Large Print titles are designed for easy reading, and all our books are made to last. Other Thorndike Press Large Print books are available at your library, through selected bookstores, or directly from us.

For information about titles, please call:
(800) 223-1244

or visit our Web site at:
http://gale.cengage.com/thorndike

To share your comments, please write:

Publisher
Thorndike Press
10 Water St., Suite 310
Waterville, ME 04901